DON'T LET THE MUSIC DIE

ANNMARIE BOYLE

DAHLIA
MEDIA

This is a work of fiction. Names, characters, places, and incidents are products of the author's imaginations or are used fictitiously and are not to be construed as real. Any resemblance to actual events, locales, organizations, or person living or dead, is entirely coincidental.

Edited by Jolene Perry

Cover by Qamber Designs and Media

ISBN 978-1-7359351-4-0

For everyone who thrives alongside mental health challenges.

ALSO BY ANNMARIE BOYLE

The Storyhill Musicians series

Love Me Like a Love Song
Off the Record (coming Fall 2022)

Storyhill Novellas

Fine Tuned
Friday at the Blue Note

CHAPTER ONE

RUNNING OFF STAGE, MATT TAYLOR SNATCHED A TOWEL from their tour manager and scrubbed it over his face. The crowd was on their feet. The applause rattled the wrap-around pews and the vintage red, yellow, and blue stained glass that comprised the back walls of the Ryman Auditorium.

He sucked in a breath. The Ryman. His band had just debuted their new album at the mother-fucking Ryman. Reserved for the likes of Elvis, BB King, and Emmylou Harris, this wasn't where a five-man country *a cappella* group, like Storyhill, performed. This is where Johnny met June. And yet, here they were—with a sold-out show.

He stared out at the dark silhouettes filling the seats, their rhythmic clapping a wordless request for more music. Had it only been eight months since the label threatened to drop the group if they failed to write an all-original album? He sighed. That would have been the perfect time to tell the guys about the songs he'd written. But he kept quiet. He knew the songs were good, but they exposed raw and painful parts of his past. A past that didn't match his present.

"You ready to wrap this up, Mattie?"

Matt turned to Storyhill's manager, Brad Rodgers, and bit his bottom lip. Was he ready? Not really. Matt loved performing, but sometimes it was exhausting. He was literally the face of Storyhill. The charmer. The grown-up version of the class clown. The guy who introduced everything—and everyone else.

He was always 'on.' There was never a down moment.

So when Andrew came up with this harebrained idea, everyone assumed he would take the lead. No one asked. No one even contemplated someone else doing it.

No one imagined this would be the last thing he wanted to do. But he couldn't admit that. He didn't dare signal he was uncomfortable or anything but entirely confident.

"Never mind," he muttered to himself. Matt Taylor didn't sulk. He didn't grimace. He didn't do anything that broke from his image. Ever.

He shook the thoughts from his mind and plastered on an all-too-practiced smile. "I'm ready," Matt said to their manager, "but is he?"

The two men glanced over at Andrew, the group's bass. He was standing at the edge of the wings, head dipped, fingers jammed into his hair, looking green around the edges.

Blake, the group's tenor, stepped up behind the men, pointing at Andrew. "I got five bucks on Andrew leaving his dinner all over the stage."

Matt laughed. "No way I'm taking that bet. He looks like he's going to pass out."

Brad nudged their shoulders. "It's time. Go give that crowd what they want. Knock the encore number out of the park. I'll make sure Andrew makes it out there."

Matt nodded, tapped his microphone against his thigh, and ran onto the stage. His oversized belt buckle jangled as the heels of his boots hit the well-worn pine floor. The boots, the buckle, the jeans, all carefully chosen. An industry insider would call it 'personal branding.' He knew the truth. It was a costume, a disguise. The outfits. The jewelry. The $100 haircut. The smile. They were nothing but a mask.

He'd become a caricature, a sum of every wink, every smile, every forced bit of southern charm. He wanted more. He wanted to show everyone there was more to him than pretty packaging. But he understood what people wanted from him and, much as he craved more, he didn't dare mess with a winning formula.

A shrill whistle yanked Matt from his thoughts. How long had he been standing there? His eyes flashed to the other men on stage. Couldn't have been too long, Andrew was just wobbling into his spot between Blake and Nick. Blake threw an arm around the bass, steadying him. Andrew didn't look great, but he managed a weak smile, nodding at Matt.

Matt turned back to the crowd. "How about one more song?"

The crowd roared in agreement, and Blake blew into the pitchpipe. Matt had eighty-one bars to lose himself in a song they'd performed hundreds of times. Three hundred and twenty-four beats before having to emcee tonight's addition.

Three bars. Four bars. Muscle memory took over and he stepped to the left and turned—and ran into Andrew. Andrew tapped his chest and mouthed, "My bad." Matt nodded and pushed a finger into Andrew's shoulder, directing him back into step with the other members of the group. Seemed Andrew's rare mistakes only happened when there was a woman involved. That's why tonight's little post-encore plan was a bad idea.

Sliding into perfect four-part harmony, the closing notes of the encore number floated over the rows of clapping fans. And on cue, Matt raised his microphone to his lips.

"Hey y'all," Matt called out. "Thanks again for coming to our CD release concert. You've been an incredible audience."

The crowd quieted but remained standing. "Before we go, let's give credit where it's due."

He turned and motioned Andrew forward. "Y'all know this guy, right?" he said, slinging an arm around Andrew's shoulders. "Sexiest voice east of the Mississippi—hell, west of it, north of it, south of it."

A decidedly female cacophony of 'whoops' filled the historic auditorium.

Andrew shot him a look and wheezed, "Get on with it."

Matt nodded. He hoped Andrew knew what he was doing. "If you liked tonight's songs," he said to the audience, following the script in his head, "then give this man an extra round of applause. He's responsible for writing eleven of the twelve songs on this album." The crowd erupted in cheers, and Matt yelled into the microphone over the uproar. "Well, he co-wrote the songs, along with one of the best songwriters in the business."

Matt lowered the microphone and whispered in Andrew's ear, "You ready?" Andrew nodded, and Matt turned to the wings.

"Grace O'Connor, come out here and join us on stage." Matt chuckled at Grace, who was madly waving her hands and mouthing, "NO!"

"C'mon Nashville, if you loved our music tonight, put your hands together for the woman who made all this possible."

Grace slinked into the stage lights and waved weakly to the crowd. "What are you doing?" she hissed, sidling up to Matt.

"Baby, it ain't what I'm doing, it's what he's doing." He turned her one hundred and eighty degrees to Andrew, who was down on one knee.

Grace gasped, and Matt felt like someone had punched him in the gut. Instantly, the applause and flashing cell phones faded away and a memory as fresh as if it happened yesterday dragged him back to the single moment, nine years ago, that blew his future into a million tiny bits.

He'd been down on one knee—just like Andrew—and snapped open a small black velvet box. The woman standing across from him had frozen and for a single moment her beautiful hazel eyes filled with joy before clouding over, closing off.

He'd waited for the happy tears, just like the ones flowing down Grace's cheeks right now. They hadn't come. What had come was a terse, "No." After six years of dating—and planning a life together—she had walked away, leaving him confused and heartbroken. He'd been over that moment—the unexpected no —a million times. Two letters shattering his heart and sending shards into his future, hidden landmines just waiting to be stepped on. He was never sure when they would explode.

He backed out of the spotlight that captured Grace and Andrew in its golden halo, trying to regain his equilibrium. He could not be Matt Taylor, rhinestone cowboy, right now. He could hardly stand. The memories kept ripping through him, washing over him with the subtlety of a tidal wave.

He bumped against a waist-high speaker and reached to steady himself. *Focus, Mattie.* One of your best friends just asked the biggest question of his life. *This is not about you.* He was thrilled for his friends. And gutted by the memories. The sadness coursing through him mixed with the happiness, poisoning it.

No. No. Just no. He squeezed his fists and willed away the messy memories.

He stepped toward center stage and caught the tip of his boot in the speaker's power cord. He lurched forward, trying to regain his balance, failing miserably and landing in Blake's arms. He felt five sets of eyes land on him. He forced a smile because that's what people expected of him, wasn't it? He was always the happy one, the easygoing life-of-the-party dude.

"Got a little carried away in the moment," Matt said into his microphone. "Blake, will you marry me?" The audience laughed on cue.

"And disappoint the legions of people in line to get a chance at marrying you?" Blake quipped. "No way. I'd fear for my life."

Matt didn't care about the legions. There was only one woman he'd ever wanted to marry, and she wasn't interested. "Storyhill's resident commitment-phobe," Matt said, pointing at Blake.

Cue the laughter. Again.

Matt shrugged. "Can't blame a guy for trying."

He needed to get off the stage. Now.

He looked down at Grace's hand. Had she said yes? A twinkling diamond, triple the size of the tiny one he'd purchased on his college student budget, danced on her finger. Yes, then.

Swallowing, he turned back to the audience and dialed his smile up another level. A move so practiced it hardly took effort. "In the immortal words of Porky Pig, that's all, folks. Really. There's no music that can top a proposal like that." He waved at the audience. "Good night Nashville!" To his ears, his voice sounded even. Nothing like the tsunami raging in his chest.

The house lights came up and he nearly ran for the wings. He hit the darkness and his smile fizzled and faded.

"Whoa, hold up," Andrew said, clapping a hand on his shoulder. "Thanks for your help, Mattie."

"Yeah, yeah," Matt said, waving off Andrew's gratitude. "Congratulations," he forced out.

"It's time to celebrate," Andrew said, addressing the band. "Grace said yes, and Mattie kept a secret. I had good feelings about the first. I was less confident about the second."

The four other men of Storyhill laughed and Matt tried to join in, but a tepid chuckle was all he could manage.

"I think I'm out for tonight." He could be happy for Andrew

and Grace and still not want to celebrate. That just made him human and not a total jerk, right?

Six sets of eyes turned to him, incredulity plastered across their faces. Shit. Talk about off-brand. He needed a plausible excuse for why the party king was begging off, and fast.

"No way," Grace said, sliding an arm through his. "It's your rule that post-concert drinks are not optional."

Matt pulled a face. "It's not nice to throw a man's own words back at him."

Grace laughed. "C'mon Mattie, it won't be the same without you."

Matt softened at her kind words. Joining his friends sounded more appealing than skulking home to a dark, silent apartment. He wasn't that twenty-two-year-old kid anymore. He should have a beer with his friends, not let the Ghost of Proposals Past dictate his present.

"Plus, you can't expect me to believe that you're going to deny the ladies at the bar the opportunity to enjoy your pretty face?" she added with a wink.

And there it was. The truth of what everyone thought of him. All flash, no substance. Good for a flirt and maybe a fuck, but nothing more. It was the reason for so many rejections in his life, including his marriage proposal.

She'd given him some lame mumbo-jumbo about not wanting to be married to a man who'd be traveling for a living. But he knew the truth. He lacked substance. He wasn't enough for her.

Why couldn't anyone see past the surface?

Maybe because you don't let them, a little voice whispered.

What was with him tonight? Matt Taylor didn't do pity parties or whatever this was. "You're right, Gracie-girl, that would be a darn shame. Let's go."

He could fake his way through this. That was his specialty, after all.

"Matt, before we go," Brad called after him. "I need a minute."

Matt turned back to their manager and mentally shook off the last dregs of his melancholy. "Yeah?"

"I need a favor."

Matt arched an eyebrow. "From me?"

Brad nodded. "Ever heard of the Avery Lind Show?"

A billboard flashed through his mind. "That's the big deal country radio morning show, right?"

"That's the one. And it's about to be an even bigger deal. The station just penned a syndication deal, and the show goes national tomorrow."

"And this has something to do with me?"

Brad's lips twisted and tightened. "I'm in a bit of a bind. Addison May was scheduled to be the first guest on the show."

Matt pushed his hand through his hair, watching his friends leave through the stage door. "Was?"

"She has laryngitis, and I told the station I'd get another one of my clients to fill in."

Matt's eyes widened, understanding dawning. "Radio's not really my medium." Matt sighed. "It's been mentioned once or twice that I'm only helpful if you can see my face. Why not one of the other guys?"

Brad laughed, clearly taking Matt's sarcasm for self-deprecating humor. "You're the best on your feet. You can make conversation with anyone."

Not exactly praise. "And I don't have a wife, fiancé, or child to deal with? Why can't Blake do it?"

Brad's eyes narrowed. "This couldn't come at a better time if I'd planned it myself. A feature on a nationally syndicated show the day after Storyhill released its first all-original album at the

Ryman? The promotion gods have laid a golden egg in our laps. Plus, Andrew's proposal will be all over social media by tomorrow morning. All things to capitalize on."

"Great," Matt grumbled. "Talking about someone else's love life sounds awesome."

"Are you okay?" Brad said, his brow squeezing into taut lines. "You're acting so . . . un-Matt like."

How was he supposed to react to that? If he answered honestly, Brad would think he'd lost his mind. *I had no idea that the minute Andrew got down on one knee I'd be transported to the exact moment, nearly a decade ago, when I was unceremoniously dumped.* Yep, that made him sound crazy—even to his own ears.

He gave his head a tiny shake. Enough. "I'm fine. Just a little more tired than usual." That was only a half lie.

Brad flipped his wrist, checking the time. "What do you say? Station manager needs an answer tonight."

Matt's stomach tightened. Could he do this? All his other jobs from high school to college to now—busking, summer stock, modeling, performing—were all face dependent. Radio was faceless.

But isn't that what he so desperately wanted? To do something more than sing melodies and smile in all the right places?

"Fine," he said, meeting his manager's questioning stare. "Tell him I'll do it."

"Her."

"Sorry?"

"The station manager is a woman. Making you an even better choice. Never seen a woman unaffected by the Matt Taylor charm."

Matt rubbed a single finger over a throbbing temple. That made him sound like a trained golden retriever . . . and wasn't exactly flattering to women, either.

But if this was his chance to prove himself, to bury the specters of the past, he needed to show Brad he would take this seriously. "Any prep I should do?"

"Station manager's name is Celeste Yoon and"—Brad consulted his phone— "she'll meet you in the lobby at 5:00. She'll give you the info you need before taking you to the studio to meet Avery."

Matt's eyes went wide. "Five *A.M.*? Whoa. I'm not sure I can talk at that hour."

Brad smirked. "Celeste assured me she'd have coffee waiting. And you don't go on until a little after six."

"Then why do I have to be there at five?"

"It's my understanding that Avery is particular and wants to prep all her guests personally."

Matt grunted. He had no problems with high maintenance at noon, but exacting and demanding before sunrise? Didn't sound like much fun. "I thought you said Celeste was prepping me?"

"Better over-prepared than under, I guess."

Matt pushed a hand through his hair. "I've done media before."

"And they'll understand that as soon as you go live. Until then, just play nice." Brad swiped back to his home screen. "I'll email you the station address and some links to previous shows. If you're not a regular listener, it'd be good to listen to a couple."

Matt flipped the watch dangling from his wrist. "In the next seven hours?"

Brad grimaced. "Better make the beer a quick one."

"Quick and free," Matt said, slapping a hand on Brad's shoulder.

"Free?" his manager asked.

"Yep, you're buying."

"How do you figure?"

Matt smiled—the first real one in over an hour. "I recall you saying you were in a bind—and I just helped you out." A deep knowing quivered in Matt's chest. If he played this right, he'd be helping himself out too.

The past didn't matter. It's where he went from here. He'd grab this opportunity by the horns and show everyone he was more than a pretty face.

CHAPTER TWO

AVERY LIND SET DOWN HER COFFEE CUP AND PLACED THE second plain white ceramic mug directly across from it. She moved the guest microphone a centimeter to the left so it was in a direct line with her own. She tapped her notes so that every paper squared up and set them down next to her pens—one blue, one black, one green, left to right.

"Relax, love," her longtime producer called in his crisp British accent through the intercom. "A few more people might hear this show, but we won't do it any differently than we have for the last three years. I know Celeste threw you a curve ball, but you're a professional. You'll roll with it like always."

Avery's eyes snapped up to the man behind the glass. "Wait, what? Ajay, what curve ball?"

Ajay held up a hand and walked from his space to hers. "The email she sent last night? About Addison May not being here?"

Her heart rate ticked up and a bead of sweat formed at the base of her neck. She rubbed the dip between her collarbones, trying to stave off the anxiety that was already climbing up her spine. No, no, no. She'd planned every part of this show, down to the very last minute.

She fumbled for her phone, attempting to open the mail app. "I've been up every night for a week prepping so I turned off my phone last night hoping I'd sleep better." She turned to Ajay, eyes wide. "We really don't have a guest? What are we going to do?" she nearly shrieked.

She yanked open the tiny desk drawer below the control panel and popped three antacids. Focusing on the peppermint flavor and the way it dissolved on her tongue, she counted down from ten.

"We have a guest, love," Ajay said, placing a steadying hand on her shoulder.

"We do?" She finally located the email from Celeste with the subject line, Change of Plans. "I'm never turning off my . . ." she trailed off, skimming the email. Laryngitis. Her manager sending another one of his clients. Performed last night at the Ryman. She stopped short at the next five words, country *a cappella* group Storyhill. The anxiety she'd barely tamped down moments ago bolted up her neck.

"Avery, you're flushing." He reached his arm around her shoulder. "I need you to breathe."

"Please, please, please," she whispered, flopping into her chair. *Please let it be someone else. There are five men in the band.* The next two words jumped off the screen. A nightmare in black and white. *Matt Taylor.*

This wasn't happening. This was her big shot. She'd clawed her way up in an industry dominated by men to stand atop the heap and now, at the precipice of achieving all her dreams, a giant wrench was hurtling toward her head. *Not funny, universe. Not funny at all.*

She dumped one more antacid on her desk and popped it in her mouth.

"Four?" Ajay asked. "This hardly seems like a four situation."

Avery turned to the man who'd produced her show since she'd arrived in Nashville. They'd come up together, a packaged team. "Ajay, you don't understand. This guest . . ."

"Is Matt Taylor," her manager announced from the studio door, "the high tenor from the up-and-coming *a cappella* group Storyhill. Fresh off an unbelievable concert at the Ryman. Not to mention an epic proposal."

He'd proposed to someone? Seriously, Avery, that's none of your business. Focus on not letting this speed bump turn into a full-blown car crash.

Avery should have known something was up when Celeste was already in her office when Avery arrived. But why hadn't she said anything? Because she'd assumed Avery had seen the email. Fastidious Avery, who required a certain brand of pens, who did impeccable research, and who never missed a thing.

Plus, Celeste would have no way of knowing she'd detonated a bomb.

Avery gripped the edge of her desk with both hands, knuckles immediately white, and turned her chair toward the door. Maybe he wouldn't recognize her. Nine years had passed. She had a new name and a new hair color. Sucking in a breath, she lifted her eyes to the man standing next to Celeste, towering behind her like some sort of Norse god. They locked eyes and she sent up a silent prayer for anonymity.

His hand, braced on the door frame, slid down while he searched her face, finally settling on her eyes—about the only thing she hadn't changed since leaving the University of Oklahoma.

"*Amy-Lynn?*" he asked, his voice barely audible.

"Amy-Lynn?" Celeste said, her eyes moving between Avery

and Matt. "I didn't know anyone other than your mother and the government called you that."

"They don't." Avery forced the wobble from her voice. She hadn't been in radio for nearly a decade for nothing. Ajay might know about her anxiety, but Celeste would find out over her cold, dead body. "Unless they've known me since I was a kid," she said with a laugh that sounded as fake as it felt.

Avery rose from her chair, using the movement around the desk to rub her palms down her pants. She stuck her hand out to Matt, hoping no one noticed the slight tremor in her fingers. "Nice to see you again," she said with every ounce of crisp professionalism she could muster.

He stared down at her hand like it was covered in something smelly and rotten. She inched it closer to him, willing him not to make a scene, and he took it reticently. A bolt of electricity started in her fingertips and streaked up her arm. She dropped his hand as if burned.

"It's *nice* to see me again?" Matt asked, rubbing his hand down a very muscular thigh.

Huh. So he'd felt it, too.

"I didn't realize you two knew each other. How delightful."

Either Celeste was trying to smooth over the discomfort radiating off both of them, or she was oblivious. Avery hoped for the latter.

"That'll make this last-minute change easier," Celeste added.

Avery wrenched her gaze away from the man making her heart ram against her rib cage. "I have to admit that I missed your email last night, but I don't think this is a great idea, Celeste. I've had no time to research Mr. Taylor or his band."

Celeste looked at her, narrowing her eyes. Was Celeste surprised over her admission or was calling him Mr. Taylor a bit too much? She gave Avery a last glance before flashing a smile at Matt.

"Nonsense," Celeste said. "Clearly you've known each other for a long time. You can use the interview to reconnect."

"Celeste, is this really the way you want to kick off syndication?" Avery knew she was drawing too much attention to this. On the surface, she always rolled with things. Begging was out of character.

Celeste sighed and pinched the bridge of her nose. "I understand your concern, Avery, but what would you propose we do? We've been billing this show as THE place for country music interviews. I cannot let you go on without a second."

"Maybe we could call in a favor and . . ." The beginning of her next excuse leaked out of her mouth.

"The time to express your concerns was last night when I emailed you," Celeste said, cutting her off and effectively shutting down the conversation. "Ask your standard interview questions or go with the fact that you knew each other as kids. I'm not sure what the big deal is, Avery."

Avery fingered the soft spot at the base of her neck and nodded. Celeste had spoken. Continuing to argue would be fruitless. "Give me a minute." She walked toward the door that Matt filled. He no longer possessed the body of a boy. Or a mortal human. Clearly, she had missed the fact that he shared DNA with Thor.

He reached out and placed a hand on her shoulder. A surge of awareness shot through her. Nine years and her traitorous body still recognized his touch.

"Mac," he breathed.

Her eyes ricocheted from his hand to his eyes. Suppressed memories threatened to burst forth. She pushed them back into the box she'd kept them in all these years—unable to let them go but unwilling to revisit them.

"I need to collect a few things from my desk," she forced out. Everyone in the room, except Matt, would know it was a lie, but she didn't care. "Please move."

He turned sideways, letting her exit, and the pressure of his gaze sunk into her back as she moved down the hall, away from the studio.

This was cosmic penance for her sins. It was the only explanation.

Matt's eyes stayed fixed on the door. The studio fell silent if one didn't count the way his heart hiccupped in his chest.

He pressed his lips together. Though he was pretty sure that wasn't a good idea because he'd been holding his breath since he'd locked eyes with her.

He couldn't believe it.

Amy-Lynn McWilliams was country radio superstar Avery Lind.

That explained why all his Google searches had come up empty.

He forced out a breath and wheezed a ragged gulp back in. Until Andrew's proposal, he'd kept thoughts of her locked away —except on melancholy nights when he'd had a little too much to drink or the occasional cold pre-dawn hours when the lonely silence sucked all other thoughts from his mind.

He'd tried to do his homework. He really had. Last night, before falling face first into bed, he'd pulled up the station's website. He'd clicked on her bio. It was all about the show, nothing about her past, nothing that would have tipped him off. Her profile pic showed a woman laughing into the microphone. With the angle of the image, the bright raspberry colored hair, and the pierced nose, tired or not, he wouldn't have recognized her with a cursory glance. It was her eyes that gave her away. Eyes that were shadowed in the photo.

Everything in him told him to run. Run from the memories. Run from the pain. Run before he failed spectacularly. And he could do it. Before she returned. Feign a sudden migraine. Who cared if it made him look like an ass?

He sighed. He did. He cared. She'd taken everything from him once before. Matt straightened and fought to channel his rising righteous anger. *She left you. With a bogus excuse. And then refused to take your calls or respond to your texts. She shut you out, not the other way around.*

He wouldn't let her take this opportunity from him.

He could do this. He just needed to focus on the band, what this would mean for them—and for him.

"Matt?" Celeste said, breaking the silence.

He gave his head a shake, making sure not to dislodge any bit of the anger, and re-focused his attention on the diminutive station manager. "Is there anything else I need to know before we go on?"

Celeste's eyes flitted back to the door. "Ajay"—she pointed at the man hovering in the back of the booth — "will get you set up with headphones and explain what all the lights mean."

"I've been on the radio before." He wasn't a rookie—at interviews or at hiding his emotions. After years of practice, both came naturally.

"Great, great," she said absently, backing out of the studio. "I'm going to see if Avery located what she needed. Ajay, you're up."

The producer nodded to his boss and turned narrowed eyes on Matt. As soon as Celeste walked out of earshot, the man turned to him. "Do not mess this up for her. I don't know what your history is, but it doesn't take a genius to see it wasn't good—

or didn't end well, at the least. She's worked her arse off for years and this is her big shot."

Matt bristled. "I can play nice for one show. Can she?"

Ajay's eyebrows climbed his forehead. "One of you of is a nine-year veteran of the industry. One of you is not."

Matt held his gaze. "And one of us fled the room and one of us did not."

Ajay pulled out the chair opposite Amy-Lynn's and spun it toward him. "Sit."

Matt bit back a retort and lowered his frame into the chair. Ajay swung it back around a little too quickly and placed the headphones over his head, letting them slap over his ears.

"Easy man," Matt said, pulling the ear cup off his right ear.

"Don't screw up," Ajay said again, as if Matt was witless and needed another reminder.

"I'm not about to let my band down by making an idiot of myself."

Ajay left the room, only to reappear on the other side of the glass. He shot another glare at Matt before turning to his computer.

Matt ran his hands over the desk and stared at the empty chair across from him. Four hours of surface-level chatter. It was only one show, and then she'd slip back into the ether.

Brad was right. The promotion gods had dropped this in their lap, and if he wanted to prove he was more than a pretty face, this was the perfect place to start. He'd be witty and fun, like always, but even more, he'd be smart and articulate and show everyone the man underneath the 'million-watt smile.'

No matter the person sitting across from him.

CHAPTER THREE

AVERY FACED HER REFLECTION IN THE LADIES' ROOM mirror. She'd changed everything about herself. She'd packed up that small-town Oklahoma girl and reinvented her into a ball-busting, take-no-prisoners professional. She struggled and pushed herself to one of the top names in country music radio. She'd proven that women could survive—and thrive—in this male-dominated profession.

And for what?

To have her past run straight into her future on the biggest day of her life?

She shook her head. No, this was her world, and he was just a visitor here.

She straightened her spine, shook out her hands, and drew a steadying breath. "Amy-Lynn McWilliams is your past. Avery Lind is your future. You created her. He can't take her away," she whispered, reassuring her reflection.

If only that single, casual touch hadn't immediately obliterated the last nine years. An electric current arced between them, illuminating a flood of memories—recollections that all led to the same conclusion—that he was her forever.

But life had other plans.

"Avery?" Celeste stood just inside the door, taut lines of concern and grim determination co-mingled on her face. Her boss stepped up to the sink, studied her reflection in the mirror, and ran a hand over her blunt, black bob. If there was a hair out of place, Avery couldn't see it.

She wiped at the corners of her mouth assuring no lipstick had dared escape her perfectly lined lips. "I'm going to take a wild guess and say Matt Taylor was far more than a childhood acquaintance."

Avery titled her chin up. "Why do you say that?"

Celeste raised a single, perfectly arched eyebrow. "Because you are hiding in the bathroom and he looks like he's seen a ghost."

A ghost. Something you thought was dead.

She pulled her fingers into a fist to stop from rubbing the burning spot on her chest. "Fine. Yes. We have a history. But that is exactly what it is, history. We haven't spoken in nine years. It's not an issue."

"You're sure?"

"Of course." *As far as lies go, that's a whopper.* "Just surprised, that's all."

"You've thrown me for a loop, Avery. I've never known you not to read an email. Or flee to the ladies' room."

"You have nothing to worry about." Avery squared up her shoulders. "Nothing is going to stop me from making this the best show we've ever done."

"I believe that . . ."

"But?" Avery asked.

"But nothing." Celeste met Avery's gaze in the mirror. "Do you know why I hired you?"

"Because I never ask for overtime pay?"

Celeste snorted. "I have always appreciated that about you.

But no. I hired you because I knew you wouldn't stop until you got here."

Avery bit back a glimmer of a grin. "Here? You mean the bathroom?"

"To the top of the industry. I knew you would never let your personal life compromise your professional life."

That's because I don't have one.

"We have that in common," Celeste added.

Avery studied her boss's reflection. She'd always admired her. Celeste was fair, kind, and just tough enough not to take bullshit from anyone. She recently joked with Momma that she wanted to be Celeste when she grew up.

"Avery?"

"Hmm?" Avery said, her eyes popping up to meet Celeste's.

"I'm proud of you. You're one of the youngest women to make it to this level. This show puts both of us on the map. We've *both* worked our entire careers for this opportunity. Chances like this usually don't come around more than once in a career."

With a shaking hand, Avery pulled a paper towel from the dispenser and wiped it over the sprinkle of water droplets dotting the counter. "Great. No pressure."

Celeste placed her hand on top of Avery's and squeezed. "No pressure. Just go knock it out of the park like you've done every day since I hired you." Celeste crumpled up the towel Avery had been pushing around and threw it into the trash. "We good?"

Avery nodded. "Yes. We're good."

Celeste laughed softly, shaking her head. "I'm glad to hear that. I didn't have a plan B. I wasn't sure what else to say."

People often didn't know what to say to her. Because few people knew the real her. The one that battled unease, fear, and doubt every day. Only one person knew all of it. But Matt

Taylor knew Amy-Lynn McWilliams, he didn't know Avery Lind. And that's how it would stay.

She forced out a smile. "How about something like I've never let a man stand in my way and I shouldn't start today? That probably would have worked."

Celeste matched her smile and pivoted on her three-inch heels toward the door. "I thought that went without saying." She held the door open for Avery to pass through.

Avery laughed. It normally did, but she wasn't a skilled enough liar to convince herself that Matt Taylor was just any man.

Avery pushed open the studio door and strode over to her chair, keeping her eyes off the beautiful man sitting across from her. The spot where he'd touched her shoulder still tingled, and she couldn't afford any more distractions.

She punched a button on the board in front of her. "Is he ready to go, Ajay?" she said into the intercom.

"You can ask me that. I'm right here." His voice, the soft one she'd heard in her dreams for years after she'd broken it off, floated across the desk. "And you'll have to look at me eventually."

She readjusted her already perfectly positioned microphone. She straightened the single sheet of paper in front of her. Someone, probably Ajay, had printed out some Storyhill facts.

"Amy-Lynn."

Her head jerked up. "Don't call me that."

Matt lifted his hands in surrender. "No need to snap at me. We both want this to work."

"Oh really? You've been working for this moment for the last nine years?"

He held her gaze, unflinching. "In a manner of speaking,

yes." His blue eyes flashed, deepening to the sapphire color that appeared when he was angry—or aroused.

She stared back and did everything she could to dial her expression back to neutral. "It's just you *cannot* call me that on-air. Branding and all."

"Yeah, it's about the branding," he mumbled.

"What's that supposed to mean?"

"Avery, we're live in five minutes." Ajay's voice filled the studio, interrupting their staring contest. "Everything okay in there?"

She would not be the first one to break eye contact. She held Matt's gaze while giving Ajay a thumbs-up through the window. "I know this is an unwelcome surprise for both of us, but today is extremely important to me." She pointed a finger at him. "Now is the time to pull out the infamous Matt Taylor charm. You help me get through this first show, and you'll never have to think about me again."

He stared at her. One beat. Two beats. Three beats of silence. He sighed, dropped her gaze, and fisted his hand in his hair. "That's unlikely, Mac. You're the face of my past."

Her body flinched as she sucked in an involuntary shudder. Calling her Amy-Lynn would be better than calling her Mac.

"Fifty-nine seconds, Avery," Ajay announced.

"Amy-Ly—" She grimaced. "Avery," Matt corrected, lacing the name with something cold. "I won't ruin this for you. But just so we're clear, I'm not doing this for you. I'm doing it for my band—and for me."

Why did that statement bother her so much? It shouldn't matter. It's just that at one time he'd have done anything for her.

Never mind. It didn't matter. It didn't. She was Avery Lind, the new national voice of country radio. She dug down and pulled out the persona that had gotten her here.

The man sitting across from her was just one more test. A test she would pass, just like she'd passed all the others.

She looked up at the clock and caught Matt's eyes. She made a zipping motion across her lips and counted down from three on her fingers. The 'on-air' sign lit up and her familiar intro played and faded into the background.

"Good morning country music fans," she said into the microphone, letting a little of her Oklahoma twang slither through. To her ears she sounded natural, relaxed. She'd practiced this opening hundreds of times. She glanced at Ajay, and he gave her a thumbs up. "If you're a regular listener to the Avery Lind Show, you know today is a big day. Today, we get to share our love of country music with listeners across the country.

"We might have a few more people tuned in this morning, but our commitment to interviews, concert reviews, and quality music remains unchanged. However, most days Ajay and I— Ajay Bansal is my longtime producer and friend—say hello Ajay —soak up that luscious accent—are not going to be alone in the studio anymore. Starting today, we're bringing in country's biggest and rising stars to spend more time with us. We're giving you what no other show offers, a chance to really get to know the people behind the music.

"Today we're thrilled"—she caught Matt rolling his eyes— "to have one of those rising stars. Matt Taylor, member of country *a cappella* group, Storyhill, and fresh off a sold-out show at the Ryman, joins us in studio today. Matt, good morning."

She motioned for Matt to continue the conversation.

"Good morning, Avery. Or is it still the middle of the night?"

She forced out a laugh. "I realize it is early for you musician types, but much of our audience is up getting ready for work or getting their kids ready for school."

"Poor kids. My mom had to resort to filling a skillet full of bacon and making sure it wafted toward my bedroom to get me out of bed."

She laughed. For real this time. She remembered his mom joking about investing in companies that produced bacon—and almost said so.

Her smile dropped, he followed suit.

"I know you were expecting Addison May," he continued effortlessly. "Unfortunately, she has laryngitis and now you're stuck with me. I hope I'm not too much of a disappointment."

Stuck with him. There'd been a time when that had been her dream. She pinched her thigh and willed her attention back to the show. She ran a finger down the page of bullets about Storyhill and stopped at one, tapping her finger.

"If you are one of the million people who've viewed Story-hill's videos on YouTube, you know this man is hardly disappointing."

His expression shifted to something unfamiliar, but his voice came out steady and smooth. "And I sing as good as I look."

He laughed, but not enough had changed that she didn't know it was fake.

She shook off the desire to make sure he was okay. "We're going to hear all about Matt's experience at the Ryman last night, but first let's sample a couple of tracks from Storyhill's first all-original album."

Avery clicked her mouse and slid a headphone off one ear.

"Nice crack about how I look," Matt said, scrubbing his hand down his face.

"Isn't that the secret to your success?" She meant it to be teasing, but it came out sharp.

"What would you know about my success? You bolted before I even got started."

She stiffened. She supposed she deserved that, but she didn't have the luxury of letting this conversation escalate. "Looks like we both did okay for ourselves," she said, trying to pull this conversation back from the edge. "In fact, that is a great place to start. "In"—she eyed her computer monitor— "eighty-seven seconds I'll ask you some questions about where you got your start. Okay?"

"Fine."

He didn't look fine, but she didn't have time to worry about it.

"Welcome back. I'm here with Matt Taylor from the band, Storyhill. We just listened to a couple of the group's newest songs. They sound great, Matt."

"Thanks. Written by my band brother, Andrew Hayes and songwriting royalty, Grace O'Connor."

"Well, they clearly make a good team."

Matt nodded. "So good in fact, that they got engaged onstage last night at the Ryman."

So that was the proposal Celeste mentioned. Avery quickly pulled up Storyhill's Instagram account. A screen full of pictures flashed up. Photos of the proposal at the Ryman. Photos of the group's bass and the songwriter who broke her silence after the death of her husband to write for Matt's band. She should ask about that. It would be the easier thing to do. But her curiosity about Matt overwhelmed her judgement.

"We'll get to that proposal. It's clearly gone viral," she said, sounding like she knew all about it. "But you're here, let's get to know you. Our listeners love a good origin story. Inspire us. Tell us about the path that brought your band to the Ryman last night."

"I'm a bit of a late bloomer," Matt said, pulling the pop filter and

27

microphone closer to his mouth without dropping his gaze from hers. "I didn't really get started in the business until after I graduated from college. I went to the University of Oklahoma, majoring in—wait, don't I remember reading you also went to O.U.?"

Avery narrowed her eyes. "Yes. Yes, I did. But we're not here to talk about me."

"I bet your story is inspirational too." Matt raised an eyebrow, a clear challenge.

Avery laughed. Inspirational is not the word she would choose. "I have a strict rule here at the Avery Lind Show, I don't spill my secrets until the guest spills theirs."

"Do you have secrets, Amy—Avery?"

Long ago memories wrapped their fingers around her chest and squeezed. Secrets? Oh, she had secrets all right. Was that why Matt had showed up in her studio today? So that she could finally unburden herself. She normally didn't believe in serendipity, but . . .

"I want to hear about Dollywood," Ajay interjected, snapping Avery back to the present. She'd gone silent. Thank goodness Ajay never let dead air happen.

Matt seamlessly picked up the thread, shooting Avery a look that said he'd circle back around. His voice crackled through her headphones, muted by her swirling thoughts. Single words and short phrases punctuated the fog. Pigeon Forge. Dinner theater. Buy the album. Post questions at @AveryLindShow.

She tried to string them together, but the word 'secret' silenced all the other words. Was Matt fishing? Or looking for confirmation? Had he found out? No. No, that wasn't possible. The only person who knew was Momma, and she'd be the last person to spill Avery's secrets.

"Avery?"

She jumped, her eyes flashing to the man standing beside

her. "What are you doing in here?" she asked her producer. He was on the wrong side of the glass.

"I cued up a few more cuts from the Storyhill album."

She scanned the studio, her eyes landing on Matt's empty chair.

"I sent him to get coffee," Ajay said, reading her thoughts. "What is going on with you?" he whispered. "I've never had to cover for you, much less twice. If I do it again, Celeste will be in here."

She blinked up at him. Matt and Ajay were carrying *her* show—her newly syndicated show. She needed to snap out of it. Now.

"I'm fine, Ajay," she lied. "Just first day jitters."

He raised his eyebrows at her. "Your first day of jitters *ever*?"

Avery snorted. "Maybe?" The anxiety that plagued her disappeared the minute the 'on-air' light illuminated—and they both knew it. "Don't worry, I got this. Really," she added. She pasted on a smile designed to be reassuring, but based on Ajay's expression, she failed miserably.

"Sure, boss," he said, sounding anything but sure.

She'd just have to prove him wrong. "How long is this break?"

"Two songs, one's already played, and four ads. About five minutes remaining."

"Great," she said, rising from her chair. "I'll grab another cup of coffee, and I'll be back to my normal charming self."

"Charming? You better make that coffee a double . . . or a triple," he said, poking her shoulder.

She smirked. "Hey, I do a great imitation of charming."

She moved to exit the studio and turned directly into the man who was melting her brain.

He shoved a cup at her. "A splash of cream and two sugars. Unless that has changed, too."

Her eyes traveled from his face to the cup and back again. She shouldn't be surprised, he'd always paid attention to the details.

"No," she said, taking the cup, "that's still the same. Thank you. And I'm sorry about the last segment."

"Sorry for what?"

"I spaced out there for a couple of minutes."

He smirked. "No worries. It's not the first time someone's been distracted by all this." He gestured to his face and body.

"So humble." She punched him in the arm. And ran into solid muscle. It took everything in her not to wrap her hand around his bicep and squeeze. "Plus, I've seen it all before. Nothing new for me."

He cocked an eyebrow but remained silent.

Why had she said that? Fire rushed up her chest and warmed her face. *Way to keep it professional, Avery.*

"I guess the magnitude of going national got to me for a bit," she blurted, trying to backpedal.

"Forty-five seconds," Ajay announced, saving her *again*.

Matt reached for her, wrapping his fingers around her forearm.

She fought the urge to yank her arm away. He really needed to stop touching her. Why did he still have this effect on her?

"You're doing great, Mac. I'm sure no one noticed."

She noticed and that was all that mattered. She needed to shut down the Matt Taylor memories. And the touches. And the nicknames.

She ignored his compliment and dropped into her chair. A long list of listener questions popped up on her monitor— enough topics for the balance of the show. *Thank you, Ajay.* She could follow this trail of breadcrumbs, no heavy thinking required.

She pushed the slider to bring up her microphone. "Welcome back. If you are just joining us or are new to our program, I'm Avery Lind and in the studio with me today is Matt Taylor, one-fifth of the country *a cappella* band, Storyhill.

"Matt, it looks like you've struck a chord—pardon the pun—with our listeners. We've received a lot of questions, but there is a clear winner. Country music fans are curious whether you have a girlfriend or boyfriend?" Much as she hated to admit it, they weren't the only ones.

He stared at her until she squirmed under his gaze.

"You're quiet, Mr. Taylor. Is it taking you that long to count all your girlfriends?"

He chuckled. "I never was very good at math," he said, expertly evading her question. "But, no, I currently do not have a significant other. Though if it would help the show's ratings, I'd be happy to set up an application process. Should interested candidates tweet you?"

Oh no, he didn't. He did not just suggest she vet his next lover. "That's sounds like a full-time job, and I already have one of those."

"Too bad," he said, clearly biting back a smile. "Maybe a less complicated question, then?"

Avery scrolled through the questions. Was it normal for him to receive so many marriage proposals? "Let's see if I can find one," she said, buying time. "Okay, here's one. How did you come to be a member of Storyhill?" That seemed innocuous enough.

"The guys found me via YouTube. I went through a bad break-up right after graduating from college." His eyes locked on hers and all the air siphoned from her lungs. "I channeled the pain and emptiness into music. I wrote a few songs, covered a lot more, and posted the videos to YouTube. They found the videos and asked me to audition."

So not innocuous at all.

Steady, Avery. "It sounds like this break-up enabled your career. Something good coming out of something bad, right?" If he agreed, her plan had worked. *Please agree.*

"I don't think that's exactly how I'd describe it."

No way she was asking him to unpack that—on national radio.

"Let's bring this back around to music. Do you have a favorite song on this new album?"

Matt's shoulders slumped, but he answered the question and talked about how the group worked with their new songwriter. Nothing loaded. Nothing hinting at their history.

And that's the way it went for the final hour, a little music followed by listener questions until Ajay announced the successful end of their first ever syndicated show.

She dropped her headphones on the desk and sighed. She'd done it. She'd taken the first step to making herself a national name. And she'd done it with Matt Taylor across the mic from her. If she could do it in this circumstance, she could do it no matter the challenge.

Celeste appeared at the door with champagne and red plastic cups. "Time to celebrate," she said, lofting the bottle. "Join me in the break room?"

CHAPTER FOUR

CELESTE SENT THE CORK BOUNCING OFF THE BREAK ROOM walls, and Avery wanted nothing more than to rip the bottle from her hands, tip it back, and let the bubbles flow down her throat. But that would signify she was out of control. And Avery Lind was never out of control. Well, not on the outside, anyway.

She'd never run a marathon, but she expected this is what it felt like at the finish line. A sense of accomplishment anchored by extreme exhaustion.

Thankfully, it was over. A couple of sips of champagne, some cursory words, and she'd escape out the back door. Matt Taylor would go back to being just a memory.

Celeste poured the champagne, the foam effervescing over the side of the first cup, pooling onto the laminate table below. She passed out the glasses and lifted hers in the air. "To an absolutely amazing first syndicated show!"

Amazing? Maybe Matt was right. Maybe no one had noticed her missteps.

"I have reservations for the four of us this evening at Chez Louis, but until then—"

Wait, what?

"Four?" Avery asked, taking a sip, and paying attention to each bubble pop on her tongue.

"Oh, yes, Matt"—Celeste turned to him—"I hope you can join us."

Avery swallowed her midday champagne. She needed to pace herself, but Celeste wasn't making it easy. "I'm sure Matt is busy this evening."

"Nope. I'm completely open," he said, turning to the station manager and blessing her with one of his signature smiles.

Seriously? Did this man have more teeth than the average person? If she had a dollar for each time she'd seen him get out of trouble with nothing more than that smile, she'd . . . she'd . . . well, she wouldn't have had to work so hard for this opportunity. At one time it was cute, now it was just annoying.

"Thank you for asking, Celeste. I'd love to join you for a celebratory dinner. Plus," he said, turning that smile on her, "it'll give Avery and me a chance to catch-up."

Oh, no, no, no, there would be no catching up. Avery bit back a retort. No need to show Celeste how deeply Matt affected her. That would lead to too many questions.

If he could paste on a smile, so could she.

"Great. You should help us celebrate. It was a team effort, right Ajay?"

Ajay opened his mouth, but Celeste jumped in. "We received more fan interaction today than we normally get in a week. I'll deny this if asked, but I think Addison May getting sick was a blessing."

"That's likely because of the larger audience, not Matt specific," Avery said.

"The fifty-two marriage proposals say different."

Avery choked on her champagne and a bit dribbled down her chin. "Fifty-two?"

"Okay," Celeste said, laughing and handing Avery a napkin,

"only twenty-ish proposals, the rest requested dating applications."

Avery rolled her eyes. "His ego doesn't need feeding."

Matt laughed. "I'm glad it all worked out."

The station manager turned to Matt. "It more than worked out. In fact,"—she hesitated, giving Avery a quick glance— "I spoke with the program director and if you're willing, we'd like you to co-host with Avery—"

Avery gasped. *Oh hell no.* "No way! What happened to girl power and all that? One day in and you're throwing a man at my show?"

"Hey now," Ajay interjected, "right here."

"You're not a man," she stumbled.

Ajay cocked an eyebrow. "Excuse me?"

Avery flapped a hand between them. "I mean, you're a show staple. You're not some random guy with no experience who just showed up one day."

Matt's smile faded. "I'm hardly random, Mac."

Avery turned her back on Matt and addressed her boss. "Celeste, this not what we discussed."

"I do travel a fair amount," Matt conceded.

Celeste laughed. She actually laughed. Apparently, the destruction of Avery's life was funny.

Celeste set her cup on the table. "You didn't let me finish. I have no intention of hiring Matt permanently. Our ad revenue doesn't justify something like that."

"Yet." It was out of Avery's mouth before she could stop it.

An eyebrow inched up Celeste's forehead. "I thought you didn't want him here?"

Dammit. "I didn't. I don't. I just meant our ad revenue will grow." She really needed to shut her mouth.

"Matt would only co-host until he left on tour. That's probably a couple of weeks?" She looked at Matt for verification.

"Three," he confirmed.

Avery dumped the balance of her champagne down the break room sink and grasped for any mental straw. "Celeste, Matt does not want to spend his mornings here at the station."

Matt cleared his throat. "Matt can speak for himself."

Her fingers curled into fists. "What will he do? We already have all the guests lined up for the next month."

Celeste shook her head. "We're not getting rid of the guests. Matt will interview them with you. It'll be fine, Avery. Most morning shows have a whole gaggle of people."

"That's what makes this show different—rotating co-hosts. Keeping it fresh and all that. Isn't that what you said?"

Celeste's lips fell into a straight line. "Nothing changes long term. We'll just use Matt to help build the initial momentum for the show, then we'll transition back to the original plan."

"Don't you think that will confuse the audience?" She tried to modulate her voice, but it kept creeping from low-radio-ready-alto to you-cannot-be-serious-soprano.

"No, I don't," Celeste answered, her voice perfectly calm, of course. "Avery, you're always the first person to jump on a marketing opportunity if it helps the show. Why is this any different?"

Celeste was not this obtuse. She knew exactly why this was different. Even if she didn't know the exact details, she knew they had a history. *I knew you would never let your personal life compromise your professional life. We have that in common.* Celeste's words from this morning clanged in her ears. Until today, Avery had always put the show ahead of everything else. And now Celeste was doing exactly that. Putting the show ahead of Avery's discomfort.

But 'everything else' had never included an ex. An ex that was hotter than should be legal. He mixed up all the wires in her head. If she couldn't stop this and had more days like today, it'd be her out of a job, not him. And that couldn't happen, not with four people depending on her salary.

"Avery?" Celeste said, breaking into her growing panic.

Her head popped up and she blinked, trying to clear the dots of light dancing in front of her eyes. "What?"

"I need you to get on board."

Celeste-speak for 'the decision is made, stop fighting it.'

"He hasn't said yes." *Stellar closing argument, Avery. Now she'll totally change her mind.*

Both women turned to Matt. Both waiting for him to do the right thing. Each having a vastly different idea of what that meant.

Matt flashed a single look at Avery before turning to the station manager. "This would be a great opportunity to get more exposure for Storyhill. Let me discuss it with my agent and manager, but barring anything unforeseen, I'm in."

All the hope flowed out of Avery, pooling around her ankles. Great. Three weeks with Matt Taylor. Whether she liked it or not. There wasn't an agent or manager in this world who'd oppose Celeste's offer.

"Perfect!" Celeste clapped her hands. "I'll draw up a simple contract and we can discuss it this evening."

"Don't worry, love, I'll sit between you and him at dinner," Ajay whispered in her ear.

She sighed. She appreciated Ajay's support, but she doubted it would matter. Despite everything, she was as drawn to Matt Taylor now as she had been at sixteen. She wasn't getting rid of him. And he'd be hard to avoid.

Meaning, for the next three weeks, she had to add three more items to her already overloaded plate: do not get sucked back into his orbit, keep all interactions strictly professional, and absolutely no walking down memory lane.

What could possibly go wrong?

. . .

Avery kicked off her shoes and threw her handbag on the sofa. What a day. What a night. And, if Matt signed on the dotted line, she had many more challenging days and nights ahead of her.

She really couldn't fault Celeste—as much as she wanted to. It was hard to determine what was bothering her the most. That he'd shown up and thrown a wrench into what was supposed to be the best day of her life or that he'd waltzed into her studio and done what he always did, flashed his big smile and gotten whatever he wanted.

"Amy-Lynn? Is that you? How was your big day?"

Avery walked into the small, but cozy living room she shared with her mother, sister, and nephew in East Nashville. Her mother sat covered in an afghan, cuddled into the plush recliner she insisted on bringing from her former house. In her lap sat the beginnings of a hand-stitched quilt.

Avery walked to the lamp beside her mother and turned up the brightness. "Momma, you know the doctor said that was hard on your eyes."

"Nonsense. I've been doing this my whole life. I barely need to look at it. I won't let this terrible disease take away all of my favorite things."

Avery smiled a soft smile and sat down next to her mother. "And people think I'm stubborn."

"You are," her mother said, patting her hand.

Avery chuckled. "Well, it's clear where I learned it. And speaking of stubborn, where are Jess and Wyatt? The house is quiet."

"Wyatt's already in bed, and I sent Jess out to pick up ice cream to have with our cake. We have to celebrate my little girl being a big radio star."

Avery pulled her hair back into a ponytail, tugged, and let it fall back to her shoulders. "Oh, Momma, did you listen to the show?"

Isabel McWilliams laid her sewing down and eyed her daughter over the top of her glasses. "Of course. You were spectacular as usual, my dear."

"Momma."

Isabel smirked. "Fine. Yes, of course I listened, though Addison May sounded a little more masculine than I expected."

Avery rolled her eyes and pointed a single finger at her mother as the door flew open and her tornado of a sister hurtled into the room—in a sequined blouse, sweatpants, and stilettos. She set a quart of buttered pecan on the small dining table and threw off her coat. "Oh. My. God. Amy-Lynn. You're finally home. Didn't you get any of my texts?"

"I saw them." Avery's eyes flashed to the ice cream, condensation already dripping down the carton. "You going to put that in the freezer?"

"It can wait," Jess said. "A few minutes won't matter."

Avery sighed. Typical Jess. Nothing was a priority for her little sister. Not even melting ice cream.

"Sissy, seriously. You go to work—to your new, big-ass gig expecting Addison May and you wind up with Matt-effing-Taylor? What the actual hell?!"

"Did someone mention cake?" Avery asked.

"It's in the refrigerator," Isabel said.

Avery walked to the fridge, pulled out a white box tied with candy cane striped string and peeked inside. Her favorite. Coconut cake with coconut frosting. She turned to her mother. "You ordered this," she said with a smile. "They don't just have these on the shelves."

"I couldn't very well let this day go by without doing something, could I?"

"Hello?" Jess yelled. "You guys are actually going to talk about cake when the great love of Amy-Lynn's life just pops up NINE YEARS LATER on her show?" She pulled the cake box from Avery's fingers.

"Hey!"

"Hey, nothing. Did you know about this?"

"I did not."

Jess's mouth fell open. "Celeste sprung it on you?"

Avery rubbed the spot between her collarbones and steeled her features in the way she had been practicing since her father passed away almost fifteen years ago. She didn't want her mother or sister to see how unsettled today's show made her. "In fairness, Celeste sent me an email last night—which I didn't see. And, she would have no way of knowing that Matt and I have any sort of history."

Jess walked into the kitchen and rummaged through the cabinets and drawers for plates and forks. She returned holding a large chef's knife and pointed it directly at Avery. "Sort of history? The one great true love of your life is now just *some sort of history*? I will cut you a piece of cake, but I demand all the juicy details."

"Nothing to tell. We didn't really talk." Avery shrugged. "I guess the only thing you didn't hear was Celeste asking him to co-host with me until his band leaves on tour again."

Jessica spun, knife still in hand, and her mother stopped midway in her rise from the recliner.

"I'm sorry mi hija, what did you just say?"

"Momma, it's your eyesight that's going, not your hearing. He did a good job. Celeste asked him to stay." Avery snuck into the kitchen and pulled out her secret stash of extra-strength antacids and popped a handful before returning to her mother and sister, who were now sitting at the table staring at her.

"What are you going to do?" Jess said. "And remind me,

why did you break up with the hottest man in Oklahoma, the man who wanted to marry you?"

Avery ignored the second part of her sister's question. That information was strictly on a need-to-know basis, and as far as she was concerned, her sister never needed to know. "I'm going to do my job, just like always. The job that pays for this house and all our bills. This is just another challenge—and one I plan on facing and then moving on. And I will hold him to the same standards I expect of everyone and if he can't take it, then he can just leave."

"Amy-Lynn." Her mother's brow furrowed with concern. "It might not be that easy."

"I'll be fine. Like always." She waved her mother's concerns off. "I didn't work this long and hard to let the likes of Matt Taylor ruin it for me. I'll do it so well, in fact, that Celeste will realize I don't need a co-host."

Her mother didn't seem convinced, but her sister bought it. "Damn, Amy-Lynn, if it was me? I don't think I could do it. If it was my ex, and he looked like Matt Taylor, I'd spend every minute flip-flopping between yelling at him and wanting to throw him on the floor and screw him right there."

"Jessica!" Isabel shook her head.

"Sorry, Momma," Jess said, pulling a face and rolling her eyes. "But it's true."

"Sometimes I wish I could put the two of you in a blender and hit mix."

"I'm sorry?" Avery asked.

"Then I'd have two balanced girls. Jessica would be a little less impulsive—and forthright—and you'd let loose once in a while."

Avery blew out a breath. It was her turn to roll her eyes. "I let loose plenty."

Jessica nearly snorted cake out of her nose. "Uh-huh. That's you, the family free spirit."

Avery whirled on her sister. Matt Taylor—and Celeste—had exhausted her normal filters. "I'm sorry, but when you want to help around here financially, maybe I can."

"Girls."

Jessica raised her hands in defeat. "Fine, Momma." But then she turned to Avery. "I watched a few Storyhill videos a while back and damn, but that boy grew up nice. I don't know how you're going to keep your hands off him."

"Jess, we haven't seen each other in nine years. Any spark that existed is long gone."

Jess cocked an eyebrow. "If you say so. But, if I remember right, there was a lot more than sparks between the two of you. You two were a full-on, raging out-of-control, forest fire."

She remembered. No matter how much she tried to forget. But no way was she admitting that to her nosy sister. Matt Taylor was only an issue if she let him be one. "Give me a piece of that cake and let's celebrate."

Avery carved out a large chunk of cake, and her mouth watered as she raised the sugary goodness to her lips. "Mmm," she said, licking the frosting from her fork. Maybe cake really was the answer to all life's problems. "Wyatt's not going to like that we ate this without him."

At the sound of her son's name, Jessica startled. She looked to the stairs, staring briefly, before dropping her gaze to the empty plate in front of her. "So. Everybody happy? All full of cake?"

Isabel nodded and Avery turned to her sister, an eyebrow cocked. She recognized that tone of voice. "Why?" she asked.

"Well," Jess said, adding extra 'e's' into the short word.

"Oh my god, Jess," Avery said, letting her fork clatter to the plate. "Please do not tell me you got fired again."

"No," Jess said, "not exactly." Avery gestured for her to go on. "I quit."

"Why? Why? Why?" Avery begged. This would be the third job Jess had lost in the last six months. Her sister was only eighteen months younger, but they couldn't be more different. Where Avery was planned and steady, Jessica was flighty—she called it spontaneous. Insert eye roll. She wondered if Jess realized she got to be the "free spirit" because Avery paid the bills, filled the cupboards with food, and cleaned up Jess's messes?

Jessica wiped a smudge of frosting from her plate. "It stifled my creativity," she said, her finger still in her mouth.

Avery pressed her fingers into her temples. "Jess! When will you learn some responsibility? You are a mother!"

"Amy-Lynn," her mother chided.

"No, Momma, you're too nice to say anything, but this has to stop. I don't want to work with Matt Taylor, but you don't see me quitting." She turned to her sister. "If it wasn't for Wyatt, I'd throw you out right now." She started for the stairs and swiveled on her sister. "You have six months to figure things out and then you are out of here."

Jess gasped. "You can't do that!"

"This is my house. I most certainly can." Anxiety and guilt blossomed in her gut, but she ignored it. Her sister needed some tough love.

"Don't take your frustrations with Matt Taylor out on me."

Her twenty-nine-year-old, job-quitting sister had the audacity to act like this was Avery's problem.

Avery pointed a single finger at her sister. Jess wasn't wrong. She was taking the day's stress out on her, but her message was still on-point. It was the delivery that lacked finesse. Enough was enough. "Six months."

"Momma!" Jess said.

Isabel looked at Avery. "What if she pays rent?"

"And how is she supposed to do that without a job?"

"I'll get one. I'll pay rent."

Avery's shoulders fell in defeat. "We'll talk about it tomorrow." Didn't Jess see that quitting yet another job put more stress on Avery? Now, because of Jess's actions, Avery would have to earn even more money and put in extra time to get more stations to syndicate the show—all while trying to avoid the all-too-sexy Matt Taylor.

A clear recipe for disaster.

CHAPTER FIVE

MATT SWUNG A DENIM-CLAD LEG OVER THE TOP OF A cracked vinyl barstool. The chair wheezed out a dramatic, malt-scented sigh as the cushion dipped under his weight. He peeled the sole of his boot off the sticky floor, hooking his heel on the lowest wooden rung. What this place lacked in ambience, it made up for in cheap beer and lack of tourists.

It was the first place he thought of when, as soon as dinner was over, he'd sent out the Bat-Signal.

For the briefest of seconds, he'd considered signing Celeste's contract before leaving the restaurant, but something stopped him. Okay, not something. Amy-Lynn stopped him, or more specifically, the look in her eyes stopped him.

For most of the awkward, uncomfortable dinner, she'd avoided looking at him. But when she did, the anxiety floating in her eyes was undeniable, making him feel like a total jerk for even considering the offer.

But.

He wanted to do this. He'd walked into that studio this morning with a chip on his shoulder. He was there to prove something. But then, even with Amy-Lynn sitting across from him, he'd started to enjoy himself. And by the end of the show, he realized he was pretty good at the whole radio thing.

But.

It was clear she didn't want him there.

Thus, the Bat-Signal.

"Nice of you guys to wait for me," he said to Nick and Blake, pointing at the half-empty pitcher on the table.

"You never send out distress signals," Blake said. "We figured we better get a head start."

Matt snorted. "Wow, you can rationalize anything, can't you?"

Blake nodded. "One of my superpowers. Lay another one on me. Challenge me. I can reframe or rationalize anything."

Matt would prefer to wait for the other guys to get here, but maybe a smaller audience would make this easier. "Okay, how about this? I had that radio gig this morning, right? Well, they asked me to co-host until we leave on tour."

Blake furrowed his brow. "I don't get it. That's not something I need to reframe, Mattie. That sounds like a no-brainer. Have Brad and your agent review the legal stuff, and if it checks out and you want to do it, do it."

If only it were that easy.

"Wait, just a second," Nick said, ever the cautious voice of reason. "Just like that? They want you to keep doing it after a single show?" Nick topped off his beer, slowly pouring from the side, trying to minimize the head.

Blake pushed a finger underneath the pitcher. "Not everything has to be perfect. Just pour the beer, mate." He looked up at Matt, pointing a finger at him. "Though Mr. Slow Pour makes a point. It does seem quick."

What did they mean by that? Did they think he couldn't do it? Did they think he would screw up given another chance?

"No one likes a guy who comes fast and peaks early,"

rumbled a deep voice from behind him. They all turned to see Andrew sliding onto an empty stool.

"Never my problem, old man." Matt scanned the bar. "Where's Joe?"

"Joe and I are not attached at the hip," Andrew said, signaling the server for a glass and a second pitcher.

"Yeah, he has a woman for that now." Blake drained his pint and smirked. "Did Joe take the break-up hard?"

"Poor Julia. If the bromance is truly over, think about how much more Joe will be at home." Nick let out a low whistle and laughed at his own joke.

"You guys are hilarious," Andrew said. "And if you want to feel sorry for Julia, you should've started years ago. Like the day she said, 'I do.'"

Matt impatiently tapped the table next to Andrew's hand. "Is Joe coming or not?"

Andrew eyed Matt with suspicion. "Does he need to be here? Your text indicated this was a personal matter. Is it about the band?"

Matt fisted his fingers in his hair. "No. It's personal. It'd just be easier to tell this story once."

"That sounds ominous," Andrew said, pouring a beer from the recently delivered pitcher.

"Ominous? You learn that fancy word from your new fiancé?" Nick said.

Matt leaned back on his stool and sighed. "You jokers about done?"

Three sets of eyes turned to look at him. Eyes widening at his sharp tone. It was totally out of character, and he couldn't care less. It had been a crazy-long day. And he was flat out of Matt Taylor charm.

Andrew's smile faltered. "Joe is having dinner with the in-laws. You didn't give us much notice."

"I don't have much time," Matt said, tapping his Apple watch awake. "I need to make a decision in the next few hours."

"Okay," Andrew said. "Catch me up. Did I overhear that the radio station wants you to be on the show again?"

Matt nodded and topped off his beer. "Not just again. Apparently, the response to today's show was so good that she—the station manager—wants me to co-host for the next few weeks."

"That sounds cool. What's the issue?" Andrew said.

Blake snapped his fingers. "Oh, I get it. It's radio. No one will see your pretty face. You're worried without that you'll flop."

Matt stiffened. He knew Blake was kidding, but it hit a little too close to home. "Hey, I have more going for me than just my looks."

They all laughed. "Sure," Blake said. "Sure, you do."

"To be fair," Andrew started.

"Thank you." Matt clapped his hand on his bandmate's shoulder.

"He can sing a little too—when the rest of us aren't carrying his sorry ass."

Matt forced out a laugh. "Funny." *Not.* He knew the guys were just yanking his chain. They'd have no way of knowing how deep those jabs cut. He'd certainly never told them. He learned a long time ago that when you looked like he did, people assumed you couldn't possibly understand pain and difficulty—like good looks were some sort of magical shield.

"Mattie, what's wrong?"

Matt turned toward the decidedly unmasculine voice to find Grace standing next to him.

Blake groaned. "I thought this was guy's night. Andrew, I do not need to see your sickening bliss again tonight. Let us single guys have our peace."

Grace chuckled and kissed her fiancé on the cheek. "Don't worry, I'm meeting some friends over there. We're doing a little preliminary wedding planning before Bridget leaves town." She pointed to a group of women huddled in the corner. "But, if you tamp down the testosterone a notch, you'll see that something is really bothering Mattie. It's written all over his pretty face."

Matt sighed. There it was again.

"Grace," Bridget called, waving. "Over here."

Grace turned to her friends and raised a 'one-minute' finger. "I can't very well keep my future sister-in-law waiting," Grace said, squeezing Andrew's shoulder. "But seriously, one of you needs to help erase that terrible expression from Matt's face."

"When did Bridget get into town?" Blake asked. "She's a little far from home, isn't she?"

Andrew wrenched his gaze away from his fiancé, and his forehead wrinkled. "She's as far away from home as you are."

Blake shrugged and traced a drop of condensation down his glass. "Yeah. But I was here to perform."

"I got her tickets for the concert. She insisted on being here for the proposal." Andrew turned in his chair to face Blake. "Wait. Why do you care?"

"I don't. Just curious." Blake's alabaster skin flushed pink around the edges, matching his auburn hair.

"That better be all," Andrew said, raising his eyebrows at Blake. "My sister is off-limits, Casanova."

Blake raised his hands in surrender. "Sue me for being interested in your family."

Matt rapped his knuckles on the table. "Guys, I have a real problem here."

Andrew stared at Blake for a beat longer before spinning toward Matt. "Okay, Grace's intuition is always spot on, so I'm guessing this is more than run-of-the mill nerves?"

"That's probably why he sent the Bat-Signal," Nick said, rolling his eyes.

"Are there parts of the gig you're not comfortable with?" Andrew said, probing deeper.

Matt wiped the condensation off his glass and rubbed his hands down his pants. "Yes, but it's not the job duties."

"Yeah, cause god knows how much you like to talk into a microphone," Blake teased. They broke into laughter again, but sobered when Matt didn't join in.

"Okay, now you're freaking me out. What's the deal?" Nick said, setting his glass on the tabletop.

Matt traced the outline of the beer coaster resting in front of him. "Any of you know Avery Lind? The show's host?"

"I've seen some pictures of her," Blake answered. "Hot. Hair like a red-velvet cupcake. A big deal in the Nashville radio scene."

His stomach turned over at Blake's description. He did not get to call Amy-Lynn 'hot.'

Was he jealous?

Really? After all these years?

He pushed the thought away. "Soon to be a big deal *nationally*—after this morning."

"You're nervous because it's a national show? Because, dude, Storyhill could really use that kind of exposure." Andrew brought his beer to his lips and held it there, waiting for Matt's answer.

Matt nodded and bumped his fist against the table. "I know. That's why I'm leaning toward saying yes, but . . ."

Andrew set his glass back on the table. "But?"

Matt cringed. "But Avery and me . . . we have a history."

Blake snorted. "Is that it? Don't you have a 'history'"—he made air quotes— "with half the ladies in Nashville? Tennessee? Oklahoma . . ."

He didn't. But that wasn't the image he'd cultivated. Or rather, the image others had cultivated for him. Through the years, people talked—and he'd never corrected them. Seemed 'ladies' man' was an ideal fit with the rest of his manufactured brand.

The corner of Nick's mouth kicked up and his head tipped. "And you didn't put two and two together when Brad offered you the gig?"

Matt's chin dropped to his chest. "No," he breathed out.

"How is that possible?" Nick said.

"Because to me she's Amy-Lynn McWilliams, not Avery Lind."

"This is the exact reason I don't believe in stage names," Nick added.

"You would if you had women showing up at your house all the time," Blake said, shaking his head.

Andrew scoffed. "Yeah, you hate that."

"Seriously, you guys are like a bunch of babies being offered candy tonight. Can you focus? For, like, ten minutes? I'd like to get a little sleep tonight."

"Right, right," Andrew said, turning his attention back to Matt. "So, this Amy-Lynn was—"

"The One," Matt said, finally ripping off the band-aid.

They all looked up from their beers and stared at him, unblinking.

"Whoa," Blake said, his glass floating in mid-air. "Matt Taylor had a serious girlfriend. I feel like my world has been shaken from its axis. I'm gonna need another beer. And some additional information."

"It's pretty much your standard boy meets girl story." Matt twisted his hands in his lap and shrugged. "We met in high school. She moved to Marla with her mom and sister right after her father died in the Iraq war. She was sad and lost, so I invited her to a party and that was it."

"Was what?"

Matt paused at Nick's question. He'd told these guys most everything about his life, but not this. He'd kept all his memories of Amy-Lynn to himself. Kept them sacred. "She was it for me. That party was the last time I was single until we graduated from OU."

"What happened?" Nick said.

Matt scrubbed his hand down his face. "That's the thing, I don't know. I've been over it a million times in my head, and I can't figure it out. One day it was good—so good—and the next day I got down on one knee . . . and she bolted."

Blake pushed his chair back from the table, his mouth hanging open. "Seriously, folks. First a serious girlfriend and now a marriage proposal? Skip the glass, the next *pitcher* is mine."

"Don't listen to him." Andrew put an elbow into Blake's ribs. "This is the first time you've seen her in nine years?"

"Yep. She texted me a few days after the proposal, saying she was sorry, but she couldn't be with someone who planned on traveling all the time. It would be too much of a reminder of her father's deployments."

"A text sucks, but what she said makes sense, I guess." It was the first time Blake had said anything serious since Matt sat down.

"It would, except we'd talked about it—a lot. I didn't ask her to marry me on a whim, we'd been discussing it, seriously, for over a year." Matt tapped his fist against the table. "I know it was nine years ago, but taking the job . . . honestly, it feels a little weird."

"How'd she act toward you?" Nick asked.

Matt raised a single shoulder. "Somewhere between totally

irritated and coolly professional?"

Blake chuckled. "I'd have paid big money to meet the one woman who's immune to the Matt Taylor charm."

That wasn't always the case.

Nick ignored Blake's ribbing, and as always, got to the heart of the matter. "How much do you want to do it?"

So much, a little voice whispered, before he'd even had time to consider the question. *It's my chance to prove to people that I'm more than the way I look.*

And I might finally get the answers I've craved for almost a decade.

A tremor pulsed up his spine. That hadn't even crossed his mind until this very moment. Was he considering this gig for reasons that had nothing to do with proving himself?

"Mattie?" Andrew said.

"I'd be crazy to pass up this much free promo for Storyhill."

"That's not a real answer," Nick countered. "This isn't about Storyhill." Nick held up a hand when Andrew's mouth dropped open. "It's about what *you* want."

Matt nodded slowly. "I want it," he said. "But what do you guys think?"

A cacophony of opinions rose, drowning out any decipherable words.

"One at a time, babies," Matt said. He pointed at Andrew. "You first."

Andrew knocked his knuckles together. "A national radio show with an expiration date? If it won't fuck with your head too much, I'd do it. It has the potential to help Storyhill and who knows what doors it could open for you personally."

It was like Andrew read his mind. One vote in the yes column.

"Nick?" Matt said, turning to the most cautious member of the group.

Nick drew in a breath and tipped his head back, staring at the ceiling. "I'd do it."

"Really?" If anyone would caution him not to do it, he figured it would be Nick.

"Yeah," Nick nodded. "I second all the stuff Andrew said. Especially the part about the expiration date. It's not like this is a forever thing. Plus," he said, gazing off into the distance as if the thought he was chasing was out there, just out of reach. "You might figure out why she bolted."

Matt's eyes widened. Maybe he'd been underestimating these idiots. Maybe they understood him better than he thought.

"Okay," Matt said, turning to the final member present. "Blake?"

"I don't think I'd be comfortable working with an ex. My vote is a 'thanks, but no thanks.'"

Andrew rolled his eyes. "Don't listen to him, Mattie. He's only saying that because his relationships always end badly."

Blake scoffed. "Dismiss me, if you will, but I have two words for you—Restraining Order."

Matt laughed. He loved these guys. They were the best brothers he could ask for. "I will keep that in mind, Blake." He tipped back the remains of his beer. "What do you think Joe would say if he was here?"

All eyes turned to Andrew.

"You're probably glad he's not here," Andrew said, pulling a face.

"Because?" Matt asked.

"That dude is a hopeless romantic. He'd likely to tell you to take the gig and woo back the lady while you're at it. And while I'm the last person to warn you away from mixing business and pleasure, following that advice has the very real possibility of blowing up in your face," Andrew said.

"When do you have to let the station manager know?" Blake

asked.

"By tomorrow morning."

"Sleep on it. It'll likely be clearer in the morning." Nick clapped Matt on the shoulder. "Now, sorry to advise and run, but I gotta get Henry from my mom's before it gets any later."

"And I need to extract Grace from that booth before Bridget convinces her to plan some larger-than-life New York City wedding-shenanigan," Andrew said, rising from his barstool.

"And I have to extract Bridget—"

Andrew whirled on Blake, thrusting a finger into his chest. "Don't even joke about that."

Blake laughed and put his hands up in surrender. Again.

"Blake. Andrew. Opposite sides of the crib," Matt said, chuckling. "And, guys, thanks for coming."

"I hope we helped," Nick said.

Matt nodded. "You did."

"Walk out together?" Blake said, dropping a few bills on the table.

Matt followed Blake and Nick, weaving through the sparsely populated tables, and stepped out into the humid night air. He thanked them again and slipped into his car. The contract laid on the passenger seat, illuminated in a flickering beam of yellow light from the parking lot lamp post.

Should he sign it?

He wanted Andrew to be right. He wanted this to be something that opened doors for him.

He wanted Nick to be right. He wanted answers.

He couldn't have either if he didn't at least try.

And when was the last time he really tried?

Without further thought, he grabbed the contract and scrawled his signature on the black line. And before he could second guess himself, he snapped a picture of it and texted the pic to Celeste.

CHAPTER SIX

AVERY SLIPPED A HAND FROM UNDER THE SHEET AND turned off her alarm. It hadn't rung. It never did. She didn't need it anymore. Five days a week, for the last five years, her schedule was the same. Get up at 4:00 a.m. Shower. Get dressed. Make her lunch. Set out Momma's medications. Fill her insulated coffee mug. Lock the door. Check the lock. And arrive at the studio promptly at 5:30 a.m.

It wasn't clear how her body knew the difference between Sunday and Monday, but she was certain of one thing, schedules meant stability.

She rolled over and blinked until the swirls in the textured ceiling came into focus. If setting her alarm wasn't part of her bedtime routine, she'd likely never turn it on again.

After her father died, a routinized schedule had been a necessity. She needed to maintain her 4.0 GPA to get a college scholarship. She picked up a job at the local grocery store to help Momma cover the bills. She designed spreadsheets to manage her father's military benefits. She set her alarm clock ten minutes early to rouse her rule-phobic sister.

She stepped into the vacancy her father's death created.

She quickly learned that following a carefully crafted agenda ensured no surprises.

How'd that work out for you yesterday, a little voice mocked.

Yes, Matt Taylor was unexpected—and about as welcome as any other surprise in her life.

She threw back the sheet and twisted to an upright position. There was no room in her schedule to think about the man who'd danced (unbidden) through her dreams last night. She would deal with him when—if—he showed up at the station this morning.

5:25. She'd checked off all her morning duties and still arrived at work five minutes early. That had to be a good sign, right?

A rap sounded on the car window, and her hand flew to her heart. Turning, a face both familiar and foreign stared at her.

Fifteen days, she reminded herself. Only sixty hours of studio time and then they'd go their separate ways. Again.

It was just a small deviation from her plan. Nothing more.

She motioned for him to step back and swung the car door open. "I guess this means you signed the contract?" she said instead of the easy, nonplussed 'good morning' she'd planned. This would not work if her mouth continued to have a mind of its own.

The smile faded from his face. "I did."

She collected her bags from the backseat. *Why is he here? Why?*

"For my band," he said.

She spun on him. Had she said that out loud?

"Let me take those." He reached for her bags and slung them over his shoulder.

Guilt swamped her. He had every reason to hate her, and yet he was being as kind as ever. Kindness she didn't deserve.

Panic coiled through her chest. *Calm down, Avery. Passing out in the parking lot is not a good way to start the day.*

"Hey, you okay?" he asked, leaning down to look into her eyes.

No. No. No. She couldn't bear his sympathy. *Say something. You speak for a living.*

She cleared her throat. Or tried to. "I'm just tearing up from the smell of your hat."

He bit back a smile and squeezed the brim of his ball cap. "That's blasphemy. My lucky hat does not stink."

She looked up—way up. The stitching that once read 'Marla Wildcats' had frayed. Only six letters remained. 'La Cats.' Like he was some fancy French foreign exchange student instead of a boy athlete from the middle-of-nowhere, Oklahoma.

"Are you telling me that's *not* the same hat you wore when your baseball team went to the state finals in high school?"

Matt placed a hand over his heart, feigning indignation. "It is. But I have learned how to do laundry since then, Mac."

She smirked and shot him a look. "There is not a detergent strong enough to rinse out eighteen-year-old flop sweat. *Boy* flop sweat."

"Just for that"—he whipped the hat from his head and squashed it over her hair— "you need to smell it up close."

She laughed as it slipped down over her eyes. "Matt, take it off!"

"Not until you admit it doesn't stink."

She inhaled a deep breath. It didn't stink. It smelled like her memories. Cinnamon. Leather. Sunshine. Matt.

"Say it," he goaded.

Her smile faltered. She pulled off the hat and handed it back to him. "Matt, what are we doing?"

He settled the hat back on his head. "I don't know about you, but I'm defending my honor. No part of me stinks."

"No, Matt, how is this going to work?" She grabbed his forearm, and his gaze flashed to where her hand rested. Her fingers buzzed, and she withdrew her hand before the tingle worked itself up her arm and into her heart. "We can pretend all we want, but this"—she motioned between them— "will not be easy. I've worked so hard for this opportunity. I can't afford any distractions. I can't let anything screw it up."

His blue eyes turned to ice. The laughter replaced with instant irritation. "Anything? Don't you mean *anyone*? It's been nine years, Amy-Lynn, maybe give the man I am now a chance to prove himself before assuming he's the same boy you discarded."

She pulled her keycard from her pocket and flashed it in front of the reader. "I did not discard you."

Liar. She had. It didn't matter if she did it for all the right reasons. She had *discarded him.*

She attempted to temper her voice. "I only meant you haven't done this before." That's not at all what she meant, but she needed something, anything, to hold on to before she succumbed to the black hole of a panic attack.

Matt stopped and turned into her. Her heart kicked against her rib cage. Had he always been this tall? He sucked in a breath and his chest inched closer to her face. Or this muscular?

"I was here yesterday and did just fine. I'm a performer, Amy-Lynn. I studied acting in college, which you know. I think I can get through your little show without making an ass of myself."

"My *little* show?" Who knew anger stopped a panic attack—and lust—in its tracks? "I'll have you know I built this 'little show' from nothing—all while stepping around giant, steaming piles of misogyny and you have the—"

"Hey, there are my two stars," Celeste called, walking down the hall. "Whoa," she said, reaching them. "I don't know what's going on here, but you cannot take this energy into the studio. We need more of yesterday's magic, not this . . . this . . . whatever this is." She fluttered her hands between them. "Ma-gic," she reiterated, pointing a finger at each of them.

Avery sucked in a deep breath and dropped her eyes to the floor. She couldn't regain her equilibrium while looking at him.

Could they make the magic Celeste demanded?

They had once.

Sixteen-year-old Matt Taylor personified magic. He'd saved her from being the 'new girl.' Then he opened his heart to her. Wrapped in his embrace, she'd never felt safer. He'd given her exactly what she needed at the time—a place where she could be herself, where she didn't have to be the second adult in the household.

Avery sighed and rubbed the space between her collarbones.

Celeste was right. They couldn't take this energy into the studio. They weren't lovers anymore—hadn't been in a long time. They were colleagues. Two adults chasing success. She threw her shoulders back and channeled the scrappy, determined woman who pushed aside all the naysayers.

"Truce?" she asked, holding out her hand to Matt. There was so much at stake, and fighting would only make it harder.

He narrowed his eyes at her. Like he thought she was playing some sort of game, but eventually covered her fingers with his own. "Truce."

She nodded and turned toward the studio.

"Amy-Lynn," he said.

She stopped but didn't turn around. "Yes?"

"I won't screw up," he said, barely over a whisper. "You're safe with me. You've always been safe with me."

She squeezed her eyes shut. *But you wouldn't have been if we'd stayed together. I would have dragged you down.* Shaking her hair back, she turned, forcing a smile that she hoped hid the swirling cocktail of emotions currently coursing through her veins.

"C'mon Calico Jack. Let's do this thing."

He cocked his head. "Calico Jack?"

She nodded. "Isn't that the character you played at the Dollywood dinner theater?"

A slow smile curved his lips northward. "Mac, have you been Googling me?"

Yes. At least four times a year for the last nine years. "No." She moved a step ahead so he couldn't read her expression. "You mentioned it in your interview."

His smile grew. "I most certainly did not."

Shit. Shit. Shit. She lifted her shoulders nonchalantly while willing her stomach to stop its Olympic-level backflips. "After yesterday's show, Momma asked what you'd been up to, so I pulled up a couple of things for her. That must have been where I saw it. Though I swear you mentioned it." Another lie. Momma had done nothing of the sort.

His lips twitched. "That's pretty old info. I'm surprised it still came up."

He knew she was lying. He'd always been able to read her better than anyone. She braced for him to call her out.

"How is Isabel?"

Her head popped up. "What?"

"Momma Isabel? How is she?"

Momma Isabel. No one called her that. Except Matt. She needed to get into the clean, orderly confines of her studio. This trip down Memory Lane was killing her.

"Oh. Momma. Right. She's good. Considering."

He opened the glass and metal door leading into the studio, holding it for her. "Considering what?"

She dropped her bag on her chair and rustled through it,

trying to find the notes for this morning's interview. "Um," she said, studying the bottom of her bag and questioning how much to tell him.

Not everything has to be a secret, Avery.

She looked up and met his gaze. "Yeah. So. She was diagnosed with MS a few years ago. Thankfully, most of the symptoms are mild and manageable, though it has affected her eyesight. Not great for a tailor."

"I'm sorry. That must be tough—especially after everything else she's been through."

His gentle words felt like a warm hug. She missed having someone who understood. Someone she could talk to. She'd done such an effective job burying her past that none of her current friends knew about her father. Who was she kidding? She didn't have friends. She had acquaintances. *That's what happens when all you do is work.*

"Thanks," she murmured.

"My mom said she left Marla a few years ago. Does she live here in Nashville now?"

Avery nodded. "She lives with me."

His eyebrows rose. "With you?"

"Yes." *She's my responsibility. Taking care of her is the least I can do after all the pain I've caused her.*

"That seems—"

"Avery, love," Ajay called, through the intercom, interrupting whatever Matt was going to say. "Luke Wallen is patched in. He's standing by and ready to go when you are."

Avery motioned for Matt to take a seat. "Luke Wallen is—"

Matt shook his head. "Give me some credit. I know who Luke Wallen is. I read the notes you sent me last night. And I've been in the industry for a while now and Luke Wallen has hardly been inconspicuous. I'm ready."

He'd read the notes? Color her impressed. The Matt Taylor

she knew played things loose, flying by the seat of his pants, charming his way out of, and into, any situation. Was he right? Was she not giving him a fair shot?

Maybe. Maybe not. She needed a little reassurance. "Dazzle me. What was Luke's first hit?"

He shot her a look that clearly said *challenge accepted.* "Anybody but Her."

She nodded. "Where did he go to college?"

The corners of his lips pulled up. "Trick question. He came to Nashville right out of high school and co-wrote a few songs before releasing his first solo EP. Are you dazzled?"

Always.

She'd have to be dead not to be dazzled by every part of him.

She smirked and quickly pulled her lips back into a flat line. "Maybe not dazzled, but less worried."

"Tough crowd." He smiled at her—and damn if the tingles didn't start again.

"Fifty-nine seconds," Ajay announced through the intercom.

She nodded through the window between the studio and production booth. Her fingers twitched. She tried to quench the need to straighten everything on her desktop. She didn't want Matt to notice, but this is what she always did immediately before the show started.

She looked up through her lashes. His head was down over the production notes Ajay had left on the desk. She quickly moved her mug two inches from the microphone arm. Straightened her pens, blue, black, green. When everything was in its proper place, she picked up her headphones and rotated them three times in her hands before sliding them over her ears.

"Matt . . ." she said.

"That's Calico Jack to you," he said, not raising his head.

"Ajay said—"

"I heard him."

He looked up and his soft expression nearly melted her. Tears stung behind her eyes. He hadn't tuned out. He'd given her the space she needed. The space *he* knew she needed.

She swallowed back the emotion. "It's almost time to go live. Get your headphones adjusted. After Ajay plays the intro, I'll jump on, welcome listeners, talk a little about Luke, and then let listeners know that you'll be co-hosting—for a while. And then you jump in and say something."

"Like what?"

She shook her head. "You wanted this gig and said you were ready. I don't have time to spoon-feed you. Just turn on the famous Matt Taylor charm."

"Aye, matey."

"Yes, like that—but without the pirate dialect. And remember, whatever you do, don't call me Amy-Lynn on air."

Matt rolled his eyes as Ajay counted down from five in her ear.

The familiar intro played in her headphones, calming her. "Good morning, country music fans. I'm Avery Lind, and I'm so happy to be here with you. Whether you're on the road, getting ready for work, or feeding the baby, we've got a great show for you. In a few minutes, we're going to chat with the incomparable Luke Wallen. He's just released another chart-topping hit. We'll talk to him about that and why he's donating all the proceeds of the song to World Central Kitchen.

"But before we do that, you might have noticed that I keep saying 'we.'" She paused, mustering every bit of her acting ability. "After receiving such a positive response yesterday, Ajay and I invited Matt Taylor to join us for a few more shows."

She pointed at Matt, held down her mute button, and let out a giant breath. She'd done it . . . and to her ears it sounded like she sold it. Was she getting too good at lying?

The question reverberated in the silence. Wait, why was there silence? She looked up and Matt wasn't talking. Dead air was her worst nightmare. Okay, maybe not the worst, but it ranked in the top five. She circled her hand frantically.

His eyes widened, and she lifted her finger from the mute button.

"Matt is clearly still overwhelmed thinking about the number of marriage proposals he received yesterday. Is that right, Matt?"

"Yes, that's it, Am—" He squeezed his eyes shut and tapped his fist against his forehead. "Avery," he enunciated. "That and getting the chance to talk to Luke Wallen. He's been such an inspiration. Storyhill covered one of his songs a few months back and it's one of our most watched YouTube videos. Did you know his father packed his truck, pressed the keys into his hand, and told him to get out and go to Nashville?"

She did not know that. She scanned the pages in front of her. That factoid was nowhere to be seen. She looked up as Matt tapped his temple. She shook her head. One piece of trivia did not compensate for dead air.

"I think that's a great place to start." See? She could play well with others . . . when her back was up against the wall. "Luke, welcome to the show. Don't know if you were listening, but Matt just mentioned that you have your father to thank for your success. Is it true that he basically threw you out?"

Luke Wallen's deep laugh rumbled through her head-phones, and her anxiety fell from full boil to a gentle simmer.

Matt sucked in a couple of quick breaths, trying to replace the air siphoned from his lungs during that first segment. He'd been so cocky, telling her not to worry, that he had it all under control. Except he didn't.

He talked to the audience at every Storyhill performance. Stage fright had *never* been an issue. Until today. She'd pointed to him, and he'd sat there, his mouth gaping like a fish out of water. Hopefully, the guys weren't listening or he'd never hear the end of it.

If he screwed up on stage, the audience laughed. They were there for the music, not his funny anecdotes. But here? This was different. And much harder than he originally thought. Yesterday Amy-Lynn and Ajay had pressed all the buttons— basically leading him by the nose through the show. Maybe a good guest didn't translate into a good co-host.

No. He would prove to her he was a worthy partner . . . professionally.

He turned his attention back to her. She was fluid, graceful, and clearly in her element. That shouldn't surprise him. From the time he'd met her, one thing had been consistent: when she set her mind to something, she didn't stop until she was the best.

Shit. She was pointing at him again. The universal sign for 'Speak, stupid.' What had Luke just said? Something about Storyhill's cover?

"Thanks," he pushed out, hoping he heard correctly. "Means a lot coming from you. Where'd you get the inspiration for the song?" he asked, praying Amy-Lynn hadn't already asked that question.

She tapped her fist against her forehead. Not a good sign.

"Luke, Matt asked where the inspiration came from."

She scrawled a note on an index card and held it up. 'Turn your mic on.'

He closed his eyes. The 'dumb ass' was implied. Luke answered and Matt jumped in—with his mic on—"Sorry, Luke, forgot to turn the mic on." He deployed his (over) practiced self-deprecating laugh. "Reminds me of some of my first times performing live. You got any of those stories, Luke?"

Based on Amy-Lynn's expression, he'd saved himself. Barely.

She expertly wrapped the interview, and the on-air light flashed off. She pulled her headphones down around her neck. "Not as easy as it looks, is it?"

He flashed his puppy dog eyes. "Am I fired?"

"Not my decision," she deadpanned.

"Great," he mumbled.

She tossed a few papers into the recycling bin, and he could swear she was smirking, but when she turned back to him, any hint of humor had disappeared. "Why don't you take a break. Stretch. Get some coffee. We have about five minutes of commercials, and then we'll play music until the bottom of the hour."

He placed a hand on his heart. "Look at you, looking out for my welfare."

She cocked an eyebrow. "Hardly. I'm not about to let you kick my house down in one day."

Matt stood and rubbed his eyes. "Was it that bad?"

She shrugged. "It could have been better."

He nodded and glanced away. "There was a time when you were the one person who believed in me, no matter what."

A sadness flickered in her eyes, but it was gone as fast as it had appeared. "Mind getting me one, too?" She lifted her cup, ignoring his comment.

"Sure," he said, grabbing her mug and turning toward the door.

"Nice save on the microphone thing," she said, barely audible.

Not high praise, but he felt like she'd thrown him a lifeline.

· · ·

"Great show," Celeste said, entering the studio when the on-air sign went dark for the last time.

"But?" Matt said. Certainly, the station manager had something to say about his less than stellar debut.

"But nothing," Celeste said.

"Really?" Amy-Lynn said, her eyes rising from the stack of papers in front of her.

Huh. He wasn't the only who was nervous about Celeste's reaction. Good to know.

"Yes," the station manager said. "Sure, you had a few bumps at the beginning. That's to be expected. But you covered well—even made the snafus funny."

Matt exhaled a breath he didn't realize he'd been holding. If Celeste was happy, he was happy. Okay, it would be nice if Amy-Lynn was also happy.

"I'll collect my things and get out of the way," he said, rising from his chair.

Celeste put a hand on his shoulder, pushing him back into the chair. "Do you have commitments this afternoon, Matt?"

Just a recovery nap. And likely a shitstorm of texts from the guys offering remedial microphone training. But he figured those were not what Celeste meant by 'commitments.'

"I have a conference call at three. I'm flexible until then." Maybe she was also going to suggest microphone training?

"Great," the station manager said. "I'd like you to stay around and record some promos with Avery."

Amy-Lynn's eyebrows slid to the center and crinkled up. "This week's promos are already in the can."

"That was before Matt joined the show. I want some new ones with the two of you together."

He could almost hear Amy-Lynn's teeth grind. "Is that really necessary? He's only here for thirteen more shows."

"But who's counting?" he muttered under his breath.

She shot him a look that was already becoming all too familiar and drummed her fingers on the desktop before lifting them to rub the spot under her collarbone.

How many people knew that was her tell?

"You're sure you'd rather have me re-record promos than contact stations about picking up the show?"

"Three to five promos should do it," Celeste said, her voice carrying as she exited the studio. "Shouldn't take you more than 60-90 minutes. Plenty of time to get them in the can and still reach out to a few stations."

It was clear Amy-Lynn was stressed. It had been a long morning. He wasn't giving up his spot on the show, but he could give her some space and time.

"How about I get us some food? I noticed a sandwich place right across the street."

She nodded, and her shoulders dropped in relief. "That sounds good. I'll make a few copy changes to the promo scripts and meet you in Studio B in twenty minutes."

"Turkey club, no tomato, extra mayo?"

Her eyes flew to his. "Is there anything you don't remember?"

"Only how to turn a mic on and off," he said with a laugh. If she kept looking at him like that, he couldn't be responsible for his actions. "Is that a yes on the sandwich?"

She cleared her throat. "Yes."

He nodded and turned toward the door. "See you in a few."

"Matt," she whispered. "Thank you."

He tipped his ball cap toward her. "You're welcome, *Avery*."

CHAPTER SEVEN

MATT GINGERLY LAID THE STRIPED PACKAGE ON THE SMALL desk in the corner of Studio B, the dressing from Amy-Lynn's sandwich already oozing through the now translucent corner of the bag.

He ran his hand over the console, half the size of the one in Ajay's studio, marveling at the fact that he was here. He'd wanted an opportunity like this for as long as he could remember. A part of him thought it would never happen, while other parts wouldn't let the dream die.

Despite his doubts, he knew with absolute certainty that not a single dream-career scenario included Amy-Lynn McWilliams. "Or Avery Lind." He let the name roll over his tongue, testing it.

In some ways, it fit her perfectly. She'd jettisoned the reticent girl that moved to Marla just weeks after her father's death. Avery Lind was strong and driven, capable and incredible at her job.

But Amy-Lynn still existed, too. The lines fanning from her eyes, too early to be wrinkles, revealed the burden she shouldered. Maybe everyone didn't see it. But even nine years later, he was still tuned to the frequency of her emotions—sensing her moods and understanding the way her body moved like no time had passed.

She was tired. And as much as he didn't want to let her get close again, he wondered how he might make things easier for her. Like he used to.

"You ready to move into the producer position already?"

Matt turned to find Celeste standing in the door.

He laughed softly. "Hardly. I think I have to master the mic's on-off switch first."

Celeste cocked her head and studied him. "I don't think you give yourself enough credit. If you ever give up the singing gig, you'd make a great host. And I don't hand out compliments lightly."

Matt felt a warmth climb his neck. A compliment that had nothing to do with the way he looked. "Thank you. Avery makes everyone around her look better. She's very good at what she does."

Celeste tucked the corners of her perfect bob behind her ears. "She is. One of the best. Which is saying a lot because a woman in this business has to work twice as hard as a man to be taken seriously."

"And then I come in, on the first day of syndication, and throw her a curve ball." Amy-Lynn had said as much, but for the first time it really sunk in. How would he have reacted if Amy-Lynn had waltzed backstage minutes before the concert at the Ryman? Like a memory made human. Would he have made it on stage? She did. Making her debut show even more impressive.

Celeste wiped a finger over the top of the console, flipping her hand over and blowing off the dust. The puff of air brought Matt back to the present.

"I wouldn't worry too much. She's given her life to this job.

She's dedicated—and resilient. It's going to take more than an unexpected guest to throw her off balance."

He nodded. "I hope so."

"What are you two talking about?" Avery said, appearing behind Celeste and shimmying around her.

"I was telling Matt he'd make a great radio host."

Avery whipped around and stared at her boss. "Are you offering him a job?"

Celeste held her hands up in surrender. "Nothing more than we've already discussed. I only mentioned that if he was ever looking for a second job, he should give hosting a shot. Maybe multi-media like Ryan Seacrest."

Avery rolled her eyes. "He does have a face for TV."

His jaw ticked. Enough with the face for TV thing. Apparently, her memory wasn't as good as his—or she'd stop saying things like that. Or maybe she remembered and was trying to get under his skin?

Two could play that game. "So far, I'm really enjoying this radio thing."

"Again, you've been here two days. Maybe try it for a few more days before you make any pronouncements." Avery dropped a stack of paper on the console and held his gaze.

Celeste cleared her throat. "Right. I have a meeting and you have promos to record. See you tomorrow, Matt?"

He pulled his eyes from Amy-Lynn and nodded at his temporary boss. "Bright and early." He laughed. "Or at least early, not sure I can promise bright yet."

Celeste laughed and waved, exiting the studio.

"You just can't help it, can you?" Avery said.

"Help what?"

Avery sighed. Just a little a breath, but he noticed. "Flashing that pretty smile and using your country charm to your advantage."

He was not getting into this. Especially not with her. He searched for a change of subject. "I got sandwiches," he said, pointing at the table in the corner of the room. "I didn't know if they were allowed in here or not."

"I'd say, don't tell the station manager, but you've got that whole get-out-of-jail-free smile, born under a lucky star thing going for you," she said. "So, let's throw caution to the wind." She held out her hand, motioning for her sandwich.

He pressed his lips together. Hard. If history held, she only made comments like those when she was anxious and uncomfortable. As much as he wanted to fire off a retort, he knew that would only escalate the situation. And, he reminded himself, *you're the reason she's stressed in the first place.* He placed the sandwich in her hand without a word.

Amy-Lynn unwrapped her hoagie and inhaled deeply. "I haven't allowed myself one of these for so long."

"Why not?"

She shrugged. "No time."

His eyes narrowed. "They're right across the street."

"After the show wraps, I work straight through lunch so that I can get home as soon as possible."

"Is that why you look so tired?"

Avery raised her eyebrows and snorted.

Matt would not be dissuaded. "Why do you look so tired, Mac?"

She opened her mouth and let it drop shut. "We should get these promos done."

He rolled his chair over next to her. "Is something going on at home? You can tell me."

She scooted away from him. "Were you always this much of a bulldog?"

He raised his eyebrows, waiting, saying nothing.

She searched his face. "Fine. As I mentioned earlier,

Momma lives with me. She really doesn't need to yet, but I felt it would be good to get her settled now. And Jessica and her son live with me, too."

His eyes widened. "Jess has a kid?"

"Yep," she said, popping the P.

"So, they all rely on you?"

"Yes," she said, her chin rising.

"That's kind of you. I guess," he said around a bite of his sandwich.

She creased the edge of the waxed butcher paper laying underneath her hoagie. And folded it again. And one more time, until it met the side of her sandwich. "I'm not sure kindness has anything to do with it. They're my responsibility."

He stopped chewing and turned to her. "Your responsibility? How do you figure?"

"Since Daddy died, I've been the second provider in the household. You know that. Or you used to."

His eyebrow arched. "But Jessica is an adult now."

A mirthless laugh leaked out of Amy-Lynn. "Well, she looks like an adult, but doesn't always act like one."

"Could that be because she knows you'll catch her every time she falls?"

Amy-Lynn sucked in a breath deep enough to flatten her nostrils. "*Excuse me?* You think you can waltz in here after not being around for nearly a decade and know what's best for my family?"

He moved toward her and reached for her before pulling back. "You're right. I'm sorry. I overstepped. But you also don't get to act like I left your life voluntarily. That was all you."

She sighed and shuffled the papers next to the console. "Matt, I really need to get to these promos. I have a lot of other things to get done today."

He nodded. Why was he even interested? She'd left him

and made her feelings clear. He wasn't good enough for her. He shouldn't need to know anything else.

Driving home from the station, Avery ran through her never-ending to-do list, but mostly she kept wondering why she'd told Matt all that? The last thing she wanted was for him to feel sorry for her, or worse, ask more questions.

She needed to shut this down before he probed further.

If only he weren't so distracting.

When, in that tiny studio, he'd rubbed his hand over his day-old stubble, the rasp of fingers against hair did funny things to her insides. It had reminded her of . . . She shook her head. Never mind what it reminded her of. Those were thoughts that didn't belong in the workplace. Ever. Even when you were forced to sit across from a Thor lookalike—and not the comic book Thor. The full-on, leather-pant-wearing, hammer-wielding Chris Hemsworth Thor. She was pretty sure that having to share a hundred square foot room with Matt-Thor-Chris was the very definition of an inhospitable workplace. She should file a complaint.

She sighed. She could see it now. Celeste rolling her eyes so hard they'd fall out.

But Matt's proximity wasn't the only thing bothering her. To her irritation, his question about Jess kept rattling around in her head.

She needed to sit down and have an adult conversation with her baby sister. Avery needed to help Momma and get this show on as many stations as possible, and to make that happen, her sister was going to have to pitch in.

She snaked through the alley and pulled into the driveway behind her house. She'd bought this house because it was big enough to house her family. As a kid, Daddy was regularly deployed, and Momma worked late hours. She wanted to give everyone a safe, stable place to land.

She laid her head down on the steering wheel. Who was she kidding? She wanted to give *herself* a safe, stable place to land.

She rubbed her clavicle, knowing this was a conversation she had to have while simultaneously wanting to put the car in reverse and ignore the entire thing.

She never backed away from a fight at work. Why was it so hard with family?

She sighed and stepped from the car, grabbing the bag of groceries she'd picked up on her drive home. She walked toward the house, more certain with every step. It was time. No more ignoring the issue. No more enabling. She'd talk to Jess tonight.

Avery stepped into the entryway and startled. Jess was standing in the mudroom, steps away from the door, her hands on her hips.

Avery glanced from her sister to the pegs on the wall. Jess's handbag and Wyatt's schoolbag were hanging neatly in their spots. "Did you just get home?"

Jess shook her head. "No. I've been waiting for you."

"Waiting to pounce on me? You couldn't wait in the kitchen or the living room?"

Jess took the bag of groceries from her hands, and Avery followed her into the kitchen. Jess pulled the items from the bag and began putting them away.

"Okay, now you're freaking me out. You're lurking *and* putting away groceries. Clearly you want something." Avery scanned the house for sound. "Or something happened to Momma." Avery scuttled past Jess into the living room. Momma's chair was empty. "Where's Momma? Did something happen?"

"No. Chill. She took Wyatt to the park so you and I can talk."

"Let me make sure I heard you right. *You* want to talk to *me*?"

"Yes." Jess pointed to the table in the kitchen. "Sit."

Avery looked at the table. A piece of paper laid in front of the chair she most often inhabited. She shot her sister a look, sliding into the chair and reading the title, "Jessica's Plan."

"You typed out a plan?" Avery said, her eyebrows shimmying up her forehead. "Now I know there's been an alien invasion."

"Ha, ha," her sister said, sliding into the banquet seating behind the worn pine table. "I know I've been leaning on you a little."

A little? 'A little' didn't begin to cover it. But Avery knew it was as much her fault as Jess's. She invited Jess and Wyatt to live here. And hadn't said a word about their extended stay until yesterday. *Passive-aggressive, much?* She'd swallowed her irritation, letting it fester inside, instead of discussing it with her sister. "Go on," Avery said slowly, wondering where Jess was taking this conversation.

"I want you to know that I heard what you said. I know I need to take care of myself and Wyatt. It's just so scary."

Now that was something Avery knew something about. Fear of her entire life crumbling was never far from her mind. But she'd decided the day Daddy died she would be strong for her family—at all costs.

"What's scary?" she asked, trying to soften her voice.

"Being a mom. Knowing it's just me and him."

Avery melted a little, an old memory moving inside her. "It's never just you and him. Momma and I will always be here."

"Yes," Jess said, nodding. "But as back-up."

Avery's eyes went wide. She opened her mouth to ask Jess to

clarify, but before she could speak, Jess pointed at the paper in front of Avery.

"It's time for me to think about what life looks like for me and Wyatt in the future. The very near future. That's where the plan comes in."

Avery held up the paper and read the numbered items. One, get a job I love. Two, pay rent. Three, finish college. She'd had a similar list once herself. Go to Nashville. Get a job in radio. Pay off student debt. Get over Matt Taylor.

Two days ago, she would have said she'd accomplished everything on that list. Today she knew better.

"What do you think?" her sister said, pulling her back to the present.

How to answer that? She sucked a breath in. She'd decided in the car that things needed to look different around here. No backpedaling now. "It's great, but it's a little thin. How do you expect to do all of this? You've promised this before and that was before Wyatt. These are just general bullets. How do you plan on achieving all of this?"

Jess sighed out a long breath. "Wow. You're being harsh."

Avery sighed. That was the soft version. She'd started with 'it's great,' after all. She placed her hand on top of Jess's. "No, I'm not. Today somebody made me realize one reason you keep living here and quitting jobs is because I'm making things too easy for you."

Jess's mouth quirked up at the corners. "Could that person be a super fine singer once permanently attached to your side?"

"Who said it is irrelevant."

"Uh, nope, very relevant. You are extremely stubborn and rarely listen to anyone. It was Matt, wasn't it?"

"This is about you, not me. Let's get back to the plan. I'll help you flesh some of this out."

Jess leaned forward and placed her chin in her hands, a smug smirk pulling at the corners of her lips. "Is he still sexy?"

Still sexy. Still sweet. And annoyingly talented. Seems growing into a man had taken all his good qualities and amped them up. But it didn't matter. If he ever found out the truth, he'd never forgive her.

"Amy-Lynn? Has time been kind to him?"

Avery fished out her phone and Googled 'Matt Taylor, Storyhill.' When a picture popped up, she enlarged it with her fingers and turned it toward her sister.

"Whoa." Her eyes widened and flashed up to Avery. "Whoa. Who'd have thought he could get even *better* looking."

"Tell me about it."

"So you aren't completely oblivious."

"Look at him." Avery waved a hand at the phone. "I'm focused, not dead."

Jess tilted her head, assessing Avery. "You ever going to tell me why you broke up?"

Avery squirmed in her chair. How did this conversation go from her sister's plan to the last thing on the planet she wanted to talk about? "What's your plan to secure not only a job, but a job you love?"

"See," Jess said, nodding knowingly, "stubborn."

"Again," Avery said, rubbing her clavicle, "not about me."

"Never is."

"What is that supposed to mean?"

"It means you keep everything locked up tighter than Fort Knox."

"Unlike you, who shares every emotion that passes through you at every moment possible?"

"Hey, I'm not the one who single-handedly supports the antacid industry."

This had gone far enough. "Do you want my help or not?"

Jess rolled her eyes. "Fine. Yes. For item number one, I went to a career counselor this morning, and we talked through some job ideas. Things that I would enjoy, that could be like an apprenticeship until I'm in a place to finish my degree."

Avery's gaze shifted from Jess's list to her face. "You did?"

"Yes. It might surprise you, but I do realize that I can't support myself and Wyatt if I keep quitting jobs."

"Alright, but . . ."

Jess's phone blared, its signature ring tone cutting off Avery's question. Jess flipped it over, her eyes widening.

"I have to take this," she said, sliding out of the banquette and retreating to the living room.

Of course, she'd take a call. It was the perfect way to deflect Avery's questions. She looked at her sister's list of bullet points and massaged her temples. Jess was saying—and had written—all the right words, but could she trust that she'd follow through? She wanted to believe her. But history told a different story.

A story Avery helped create.

She walked to the sink and filled a water glass. She looked over her shoulder toward the living room, where she could hear Jess pacing thanks to the hundred-year-old wood floors. Avery had a choice. She could either keep enabling Jess or enthusiastically get behind her plan. It was clear which one needed to happen.

Jess wandered back into the room, her eyes dazed. "Amy-Lynn," she breathed out before sidling up behind her and wrapping her arms around Avery's shoulders.

"What's going on?" Avery stilled in her sister's arms. Jess was free with affection, but she usually saved it for Wyatt. Or Momma. Or anyone except Avery.

"You will not believe this," she said into Avery's hair.

"Mommy!" Wyatt yelled, cutting off Jess, the door banging

open. He ran toward her and circled her knees with his chubby arms.

How must that feel? To have someone love you unconditionally like that. Maybe if things had been different with Matt . . . She shook the thought from her head.

"Hey baby," Jess said to the toddler, "did you have fun at the park with Abuela?" She kissed the top of his dark brown curls. No one could deny that Wyatt looked far more like his father than any of the McWilliams. She couldn't help but wonder if they were both destined for a lifetime of screwed up relationships.

"Momma," Jess said excitedly, "I'm glad you're here. I was just about to tell Amy-Lynn my exciting news."

Momma dropped into the chair across from Avery. She smiled at her younger daughter, but Avery could see the strain around her eyes and the corners of her mouth. The time at the park with Wyatt had taken a toll on her. Maybe Avery should try to get home earlier so she could help more with Wyatt.

Isabel moved her legs under the table, attempting to disguise the fact she was rubbing her knees, but Avery noticed. "What's your exciting news, mi hija?"

"I just got a phone call about a job application I dropped off this morning."

"That was fast," Avery said, trying to hide the surprise in her voice.

Jess bounced on the balls of her feet. "It is. It's one of the jobs the career counselor helped me find! It's for a Design Assistant and Showroom Coordinator for an interior design firm! It's entry level, but the woman who called says she likes to hire apprentices and train them. I could do this without a college degree, and the pay is enough to help with the bills around here."

"Whoa, slow down," Avery said. She didn't want to crush

Jess's enthusiasm, but she'd seen it before and also saw how fast it disappeared. "You don't have the job yet."

"I have a really good feeling about this one. And I think I'd be really good at it."

Avery tipped her head and twisted her lips. "Jess . . ."

"Amy-Lynn," her mother cut in, giving her a look that could only be translated one way: stop being such a rain cloud.

Right. Just promised to 'enthusiastically' get behind Jess's plan. That lasted all of three minutes. Apparently, it wasn't only Jess's habits that die hard.

"Did the woman ask to set up an interview?" Isabel asked her younger daughter.

"Yes!" Jess said, clapping her palms together. "She wants to meet with me tomorrow morning. Can you believe that?"

"Mi hija, tomorrow morning is my doctor's appointment. You promised to drive me," Isabel said. "I can't reschedule."

Jess turned to Avery.

Avery shook her head. "Jess, no way. I host a *LIVE* show. It's called the Avery Lind show. Can't very well do the Avery Lind show without Avery Lind. You need to reschedule your interview. You promised Momma."

"I can take the bus," her mother offered.

"No, you can't, Momma. One of the tests requires light sedation, remember? They won't release you from the clinic without a designated driver. Jess needs to make good on her promise."

Avery rubbed her clavicle. Tough love was hard.

Jess huffed. "What if Matt did the show? C'mon Amy-Lynn, the woman who called said this was the only time she had free for the next ten days. You want me to get a job, don't you?"

This was typical Jess. No thought for anyone but herself. "Yes, I want you to have a job. One you love. But Matt cannot carry the show."

"I bet Celeste would run a 'best of' show." Jess nodded her head as if she did it long enough Avery would agree. "Please, please, please, big sister. I want to show you I can do this. I want you to be proud of me."

"Proud of you because you have a job interview, but not taking care of your mother?"

Jess interlaced her fingers and stepped closer to Avery. "Just this once. Please, Amy-Lynn?"

Clearly, Matt hadn't cornered the market on puppy dog eyes. Jessica was equally talented in that department. Avery felt the guilt climbing her spine and settling in the spot at the base of her neck that never seemed to stop hurting. "We both know this is not just once. What about Wyatt?"

"He can go with you?" Jessica winced, knowing this might be one thing too many. She stuck out her bottom lip and Avery caved, just like always.

"I'll call Celeste and get her take on this. She will not be thrilled. We literally just went national. At least it's Friday and we don't book guests on Fridays."

Jessica screamed and rounded the table, throwing her arms around Avery once more.

"I haven't said 'yes.'"

"But you will."

Of course she would. Momma and Jess were her responsibility, and she'd do whatever it took to help them.

"I'll go call Celeste." She stood and walked to the kitchen counter where she'd dropped her phone. She turned back to her sister. "Don't make me regret this."

Jess did a little shimmy. "I won't."

Famous last words.

CHAPTER EIGHT

The next morning, Avery found herself in a waiting room holding a wiggly three-year-old. The motion did nothing to soothe her already churning stomach. Celeste hadn't been happy to run a few 'best of' interviews from the previous year, but as Avery never asked for time off, she reluctantly agreed.

And it wasn't all bad. Being here meant getting Momma's medical information right away, and that meant she could put together a plan for her care immediately.

She'd streamed the show this morning before leaving for the clinic. Celeste and Ajay had run her interview with Carrie Harris. It was a good choice. Hopefully, the stations syndicating the show wouldn't be too disappointed. The thought of losing even one of the hard-won syndicators made the butterflies in her stomach erupt into an entire zoo.

She lifted Wyatt from her lap with shaking hands and settled him in the chair next to her. She handed him his tablet and he immediately stilled, his eyes glued to the bright colors and dancing lights.

She checked the time on her phone. Two and a half hours down on the show, one and a half to go. She shouldn't worry.

She shouldn't tune in. Ajay knew how to handle 'best of' shows. But she couldn't resist.

She laughed out loud. Open the dictionary to 'micromanager' and you'd likely find her picture. She might not be able to change it, but at least she knew it was an issue. And she could laugh about it.

She checked on Wyatt and handed him a dish of Goldfish crackers. He dipped his fingers into the bowl without taking his eyes off the screen. Maybe he had gotten something from her—that level of focus was very familiar.

She pulled her AirPods from her bag and called up the station website, clicking on the 'Listen Now' button. Commercial. She'd suggested a playlist (unnecessary) and a second interview. Her highest rated shows were as familiar as her own name.

The commercial faded, and the show's musical intro played. As soon as she heard her voice come through her earphones, she'd turn it off.

She sat ramrod straight when it wasn't her voice that came through the speakers. What the hell?

"What the hell," Wyatt mimicked. Oh my god, had she said that out loud?

"Wyatt, honey, look at Tía. Those are not nice words. Do not say them again."

The toddler looked at her and shrugged and said, "Hell."

She rubbed her forehead and tried another tactic while trying to listen to Matt. "What are you watching, honey?"

"Fucking Super Monsters."

Okay, he'd not learned *that* word from her. She should admonish him, but she had more pressing issues than her foul-mouthed nephew.

She swiped over to her text app and typed *Why is Matt talking?????* to Ajay as she heard Matt announce he would interview songwriting royalty Grace O'Connor in the next hour.

A text popped up. *He pitched the O'Connor interview idea to Celeste, and she ran with it. Don't freak out. He's doing a great job.*

A great job taking my job? she texted back before she could stop herself. She did the deep breathing exercises designed to keep her anxiety at bay. Her heart rate seemed steady, but her stomach churned.

He's not taking your job, love. In fact, if he sucked up to you any further, sugar would drip from the microphone.

Matt was praising her? Again. What. The. Hell.

Ajay texted again. *Relax. And listen. You've no worries.*

"Potty," Wyatt demanded, pulling on her sleeve.

That's one word for it.

Wyatt pulled on the hem of her shirt. "Potty now, Tía!"

She didn't know a lot about toddlers, but she knew enough to know you didn't mess with bathroom requests. She lowered the volume of her headphones and shuffled Wyatt off to the restroom.

She opened the door to the stall as Matt introduced Grace O'Connor. Wyatt immediately flushed the toilet, drowning out Matt's introduction. A flushing toilet felt like an apt metaphor for her career right about now. Why had she let Jess talk her into this?

Wyatt reached for the silver lever again, but Avery caught his chubby hand in hers. "Wyatt, honey, we don't flush the toilet until *after* we go potty."

"Why?" He looked up at her while pulling down his shorts.

Because I'm no fun. "Because wasting water is for chumps."

He giggled and lifted his arms in the universal symbol for 'up.'

She settled Wyatt on the toilet as Matt said, "I met Grace

O'Connor when she and Storyhill's bass, Andrew Hayes, wrote our latest album."

The interview continued smooth as silk. Something bubbled in her stomach. Disappointment? No. She wanted her show to succeed—at all costs. But a tiny part of her wished it wouldn't be so easy for him.

She had to work so hard. Things just came to him.

Before she could work up a full belly of resentment, she heard her name echo through her headphones. Grace had asked Matt about her.

"Yep, I've known Avery since we were sixteen. We went to the same high school and attended OU at the same time. Though we fell out of touch after college."

Fell out of touch. He was being kind. There was not a hint of anger or resentment in his voice. Both things she deserved.

"Is that how you ended up with this gig?"

Grace was also a skilled interviewer. She couldn't help feeling unneeded.

"Flush now, Tia?"

Avery snorted. Yes. Flush now. Flush it all.

Except she really wanted to hear how Matt answered Grace's question. "You go wash your hands. Use the stepstool. And I'll flush."

She missed the first few words. ". . . we'd fallen out of touch. It was happenstance. But I must admit it's been amazing to drop back into her life and witness all she's accomplished. Did you know that only about thirty percent of solo radio hosts are women?"

"Making her story even more impressive," Grace said.

"Right?" Matt said. "She's just over thirty—whoops, maybe shouldn't have announced that," he said, laughing. "And she has a nationally syndicated show and three Marconi Awards."

"When you knew her at sixteen, did you see all this happening for her?"

When did this interview digress from Grace O'Connor Grammy award-winning songwriter to the history of Avery Lind? She grabbed Wyatt's hand, leading him out of the bathroom and willing Ajay to redirect the interview.

"I did."

He did?

"She was always the most driven and composed person I'd ever met. I think the two of you would hit it off. You have a lot of similar traits."

"Well, maybe we'll get to meet sometime soon," Grace said.

"Maybe," Matt echoed. "I'm getting the wrap-up sign from Ajay. Thanks for joining us today, Grace. Avery will be back on Monday. This is Matt Taylor signing off, leaving you with a few of Avery's favorite songs from the past few years."

He knew her favorite songs? Oh. Right. The music list she'd provided.

"Mi hija?"

Avery jumped at the sound of her mother's voice. She glanced to her left. Wyatt had clambered back into the waiting room chair and had rebooted his cartoons.

She pulled the AirPods from her ears. "Momma, they were supposed to come and get me when you were finished." She pursed her lips and shot a look at the nurse standing behind the desk.

Isabel chuckled. "No need for that look, Amy-Lynn. I didn't need to be sedated after all."

"No?" *Great.* She took off work and let Matt Taylor take over for nothing. She shook her head. No, not nothing. It was important to be here for Momma.

"Nope." Her mother smiled. "The doctor held off on that test because she believes the disease is currently in remission."

Avery wrapped her arms around her mother. All thoughts of Matt and the show fading into the background. "That's great news, Momma! See? Taking it easy has its rewards. I hope she told you not to push it just because things haven't gotten worse."

Isabel smirked. "She did."

Avery's eyes narrowed. "And will you listen? You're not going back to your workaholic ways, right?"

Isabel laughed. "That's quite the question coming from you."

Avery joined in her mother's laughter. "I guess the apple doesn't fall far from the tree."

Her mother nodded, her smile drooping. "I wish I could have passed on something else. You work too much, Amy-Lynn."

Avery's eyes widened. "I love my job, Momma."

After a few moments of silence, her mother added, "I just hope you're doing it for the right reasons."

I'm doing it for you, and Jess, and Wyatt. "I am Momma."

Her mother eyed her, doubt written all over her face. "If you say so, mi hija."

Ignoring her mother's intimations, Avery leaned down to Wyatt. "How about some ice cream to celebrate Abuela's good news?"

Wyatt jumped up and yelled, "Chocolate!"

Isabel laughed, taking her grandson's hand in hers. "You don't want to get back to the station?"

"I'll get there, but this is more important."

Isabel slid another look at her daughter. "Okay," she said, suspicion lacing her voice. "Did you listen to the show?"

Avery's fingers curled into a fist. "Yes."

"And the 'best of' format worked?"

"Well, they deviated from the plan a little. They ran a previous interview first and then they let Matt do the last hour."

Isabel stopped and looked at her daughter, eyes wide. She was clearly waiting for Avery's freak out.

She shrugged. "He interviewed a songwriter—the one getting married to one of his bandmates. She's a big get. And one I'm not sure I could have secured."

"And?"

"And he did a good job." She rolled her eyes. "Great, actually. Doesn't look like I'm getting rid of him anytime soon."

"Do you want to?"

Yes. No. Maybe. She wanted her show back. But having Matt around felt . . . what? Good? No, that wasn't quite it. Comforting, maybe? Like slipping into a well-worn sweater. If that sweater looked like Thor and lit up her girl parts like a Christmas tree lighting in a Hallmark movie. One flick of a switch and, whoosh, she was ablaze.

Avery drew in a deep, bracing breath, scrubbing the thought from her mind. "Doesn't matter. Not my choice," she said, trying to end her mother's line of questioning.

Isabel stopped at Avery's car, her fingers curling around the passenger side door handle. "Are you going to tell him?"

Avery lifted Wyatt into his car seat. She didn't need to ask her mother for clarification. She knew exactly what her mother was asking.

She *should* tell him. But he was leaving in three weeks. And it was ancient history. Probably better not to dredge it up.

"Wyatt wants chocolate ice cream. What flavor would you like, Momma?"

Isabel looked at her over the top of her glasses. "Amy-Lynn."

Avery punched the ignition button. "I know, Momma. But that's not something you drop on someone after not seeing them for almost a decade."

Isabel shrugged. "You might feel better."

"I don't know what you're talking about, I feel great."

Isabel sighed and shook her head, but finally let the subject drop. "You should at least reach out and thank him for doing the show today. Thank him for me. These things are so much easier knowing one of my girls is waiting for me."

"I can do that."

Avery stared at her phone. She'd gotten Matt's number in case of emergency—a show-related emergency. She needed to say thank you, but the petulant child inside her kept saying things like, "You need to say thank you for him going against your wishes?"

"Shut up," she said to no one. She wanted to be better than all that, and normally she was. But this was Matt Taylor. And 'complicated' didn't begin to describe her feelings toward the man.

"Get over yourself." Had she always talked to herself this much?

Her finger hovered over the call button, but she chickened out at the last minute and hit the message button.

I caught your interview with Grace this morning. Nice job.
Send.

"C'mon Avery," she chided herself.

She punched the screen, popping the cursor into the text message box. *Can I take you out for a drink to say thank you?*

She hit send before she could chicken out again.

She waited for the telltale three dots, but her screen remained quiet.

Matt stared at the screen. The compliment came first, and if that wasn't shocking enough, she'd followed it up with an invitation to meet for drinks. He lifted his finger to type a response. And then pulled it back. How was it that the thought of meeting with her away from the station was the best *and worst* thing he could imagine?

Meeting at a bar felt like a date.

Should he suggest a coffee shop instead?

Or claim he was busy tonight?

Or maybe pull his head out of his ass and stop over-analyzing the situation?

He stared at the blinking blue cursor, unsure of his next move.

"Mattie," Blake called from the stage. "You planning on joining us? Clock's ticking."

Matt looked up at his bandmates, waiting for him to block the last number of their upcoming tour. "Yeah. Just need a minute." He turned his attention back to his phone. "Man up," he muttered under his breath.

Sure, he typed. *Tonight?* He hit Send, wondering if his response was too presumptuous.

The dots jumped immediately.

Yes, tonight. How about happy hour? 4pm at Dahlia Lounge? They've got good drinks and excellent apps. Or somewhere else? Whatever you'd like.

Matt chuckled. She was text babbling. At least he wasn't the only one nervous about meeting.

Dahlia's is fine. See you there.

She sent him back the thumbs-up emoji. The Dahlia Lounge was a small bar. He'd been there many times. Had she? It suddenly seemed odd that they'd never run into each other before now. Nashville was a town of nearly 700,000 people, but it still had a lot of small-town elements to it. Especially for people in the industry. Maybe she truly did work all the time?

"Matt," Andrew said. "Sometime today would be great."

"Coming," he said, depositing his phone in his back pocket and taking the stage stairs two at a time.

An hour later, with blocking complete, the guys suggested grabbing a beer. He declined.

"You have a better offer?" Blake asked.

His stomach executed a perfect somersault. Was it a better offer? Or was curiosity getting the better of him? He fisted his hand in his hair and rubbed the back of his neck. "Um, yeah, I guess I do."

Blake waggled his eyebrows. "A hot date? And does she have a friend?"

Matt rolled his eyes. "No. And I don't know."

"A better offer that's not a hot date?" Nick asked. "That seems like an oxymoron to me. Hey, Andrew and Joe, Mattie says he's got another commitment tonight that's better than sharing a beer with us, but it's not a hot date. Sound weird to you?"

Great, now everyone was waiting for him to explain something he himself didn't understand.

"A commitment on a Friday night that's not a date? You're right, Nick, sounds fishy," Joe said with a smile.

These guys were clearly enjoying Matt's obvious discomfort. But if the situation were reversed, he'd likely be doing the same thing.

"Fine," Matt said. "I'm meeting Avery."

"Oo-ooh," they chorused.

"Seriously. What is this? Feels like middle school all over again."

"They're just jealous," Andrew said, as if he hadn't just been in the center of all the ribbing.

"I'm not jealous," Joe said. "I'm headed home to the prettiest woman in Nashville."

"Fine, it's just them then," Andrew said, pointing at Nick and Blake.

"I'm not jealous," Blake said, his chin tipping up.

"So, you have a hot date tonight?" Matt said, unable to stop himself.

"No," Blake grumbled.

"Nick?" Matt asked, a smirk pulling at the corners of his lips.

Nick raised a single bushy eyebrow. "Avery's finally warming up to you, then?" the baritone asked, completely side-stepping Matt's question.

That's a good question. Was she? "Maybe. Not sure. She texted that the interview with Grace was good, but I can't help wondering if she wants to get to together to yell at me for not letting the station just run 'best of' stuff."

"Uncharted territory," Blake said with a grin.

"Sorry?" Matt said.

"Not knowing where you stand with a woman," Blake said, his smile growing. "Can I come along to watch?"

Matt blew out a breath. "You need to get a life."

Blake laughed. "Where are you meeting her, Mattie? We could get a beer there, right, guys?"

They all nodded, the bastards. "You know that dive bar on Elm Street?"

Blake's eyes widened. "I do."

"That's not it," Matt called as he bounded down the stairs.

CHAPTER NINE

Matt walked into the Dahlia Lounge a couple of minutes before four and scanned the interior. He was happy she hadn't suggested the bars or honky-tonks on Broadway. He enjoyed the hustle and bustle of the popular joints occasionally, but they weren't conducive to talking.

He meandered to a table toward the back with windows facing the street and looked over the menu. Or pretended to. The words swam in front of his eyes. Questions stacked up in his head like cars in a demolition derby.

He'd jumped from wanting to know 'why was he here' and 'what did she really want' to the questions he'd been tossing around for days. What had her life been like for the past nine years? How did she find herself in Nashville? How long had she worked at the station? Was she in a relationship? Was she married?

Wait.

Could she be married? To someone else? His stomach dropped. He'd asked her to be *his* wife.

"Hey," came a soft voice, interrupting his thoughts.

He looked up to see her standing tentatively at the edge of the table.

"Are you married?" he blurted, instead of a greeting.

She laughed. "I remember you being much more tactful."

The server set a beer on the table and winked at him.

"Now, that hasn't changed," Amy-Lynn said as the young woman sashayed away, an intentional swing in her curvy hips.

Matt grunted.

"What? Is it hard having women falling at your feet?"

"It's harder than you think," he mumbled.

"What?"

He looked back at her. "Nothing."

She slid into the bench seat opposite him and grabbed the plastic-coated menu from behind the napkins, not looking at him. "No, I'm not married. And," she said, raising a finger to stop his next question, "I'm not dating anyone."

"Why not?"

"My job and my family are my priorities. No time to date. You?"

He shook his head. "Not presently."

The server returned with an overflowing basket of fries.

"I didn't order these," Matt said to the woman.

"On the house."

Her smile dimmed as she turned to Amy-Lynn. "What can I getcha?"

She ordered a drink and chicken wings, taking a fry from the free basket. "I forgot about the benefits of being with Matt Taylor."

An eyebrow popped up. "Excuse me?"

"The fries," she said, pink creeping across her face. "So, how are your mom and dad?" she asked, quickly changing the subject. She grabbed for the bottle of ketchup and pounded the bottom. Nothing came out.

He watched her for a beat, wondering if he should ask her more about the 'benefits of being with Matt Taylor,' but he didn't want to make her more uncomfortable—or look like he needed his ego stroked. "Here, let me." He reached for the bottle, gave it one swift hit with the palm of his hand, and the ketchup flowed out.

She rolled her eyes and shook her head.

"Another benefit of being with Matt Taylor?" he asked, unable to stop himself.

She pulled a face. "Your parents?" she repeated. "Are they good?"

He bit back a smile. Turned out, she still got flustered easily —and he still loved teasing her. "Still in Marla. Filling their time bragging about their kids and grandkids."

"Having a famous musician in the family is certainly something to talk about."

His smile faded. "I don't think I qualify as famous."

"All the emails the station has gotten say otherwise." She dragged a french fry through the ketchup now covering her plate and popped it in her mouth.

Matt pulled a long draw from his beer. "I doubt my parents would be interested in electronic marriage proposals. They pay no more attention to me now than they did when we were teenagers."

She waved her hand in the air. "Oh, come on, they love you like crazy."

"I don't deny that. It's just they were tired by the time I came along. They let me do whatever I wanted. And what I wanted was for them to notice me. I made a lot of unnecessary trouble, hoping to get their attention."

"That's right"—she smiled and snapped her fingers— "what was it the old ladies called you?"

"Beautiful, but feral," he grumbled.

"Ha! That's right! Does that description still fit?"

He smoothed his hands down his chest. "You tell me."

She blushed a deep red. "I meant the feral part."

He looked down at the table. "Depends on who you ask."

She cocked her head to the side. "What does that mean?"

"It means things aren't always as they seem." He studied his beer. That might have been cryptic, but it was as close to his truth as he'd let anyone see in a long time. Likely the last time was when the same woman sat across the table from him.

"One rum and coke," the server said, sliding Amy-Lynn's drink across the table. "How are the fries?" she said, turning to Matt once again.

"You'll have to ask my date. She's tried them, I haven't yet."

"You should try them," the server said before turning back toward the kitchen. "They're delicious."

Amy-Lynn smirked. "No using me as a human shield, Mr. Taylor."

"Meaning?"

"Meaning, this is not a date."

Matt cocked a single eyebrow. "Then what is it?" He'd really like to know.

"One colleague thanking another." She held up her glass. "Thank you for filling in for me today—and bringing in Grace O'Connor. Celeste says the response was good."

He lifted his half-empty pint and clinked her glass. "To colleagues," he said. "You checked up on me?"

She didn't even flinch. "Of course. I've spent nine years crafting a following. The listeners trust me to deliver a specific product. I need to know everything that goes on and how people are reacting to it."

Because she still didn't trust him. Didn't believe in him. Even after today. His lips tightened into a thin line. "Even I couldn't ruin nine years of work in one day."

She sighed and rubbed the center of her clavicle. "I don't want to fight. I'm particular about my show. It has nothing to do with you."

He bounced a fist off his thigh. "Sure."

"Matt, you have nine shows left. I'd like it if we could get along. It would make everything so much easier. How about we put the past behind us and focus on the show? Can we do that?"

"Maybe." *For tonight*. He grinned at her, but it was his performer's grin. He didn't want to bury the past, not before he had the answers he'd been craving for nearly a decade. "Another drink?"

She stared into the cup. He could see her warring with herself. "I guess I could have one more. It's Friday. I don't have to get up for the show tomorrow."

He signaled the server for another round before turning his attention back to Amy-Lynn. "When's the last time you let go? Just let everything wash away for a while?"

She looked at him and a sadness passed over her eyes. "I don't know. 1995, maybe?"

He laughed, choking on his beer. "When you were five? Was that a joke, Mac?"

She flinched at the name but said nothing. He wondered if it wasn't so much the name as him saying it.

"Hey, I'm capable of producing a joke on rare occasions." She gave him a self-deprecating—and real—smile.

Time to test his theory. "Do your mom and Jess call you Avery?"

She chewed on the end of her straw. "No. They still call me Amy-Lynn." She shrugged. "People at work call me Avery."

"What do your friends call you?"

She squirmed in her seat. "Depends on when they met me."

Matt gazed at her, knowing he should probably let this line

f questioning go. But for whatever reason, he needed the answer. "But you'd prefer I call you Avery?"

She looked at him from under her lashes. "Yes," she said, barely over a whisper.

"What about Mac? Can I call you that?" He was really pushing things, and he wasn't entirely sure why.

"Avery, please," she said, this time with a little more force.

It didn't take a genius to know she was trying to put some distance between them. But the bigger question was why? If she didn't have any feelings left for him, what did it matter what he called her? Maybe she wasn't as unaffected as she pretended.

She cleared her throat, swung her hair over her shoulders, and wiped the condensation from the ridges of her plastic cup. "So, you joined Storyhill seven years ago?"

His eyebrows rose. The subject change was jarring, but he put that aside, happy she was still sitting across from him, not hustling toward the nearest exit. "How did you know that?"

She looked away and shrugged. "It doesn't take a genius to figure it out. I know when you graduated college, and you said you worked at Dollywood for a couple of years, I did the math."

No way was he letting her off the hook that easily. "Have you been following my career, Avery Lind?"

Her head snapped up. "You called me Avery."

"You just asked me to."

She leaned back to allow the server to place the plate of chicken wings in front of her. "Doesn't mean I actually thought you'd do it."

He reached across the table and ran his fingers over her knuckles and damn if fireworks didn't pop and crackle over them. She flinched but didn't pull her hand away. "Maybe it's because I already know Amy-Lynn and I'd like to learn more about Avery. Would that be okay?"

"Smooth," she said with a chuckle.

He grinned back at her. "I'll ask again, how is it you knew I joined Storyhill seven years ago?"

She bit into a chicken wing. "Mouth's fwull," she said, pointing at her lips.

He followed her finger and stared at her full lips for a beat too long. It might have been nine years since he'd felt them pressed against his own, but he could feel their last kiss like it happened minutes ago.

She must have sensed it because she quickly swallowed and wiped a napkin across her lips. "I told you before, Momma's kept tabs on you."

"Oh, it's Isabel that's been following my career, is it?"

"She's got mad Googling skills . . . and she's a bit of a YouTube junkie."

"Really?"

She swatted at his hand with her napkin. "Yes, really, Mr. Ego. She might be a grandmother, but she's not even fifty yet."

He nodded. "I forgot how young she was when she had you."

Her smirk flatlined. "Yeah."

"I can't imagine how an unexpected pregnancy changes your life."

She cleared her throat. "Do you think you could get the server's attention?" she said, rattling the ice in her empty cup.

He'd hit a sore spot. He reached for her hand, and this time she pulled it away. "I'm sorry. I know it wasn't always easy for you, and your parents had some issues."

"I'm going to go find her." Amy-Lynn stood from the booth and headed to the bar.

He watched her go, a little confused. She'd never been comfortable discussing her family life, but this seemed more pronounced. And nine years had passed. Things changed. He was no longer her confidant. But he wanted her to know that she could still tell him anything. Like before.

But it wasn't before. It was after.

She returned to the table with two more glasses. He noticed a little wobble in her step.

"You okay with a third?"

"You monitoring my drinking?" she snapped.

He held his hands up in surrender.

"You're right," she said with a sigh. "I probably shouldn't have a third. I'm a total lightweight. I never do this. But I'm just so tired of always being the responsible one. It's been so long since I've thought about anything other than what Momma or Jess might need or what Celeste wants." She laid her head on the table. "I just want to think about me for a while."

At least that's what he thought she said. The table muffled her voice.

"Avery?" It was so hard to call her that, but if that's what she wanted, he'd do it. For her. He smoothed a hand over her rasp-berry-colored hair. "Avery, honey?"

"What?" she said, her head still down on the table.

"I'd like to see your pretty face."

She looked up, and he brushed her hair back. "How about I don't drink this one." He pushed the beer away. "We'll order some more food and some water, and I'll make sure you get home safely. Have as many as you want."

"But what about my car?"

"I'll drive it to your house and Uber back here."

"But then you'd see where I live," she said, a slight slur inching into her voice.

"I'll close my eyes."

"Okay," she said.

He chuckled to himself.

"And a second idea. Tomorrow night, Storyhill is getting

together. It'll be the guys, our tech team, and their significant others. We do the potluck thing, have a beverage or two, play some games. Come with me."

Her chest rose as she drew in an enormous breath. "With you? Like a date?"

Stop looking at her chest. He forced his eyes to meet hers.

Yes, he would love to call it a date, but she'd never let that happen. "Not a date. I've just never known anyone who needed a night out as much as you."

She frowned and waggled a finger in front of his face. "But all your friends will think it's a date."

Would that be so bad? Women were usually clamoring to go out with him. "Grace mentioned in the interview that she'd like to meet you. How about we tell them that's why you came?"

"Okay," she said, downing the dregs of another rum and Coke.

"You'll go?" He tried to hide his surprise. He hoped she'd remember this in the morning.

"Yes. For research."

"Playing games with Storyhill is research? For the show?"

She giggled and nodded, the alcohol exaggerating her motions. "Country music singers in their natural habitat." She looked side-to-side, placing a finger over her lips. "What will they do? What will they say?" she whispered as if on safari. "There are always new things to learn."

"All right, David Attenborough," he said, laughing. "Now let's get you a little more food and some water."

"And another drink?"

"If you still want one after the food and water, sure."

"You, Matthew Benjamin Taylor, are a stick in the mud," she pouted.

Okay, not too drunk. She still knew his full name.

"Yeah, that's what people always say about me."

She giggled and then snorted. Her eyes flew wide, and she slapped a hand over her mouth.

"Classy," he said, nearly drunk himself from a few notes of her laughter.

She stuck out her bottom lip. "At least I know who David Attenborough is."

He sucked in his lips, biting back a smile. "Um. I think I brought him up."

"Really?" She looked at him, cocked her head, and squeezed one eye shut.

It was about the cutest damn thing he'd ever seen.

She brushed her hair back from her face. "Don't tell Celeste about this, okay?"

He paused. Was he not supposed to tell Celeste she'd invited him out for drinks or that she'd gotten drunk or that she didn't remember who first brought up David Attenborough? It didn't matter. He didn't intend on telling Celeste—or anyone else—about their evening. This was his memory to cherish.

He pulled into her driveway. A beautiful Craftsman bungalow in East Nashville. The perfect place for a family.

He turned to her. Her head lolled to the side, and she was softly snoring.

"Avery," he said, shaking her shoulder gently.

Her eyes popped open and focused on his face. She reached out, placed her hand on his face, and rubbed her thumb under his chin. The touch left a trail of warmth, nearly searing his skin. How many times had he dreamed of her touch?

"Matt," she breathed out.

He went still. Was she dreaming?

"Avery, honey, are you awake?"

She traced a finger along his jawbone. "Yes, I'm awake. You could kiss me right now. I'd let you."

God, how he wanted that. But if—when—he kissed her again, he didn't want it to be like this. He had to know it was something she really wanted.

"Probably better not to let Captain Morgan make decisions for you."

She frowned, her forehead creasing into deep wrinkles. "I'm sober now."

Matt pursed his lips, cocking his head to the side. "I'm not sure that's entirely true. How about this? I'll walk you to the door and if you can walk a straight line, I'll give you a goodnight kiss."

She pushed her bottom lip out in a pout. "You don't think I'm pretty anymore."

"No." His groin tightened at the sight of her lower lip on full display. "You're more beautiful than ever." He slipped out the door and opened hers before he said or did something stupid.

"Out we go." He offered her his hand and slid her from the car. "I'm putting your keys in your purse."

He wrapped an arm around her and guided her to the house. She accidentally kicked one of the solar lights lining the sidewalk and giggled.

Nope, not sober.

When he reached the door, he knocked. Isabel opened the door.

"Matt?" she said, surprise widening her eyes.

"Hi Momma!" Amy-Lynn announced.

"Hi baby," she said, her eyes flashing between her daughter and Matt.

Amy-Lynn staggered a step to the left, and he pulled her tighter to his side. "He wouldn't even kiss me goodnight, Momma. Can you believe that?"

Matt shrugged. "Think you can take it from here, Mrs. McWilliams?"

"She's drunk," Isabel said, surprise still filling her voice.

"Yep," Matt said, laughing.

Isabel pushed the door open wide. "She's *never* drunk."

Matt winced. "She had a stressful week. I think she needed to let loose a little."

"I'm right here. I can hear you guys. And I'm not drunk. Not anymore." She slipped out from under Matt's arm and ducked beside her mother, flopping into the chair nearest the door.

They both watched as she closed her eyes and let her head fall back.

"I'll see she drinks some water and takes some aspirin," Isabel said, watching her daughter out of the corner of her eye.

He stole a last glance at the woman who'd once been his entire world. "Avery?"

She opened one eye and looked at him. "Mmm?"

"Remember. Tomorrow night. I'll text you the details."

She gave him the thumbs up sign before closing her eyes again.

Isabel gaped at him. "You called her Avery."

He shrugged. "It's what she wants."

Isabel narrowed her eyes and scanned him from head to toe. "Huh."

Matt held up a single hand. "It was good to see you, Isabel."

"You too, Matt," Isabel said, her eyes still shifting from Matt to Amy-Lynn.

He turned down the walk and pulled out his phone to order an Uber. Two minutes away.

Isabel called after him. "Thanks for getting her home safe."

He turned and walked backwards. "Of course."

"And Matt," she continued, stepping out onto the porch. "I've never seen her drunk."

Matt sighed. "I bring out the best in people."

"I agree, but not in the way *you* mean it. She'd never have done this with someone she didn't trust."

A warmth flooded his chest, surrounding his heart. He wanted to sink into the feeling. But he couldn't. Not yet. Not until he got a few more questions answered.

The Uber pulled up to the curb. "Good night, Isabel. Take care of our girl."

CHAPTER TEN

A<small>VERY ROLLED OVER AND GROANED</small>. W<small>HY WAS THE ROOM</small> spinning? Last night's events filled in and came to an abrupt stop when the words, "You could kiss me. I'd let you," crashed through her brain.

Oh my god.

Not only had she let her guard down with Matt, but she'd also gotten drunk and propositioned him. Okay, she was being melodramatic. It's not like she invited him in and threw him down on the bed.

But still. She threw her arm across her eyes. He'd said *no*.

Which was more embarrassing? Asking him or getting turned down?

The door to her bedroom flew open, and Wyatt jumped on her bed. She had to swallow hard to keep last night's food down. "Tía! Pancakes and flowers!"

She tried to shake off the haze and translate toddler-speak. "Abuela made pancakes?"

"No. Mommy."

Was she still dreaming? "Your mom made pancakes?"

Wyatt nodded in that full-body way that only toddlers managed. "Get up!" He pulled on her arm.

She rubbed her eyes. Yikes. She'd slept with her contacts in. "Wyatt, baby, go tell your mommy I'll be there in five minutes."

"Okay," he said brightly, hopping down from the bed and running down the hallway, screaming, "Mommy!"

Avery grabbed her head. He really needed to stop that. She sat up and checked in with her stomach. "How about some pancakes?" she asked it. It didn't send anything spiraling upwards. She took that as a good sign.

She padded into her ensuite and without looking in the mirror—she didn't dare—she peeled the contacts out and pulled a brush through her tangle of snarls. Once she'd located her glasses, she walked tentatively into the kitchen, blinking at the bright light, and slipped onto a barstool.

Jess slid a plate in front of her.

"Eat!" Wyatt said, grabbing her arm, his sticky fingers leaving a trail of maple syrup behind.

"Inside voice, baby," she said to the child, but she couldn't help smiling at his exuberance. She could use a bit of that energy right now.

"Momma said you got drunk with Matt Taylor last night."

She looked at her sister over the top of her glasses. Good lord. Was nothing sacred in this house?

"Tía drunk. Tía drunk. Drunk. Dunk. Bunk," Wyatt sang.

Avery laughed. "Is that why you made pancakes?"

"Well, they are good hangover food, but no. I made them to say thank you for taking Momma to her appointment."

That's right, that was just yesterday. Why did it feel like she'd lived a hundred years since then?

"How'd the interview go?" She prepared herself for her sister's litany of excuses. Hopefully, she'd *gone* to the interview.

Jess ran around the island and circled Avery's shoulders and squeezed. Her second hug in as many days. "Sissy! I got the job! I start on Monday! And I even have a daycare plan worked out!"

"Momma?" Avery knew she shouldn't be so cynical, but all previous data pointed to it.

"For the first week, yes. But then he's enrolled at the Montessori on Douglas."

Avery looked up, full fork hanging in the air. "That's great, Jess. I'm very proud of you." And she realized it was the truth.

"You are?" her sister asked, a tremble in her voice.

She grabbed her sister's arms and squeezed her back. "Very proud."

"We can talk about rent," Jess said, bouncing back to the stove to flip a pancake.

"How about we wait until my head stops pounding?"

Jess laughed and shook her head. "I still can't believe you got drunk. It's so unlike you. Maybe yesterday was opposite day. I got a job and you got drunk."

"Maybe that's it." But she thought it had less to do with that and more to do with a tall, super sexy, blond musician.

"Oh, I almost forgot," Jess said, pushing a vase of daisies toward Avery. "These came for you."

"You didn't need to spend your money on flowers, Jess. The pancakes were enough."

"I didn't," she said, smirking over her shoulder.

Avery's brow furrowed. If not Jess, then who? She pulled the card from the floral pick. *"Hope you're not feeling too bad this morning. Not sure if these are still your favorites. Looking forward to seeing you tonight. M."*

"What's happening tonight?" Jess asked, slapping another pancake on her plate.

Avery glared at her sister. "You read the card?"

Jess shrugged. "Wanted to make sure they weren't from some crazy fan."

"Sure." Avery rolled her eyes. "And what would you have done if they were?"

"Left them outside."

"It's only signed 'M.'"

"But it mentions your hangover."

She stuffed her mouth with pancakes and let it go. "He mentioned some Storyhill thing tonight. I think I said yes."

"Damn straight you said yes."

"It's not that easy, Jess."

Jess poured more batter onto the griddle. "You overcomplicate everything, Sissy."

"And you don't think things through."

"Are you two fighting again?" Isabel asked, emerging from the hallway. "Or should I say 'still?'"

"Abuela! Eat pancakes!" Wyatt yelled, making them all laugh.

"I'm pretty sure we can all agree that the pancakes are delicious. Right, Sissy?" Jessica asked Avery.

"Right."

"Good," Isabel said, sliding onto the stool on the opposite side of Wyatt. "You feeling okay?" she asked Avery quietly.

Avery nodded. "Considering."

Isabel slid a fork through her pancake and glanced at Avery from the corner of her eye. "It was nice of Matt to bring you home."

Avery let out a low groan, dropping her head to her chest. "Momma, don't start."

"What?" Isabel said, feigning innocence, a small smile dancing at the corners of her lips.

Avery spun to face her mother. "It was your idea that I thank him for covering yesterday's show."

Isabel shrugged and her smile grew. "I was thinking a text or maybe a phone call. Never imagined you'd end up wrapped in his arms on our front step."

Jess turned, her eyes popping wide. "You were '*wrapped*' in his arms, Sissy? With Momma watching?"

Avery snorted. "He was holding me up, Jess. Nothing romantic—or sexy—about it." Though she'd be lying if she didn't admit it felt good to be in his arms again. Safe. Warm. Protected. And something, she realized, that she'd missed every day for the past nine years.

"Sure, Sissy," Jess said, giving Avery an exaggerated wink. "Whatever you say."

Avery rolled her eyes. "Look what you started, Momma," she said, waving her hand at Jess.

"Nope," her mother said, shaking her head. "That was all you. You started it—and now you're going to do the next right thing."

Avery choked on a bite of pancake. "Momma," she hissed through clenched teeth. She was clear on her mother's meaning, but she didn't need Jess getting clear on it, too.

"Yeah," Jess said, waggling her eyebrows. "The next right step is to get his arms around you again. And see where it leads."

A relieved sigh oozed out of Avery. Jess hadn't read into Momma's comment. And that's the way it was going to stay.

When the time came to get ready for the party, Avery stood in front of her closet, chewing on a bright blue nail. What should she wear? Should she even go?

How was she supposed to face Matt after nearly begging him to kiss her?

"See?" she said, pacing in front of her closet. "This is why inviting Matt Taylor to co-host was a bad idea." She shouldn't go to the party. She pulled out her favorite sweatshirt and yoga pants, but stopped.

She was Avery-fucking-Lind. She would not be afraid. She had the opportunity to spend the evening with country singers, a Grammy award-winning songwriter, and other industry people. This was just networking.

Except it wasn't.

Her heart slammed against her ribcage. Impending panic attack. She laid back on the bed and stroked her fingers between her breasts, reciting the mantra that calmed her.

A knock resounded through her door. "Yes?" She'd told her family that the anxiety was better. She didn't want anyone to see her like this.

"Sissy? Can I come in?"

"I'm getting ready. Not dressed. Can it wait?"

"Then my timing is perfect. I pulled something from my closet that I think will look beautiful on you. You can't go on your first date with Mr. Taylor, after all these years, and not look absolutely fabulous."

"It's not a date!" She wondered if she was telling herself or her sister. "But come in." She wiped away the perspiration that had accumulated at the base of her neck.

"What are you doing?" her sister asked, scanning her prone position from head to toe.

"And why, if this isn't a date, do you have your best bra and panties on?" Jessica tried holding back a smirk but couldn't do it. She sat down next to Avery on the bed. "And you shaved your legs?" she asked even more smugly, running a hand down Avery's smooth calf.

Avery rolled over and buried her face in the duvet. "I don't know," she said, voice muffled. "I don't know," she repeated.

"Roll over," Jessica demanded. When Avery had done so, she asked, "Is this what it's like dealing with me? I can see why it's so exhausting. Now, sit up and act like the Amy-Lynn we all know and love—balls to the walls, take no prisoners."

Avery sat up and looked at the dress Jess was holding up. It was short, black, had a deep, plunging neckline, and was totally outside of Avery's comfort zone. "What's wrong with my clothes?" she said, motioning toward her closet.

Jess gave her a look that said, I really don't need to say this, do I?

"It's basically all work wear."

Avery scoffed. "I have dresses."

Jess snorted. "Designed for Victorian ladies."

"That's not fair," Avery said, tromping over to her closet and pulling out her one sequined top. "I have this."

"Which I haven't seen you wear in years." Jess wiggled the dress hanger. "Just try it on."

Avery sighed. "Fine." She wrenched the dress from Jess and slid it on over her head. It fit perfectly and clung just enough to show off her figure, but not so much she'd be uncomfortable.

"Whoa, Sissy," Jess whistled. "If I had a figure like that, I'd never stop showing it off."

Avery rolled her eyes. "This is your dress."

"My body has changed since having Wyatt."

Avery started pulling her hair up, but Jess stopped her. "Leave it down. And how about I do your make-up?"

"I can do my make-up."

Jess's expression softened. "Let me do it, like old times."

"Okay," Avery said. "And you might as well find me some shoes, too."

Jessica clapped her hands together and squealed.

Was this all it took to make their relationship easier? She really could use one less stressful thing in her life right now.

. . .

The doorbell rang just as Jessica swiped a final coat of mascara on Avery's lashes—false lashes, Jess had insisted. She felt like a dress-up doll, but it made Jess so happy. And isn't that why she did all the things she did? To make her family happy?

"Amy-Lynn," her mother called from the bottom of the stairs, "Matt is here."

Avery turned to look in the mirror, but her sister stopped her. "Don't keep him waiting."

"But I need to see . . ."

"You look perfect."

Avery scooted closer to the mirror. "It makes me uneasy that you won't let me look. What did you do to me?"

Jess smiled and lightly patted Avery's cheek. "Relax, you're still 92 percent professional, stuffy Avery."

"What's the other eight percent?"

"Jessica McWilliams magic."

Avery snorted.

"Now go," Jess said, pushing her out the door.

Avery really wanted a mirror. What if Jess wasn't telling the truth?

She didn't have to worry long. She descended the stairs and Matt turned to look at her. His eyes widened, and his mouth fell open before he caught himself. "You look beautiful. I mean, you always do, but this is different."

"Different bad?" She nervously smoothed her hands down the front of the dress. Why did she care? Avery Lind didn't need anyone's approval. "If this isn't right for the party, I can go upstairs and change."

"It's perfect," he said, reaching for her hand and threading her fingers through his.

She looked from their intertwined hands to her mother and her sister and quickly pulled her hand free. Her mother wore a soft, enigmatic expression, but Jess's expression read *I told you so.*

"You obviously met Momma last night," she said, trying to move attention away from his touch. "And you remember Jess."

"Yes," he said, pulling his attention away from Avery. "Nice to see you again, Jessica."

Jess smiled like a Cheshire cat. "You're welcome here anytime, Matt."

Avery cleared her throat. "Still my house, baby sister."

"Momma taught us to be hospitable, big sister. Didn't you, Momma?"

Isabel smirked and arched a single eyebrow at Avery. "That I did. That I did."

Before Avery could say anything further, a streak of blue ran past her and wrapped his arms around Matt's knees. "Boy!" the little boy hollered. They really needed to talk to him about using his inside voice.

Matt laughed softly and mussed the little boy's head. "And this must be Wyatt," he said, looking at Jess. "Your auntie was telling me all about you last night."

"Boy stay. Play," Wyatt said with a stomp.

Jess pulled him away from Matt. "He has plenty of friends, but I'm afraid he doesn't have a lot of contact with adult *boys*," she explained.

Matt looked up from the child and met Avery's eyes. "Really?" he said. "Three beautiful women in this house and he doesn't see a lot of men, huh?" The question was meant for all of them, but it was directed at Avery.

"There it is," Isabel said. "The famous Matt Taylor charm. Glad to see it hasn't gone away."

"No, ma'am," Matt said, finally moving his intense gaze off Avery. "It's served me well. Can't go messing with a proven winner." He smiled at Isabel, and Avery could have sworn her mother blushed a little.

Matt bent to get eye level with her nephew. "Your auntie and I already have a playdate planned. How about I come back and play with you another time?"

"Tomorrow," Wyatt said, crossing his little arms, demanding agreement.

Matt looked up at Avery. "That's up to your auntie."

"Tía," Wyatt said, pulling on the hem of her shorter-than-she-liked dress. "Tomorrow?"

"We'll see Wyatt," she said, shooting Matt a look that she hoped communicated, don't make him promises you can't keep.

Matt stood to his full height and picked the little boy up. Seeing him hold Wyatt made her gut twist. What if they'd never broken up?

No. No. No. She'd made her choices. Crafted her life to perfection. Well, professional perfection. She would not play the 'what if' game.

Avery patted her nephew's back. "Wyatt, say goodbye to Mr. Matt."

"Bye," the little boy said, and placed a big, wet kiss on Matt's cheek.

Jess motioned for Wyatt to come to her. "I'm sorry, he never does that. He's usually shy around strangers."

"Maybe he senses I'm not really a stranger," Matt said, his attention shifting back to Avery.

"We really need to go," Avery said, without knowing if that was the truth or not. She grabbed her handbag and the door handle. "Right, Matt?"

"Yes, Grace has a thing about punctuality."

Jess leaned in and whispered, "You're wearing my dress. Maybe act a little more like Jess tonight and a little less like Amy-Lynn."

Avery screwed up her lips, rolled her eyes, gave Jess's shoulder a nudge, and stepped out onto the porch.

"We won't wait up," Jess yelled after them.

∼

Matt opened the truck door for Amy-Lynn and took her hand, helping her onto the elevated seat. Her dress slipped up, exposing the creamy skin of her thighs, and a current shot through him, gaining speed as it hurtled down his spine, settling low. He'd once known her body better than he'd known his own, and if the tightening of his pants was any indication, his body was on board to learn the curves of her body all over again.

He slid into the driver's side and started the ignition.

"Sorry about Jess. And her . . . her . . . insinuations."

Matt bit back a smile. She was so confident at work. He couldn't help liking this more vulnerable side of her. "What was she insinuating?"

"Nothing," she grumbled.

"Why apologize if it's nothing?"

She flicked him on the shoulder. "You're maddening."

He sobered. "Are you still embarrassed about being seen with me?"

"Embarrassed?" She swiveled in her seat to face him and damn if that dress didn't slide up even higher. If it inched up just a little more, he'd know exactly what she was wearing under it. Could his heart take it? Doubtful.

"What does that mean?" she asked, snapping his attention back to her comments about Jessica.

He tapped his fingers on the steering wheel and kept his attention on the road. He didn't want to see her expression. "Clearly I've never been good enough for you."

Her skin squeaked against the leather seat, and he felt the weight of her gaze on him. "That is not true, and you know it."

He signaled left, and he knew this was not the time or place for this discussion—in less than five minutes they'd be at the condo Grace and Andrew were renting until they found a second home in Nashville—but he couldn't force himself to let it go.

"That's the real reason you broke up with me, isn't it? I didn't fit into your grand plan."

He glanced her direction. She was looking at him as if he had a shark head.

"Is that honestly what you think?"

He lifted a single shoulder. "Why else?"

She twisted her hands in her lap and looked out the passenger side window. "I told you why," she whispered.

He shouldn't push. He knew that. But the truth was within his reach. Maybe she'd finally tell him? "Remind me."

"I didn't want a partner who was going to be gone all the time, like my daddy. I saw what it did to my family." Her words were even, but her body had gone stiff, and the color drained from her face.

He turned into the surface lot surrounding Andrew and Grace's condo, pulled into the first open parking spot, and killed the engine.

"That hadn't mattered for the six years we were together, and then one day it did? I might not be the sharpest crayon in the box, but I'm a long way from stupid, Mac. I deserve the real explanation, or at least why you suddenly changed your mind about my career choice."

"I don't know what you want me to say," she said, rubbing her fingers over the depression in her collarbone while her telltale blush colored the column of her neck.

No. He wouldn't cause a panic attack, especially before

meeting his friends. This was supposed to be a fun night. A night to help her forget about all her worries for a few hours.

There was more to the story than she'd tell him, but he didn't need to dig it out right now.

He grabbed her fingers and uncurled them, rubbing the webbing between her thumb and forefinger in a way that calmed her—or had nine years ago.

"I'm sorry," he said, keeping pressure on her fingers. "We—well, I—need to talk about this, but it doesn't have to be tonight. Is there anything else I can do to help with the anxiety?"

"Anxiety?" she said, clearly trying to mask what was going on.

He pushed a curl behind her ear. "I know the signs. Mac. Is it still as bad as ever?"

She dropped her head and her eyes shuttered closed. "No," she whispered.

"But it's still an issue?"

She nodded without looking up.

He placed a single finger under her chin and tilted her head up. "Look at me," he said.

She finally opened her eyes. "I'm so embarrassed."

He pulled her into a hug over the center console. Her body stiffened, but she didn't pull away. He'd take that as a win. He could feel her pulse throbbing in her neck. What had he read about anxiety attacks? Keep calm. Speak in short sentences. Help her stay grounded. "There is absolutely no reason to be embarrassed. This doesn't define you."

She reached for the hollow spot in her clavicle. Again.

"Want to do the 3-3-3 rule?"

Her eyes found his. "How do you remember that?" she whispered.

"I love you," he said. Her eyes flashed again. "I mean, I *loved* you. I learned everything I could about anxiety."

"Thank you. But I think I'm okay."

"I can take you home."

She looked out the window in the direction they came from and then back to him. "No. I committed to this, and I will do it. You told me you wanted to meet the woman I'd become. Turnabout is fair play."

He smiled. "You think my friends are going to be a window into my world?"

"Yep. And the people most likely to tell embarrassing stories I can rub in your face over the next nine shows."

"Nine shows," he repeated, "is that all that's left?"

"Yep, thirty-six hours and you'll be free of me."

Something reached out and squeezed his heart. Thirty-six hours to show his bandmates he had skills. Thirty-six hours to get the answers he wanted—no, needed. And thirty-six hours to figure out, all over again, how to live without her.

"Well, thirty-six show hours plus this party."

She smiled. "There's that."

"We better get started, then."

Her smile drooped. "Is there anything I need to know before we go in?"

She smoothed her hands down her dress and damn if he didn't watch her hands, wanting to do the same thing himself. So many emotions, but apparently lust trumped everything else going on.

"Don't worry, Mac. These people have no expectations, they are a laid back, welcoming group. Being yourself is all they expect."

CHAPTER ELEVEN

BE YOURSELF, AVERY REPEATED IN HER HEAD AS THEY RODE the elevator to the top floor. Did she still know how to do that? Was she anxiety-ridden Amy-Lynn? Or confident and capable Avery Lind? Likely a jumble of both.

The elevator doors opened directly into a large apartment. "Penthouse?" Avery asked, scanning the large entryway.

"Yep. Grace is very down to earth, but I think she grew accustomed to a certain way of living while married to Jax Jensen."

Avery wanted to know more, but at that moment, the woman herself floated into the vestibule and pulled Matt into a familiar hug. "I was wondering if you'd forgotten."

He gave Grace his biggest smile and placed a small kiss on her cheek. So he'd kiss Grace, but not her? *It's not the same and you know it.* She did, but the little green monster currently jumping on her chest didn't.

Against her better judgement, she longed to feel Matt's arms around her and feel his lips pressed against her skin. The need to touch him grew stronger every moment they spent together. How long would she be able to keep her distance?

"No chance I'd forget," Matt said to Grace. "I haven't eaten since breakfast to leave room for all this delicious food."

Avery had almost forgotten about the pie in her hands. "I hope bourbon pecan pie will fit in," she said, employing her radio voice. "My momma's nearly famous for it," she added, holding it out to Grace.

Grace turned her smile on her. "You must be Avery. I've been looking forward to meeting you."

Avery smiled. A real one. "Hi. Yes. Nice to meet you too. Thank you for being on the show yesterday. I'm sorry if you had to juggle your schedule."

"Of course. My pleasure. That's the beauty of songwriting. I can do most of it on my schedule. That's a great dress, by the way," Grace said, turning toward the archway into the living room.

Avery fought the urge to pull at the hem. "Thank you. I hope I'm not overdressed. I rarely go out, so I don't have many chances to wear something like this."

"Then I'm even more pleased Matt invited you. I can imagine your job takes a lot of time and attention. And we both know it's harder for women in this industry."

Avery nodded and sighed, releasing some of the tension caught between her shoulder blades. It felt good to have someone understand the rigors of her job—and the effort it took.

Grace led them into the adjoining room and the sound got louder with every step. Matt said there'd be fifteen people max. Maybe she should have gone home.

As if reading her mind, Grace turned and said, "There are only ten people here even though it sounds like fifty."

"My boys aren't known for their inside voices," Matt said with a chuckle.

"Truth," Grace said, setting the pie on a table piled high with all kinds of amazing looking food.

"Kinda like Wyatt," he said next to her ear.

Avery laughed, because it was true, but also because his breath dancing over her cheek lit up neurons from her ears to her toes. Somewhere in the far reaches of her brain, her body still remembered what it felt like to be touched—to be loved—by Matt Taylor. Would it be the same? Or better? The shivers running up and down her spine suggested yes.

"Hey Storyhill," Grace said in a voice that immediately silenced the room. Avery's lips twitched. There was no doubt who was the alpha in this crowd. She was going to like Grace very much. "Meet Avery Lind."

"Avery!" a cheer went up around the room, everyone lifting their glass.

"Do they practice that?" she whispered to Grace.

"You'd think so," Grace said, laughing. "Let me introduce you to everyone. Unless Matt wants to do that." Grace turned to Matt and cocked an eyebrow.

He smiled softly at the two women. "Go ahead, Grace. I'll get drinks." He winked at Avery, and a colony of butterflies exploded in her belly. She pressed a hand into her abdomen, trying to settle them, but they were a hardy bunch.

Grace escorted her around the room, helping Avery put faces to the names Matt had mentioned. Everyone was open and kind and welcomed her as if she'd been coming to these gatherings for years.

Their tour ended in the kitchen. A dark-haired man pulled a six-pack from the fridge, and Avery instantly recognized Andrew. Grace's entire demeanor changed, and her voice softened. The look they shared made Avery blush a little. What must it be like to have someone look at you like that? *You knew once*, that nagging little voice said.

"Welcome. I can't imagine what Matt had to promise you to get you to come. Meeting everyone all at once is a tough date. I think that's why he usually comes alone," Andrew said, circling his fiancé's shoulders.

Her first response was to make sure Andrew and Grace knew this wasn't a date. But the thing that fell out of her mouth was, "Matt hasn't brought other women to these things?"

"No," Grace said, surprised by her own answer. "His face might launch a thousand ships, but he's never brought any into this port."

Andrew's brow furrowed and he laughed.

"I know," Grace said, "that was a really terrible metaphor. And I'm supposed to be good with words."

Avery laughed, though the thought that a confirmed ladies' man had never introduced any of his partners to his friends surprised her. "It'll be our little secret," she said to Grace.

"What's the secret?" Matt asked, stepping up to them and handing Avery a half-full wineglass.

"Not everything that comes out of Grace's mouth is a hit song," Avery said, accepting the glass.

"I thought it was a secret," Grace said, laughing.

"Sorry. I'm normally good with secrets." *From years of practice.* Secrets that, if they came out, would ruin so many things.

"No worries," Grace said with the air of a woman perfectly at home in her skin. Unlike Avery. "And now that most everyone is here, I think it's time for a game."

"What should we play tonight, love?" Andrew asked.

"Well, Cowboy, I was thinking Song Titles." Grace grabbed Avery's hand. "And Avery and I are going to be a team."

The familiarity of Grace's touch startled her. "You want to partner with me? We've only just met."

"Song Titles is a game where a word is pulled from a jar and each team has ten seconds to name a song with that word in it—and bonus points if you can name the artist. A team comprising a radio host and a songwriter is a winning combination. I'm being totally selfish." She winked at Avery. "I'm really ready to take some cash off these boys."

"You play for money?"

Grace nodded. "It's a small pot. The real winning comes in rubbing their faces in their loss."

Avery laughed. "I have a feeling we're going to be friends, Grace O'Connor." A sadness rolled over Avery. Would she have the opportunity to see Grace again?

When was the last time she had a female friend? Someone who was more than a co-worker? She couldn't remember.

An hour later, Grace and Avery were collecting their winnings and talking a fair amount of trash. Her cheeks hurt from smiling. She hadn't had this much fun in a long time. Matt was right. She really did need a night out.

She looked across the room at Matt spread out on the sofa. He was talking and laughing with his friends, relaxed in a way that made him even more attractive. She hardly thought that was possible.

He looked up and caught her staring. His lips curved in a soft smile before winking at her with something entirely not soft. A tremor ran down her spine, heat pooling in her belly.

She'd once loved him so deeply. And she couldn't deny that some of those feelings still existed. And her body was ten steps ahead of her head and heart. He was going to be gone soon. What if she gave into her body's cravings? Would that be so bad? One night. No past. No future. Just now. Images of him, braced over her, filled her head. Heat spread through her body.

She needed some air.

She broke eye contact with Matt and spun on her heel, hurriedly moving toward the open balcony. When she stepped outside, she tried to pull in a deep breath, but her chest wouldn't expand. Whether it was the hazy, humid July heat or something else, she couldn't be sure.

She was sure of one thing, though. She would not have a panic attack in front of these people. She tried for another steadying breath and counted back, slowly, from ten.

"You okay?" came an all-too-familiar voice from behind her.

"Trying," she answered. It was the most honest answer she'd given anyone in a long time.

He stepped behind her, his chest flush with her back. She waited for another anxiety spike, but it didn't come. Instead, her breathing evened out and the pain in her chest loosened.

"Hold me," she said, barely over a whisper.

She could sense his surprise, but he said nothing, simply wrapping his arms around her middle and pulling her tighter against his chest.

"If I remember, tight is better than loose. Is that still right?"

"Yes," she breathed out. He remembered so many things about her. What did she remember? His easy laugh. His gifts on stage. How it felt to lie naked next to him. How carefully he loved her, in and out of bed.

Awareness shot through her. She wanted that again. She wanted to watch him slowly remove his clothes and climb into bed with her, kissing his way down her body and making love to her like there was no place he'd rather be.

"Matt." His name slipped out on an exhale.

"What do you need, Mac?"

Damn, that nickname. How could one syllable have so much power over her? "Take me home."

She felt his body tense. "I'm sorry. I should have known this might be too much for you. I just wanted you to meet my friends."

She spun to face him, his arms still bracketing her. "No, you don't understand. Take me home—to your place." She reached up on tippy-toes and brushed a soft kiss over his lips.

She wanted to deepen the kiss, but there was a house full of people steps away.

His eyes widened, and he ran a finger over her lower lip. "Are you asking what I think you're asking?"

She nodded. Forming the words would make her second guess herself. And for once, she didn't want to overthink something.

"You're sure? Only a week ago you wanted nothing to do with me."

That's not true. I've always wanted all of you. That's why I gave you up.

"You don't feel it?" she said, running a hand up his chest and pushing away her thoughts. Now was the time to channel Avery, not get caught up in Amy-Lynn's complicated truths.

He caught her hand. "I feel it. I never stopped feeling it."

"But?" she said, caught between embarrassment and lust. No, there was no room for embarrassment. Avery hadn't gotten where she was without asking for what she wanted.

"But," he said, twirling a piece of her hair around his finger. "There are a lot of unresolved things between us."

She looked up at him from underneath her lashes. "Maybe we could forget about all that for tonight?"

Please say yes, she pleaded silently. If they started discussing the past, this probably wouldn't happen.

All she wanted was a single night before he left on tour and walked out of her life. Was it wrong to ask for sex with a secret hanging between them? Yes. Did it make her want him less? No.

"I'd like to, Mac, so much. But it broke me when you left. I don't know if I can survive that again. Lust and logic are having a knock-down-drag-out fight in my brain right now."

She knew exactly what he meant. It's not like she broke

up with him because she'd fallen out of love with him. She'd been facing the same battle since the morning he'd followed Celeste into the studio. But right now, all she wanted was to forget about her momma, Jessica, her father's death, the radio show, and even the secret that stood between them for a little while. And it wasn't just sex. She wanted to be held. She wanted to be in the arms of someone she trusted. Someone she loved.

The word rattled through her with the subtlety of a spring thunderstorm. She still loved him. Did that make this a good idea or a careless one?

"You don't want me," she said, giving him an out.

He pulled her closer, and the hard line of his erection pressed into her belly. "Does that feel like I don't want you?"

She slipped a hand between them and ran a finger down his length, causing both of them to shiver in response.

He leaned down, mumbling something about 'questionable choices' and kissed her. Not a brushing kiss like hers, but hard, nipping at her bottom lip. She gasped and his tongue swept against hers.

It was like no time had passed. He remembered what she liked. She remembered the taste and feel of him. And she wanted more.

He pulled back, his chest rising and falling like he'd just run a flight of stairs.

"You sure about this?"

She nodded. "Yes."

"Okay. Find your handbag and let Grace know we're leaving. I need a minute to take care of this situation." He waved his hand in front of his zipper.

She licked her lips and looked down. "I could help."

"No," he laughed softly. "Not here, you can't. And when did you become so bold?"

"Years of fighting the patriarchy will do that to a girl." *Screw you, Amy-Lynn. Avery Lind for the win!*

A slow smile crept across his lips. "I like it."

She smirked. "Yeah?"

"Yeah. Now go." He gave her shoulder a playful shove. "I'll come shortly."

"Yeah you will." Her eyes widened at her brashness. Where was this coming from?

Matt snorted, shaking his head, and biting back a smile. "Go."

She turned and chuckled under her breath. This new fearless attitude could really grow on her.

Matt watched Amy-Lynn zigzag through outstretched legs and displaced furniture. Everything from the neck up told him this was not a good idea, but everything from the neck down held an opposing opinion.

Maybe this was a good sign? Maybe her wanting him physically was her way of showing him she saw his potential.

That could be it, right? She'd noticed his band was on an upward trajectory. He'd handled the show well yesterday. She'd said so herself.

Or maybe it was just his dick talking.

Either way, he couldn't bring himself to turn down a night with her. He dreamed of this for over nine years.

And if it was only one night? Could his heart sustain it?

Did it matter? He was leaving in ten days. Nine shows and ten days. Professionally, this was likely a stupid decision.

Or maybe not? Maybe it would help to get her out of his system. He laughed. Yeah, there was no part of him that bought that story.

He followed her path through the living room and stopped where Grace and Avery stood talking.

"Sorry to hear you're leaving. Maybe the four of us could get together before you leave on tour?" Grace asked.

"I'd like that," Amy-Lynn responded, surprising Matt. Voluntarily getting together with people? Very unlike her. Well, unlike Amy-Lynn. Maybe Avery Lind was different? There was still so much he didn't know about her current life.

"Great," Grace said, pulling Amy-Lynn into a hug and winking at him over her shoulder. "Get some good rest."

Matt rolled his eyes at Grace. The woman missed nothing.

Grace reached for Amy-Lynn's hand and squeezed it. "I'll get your number from Matt and text you."

Avery thanked Grace again and Matt yelled to the remaining band members as they stepped into the entryway, but not before he heard Joe say, "So that was the infamous Avery Lind."

He hoped she hadn't heard.

As they walked to the car, he felt the need to close the gap that the last nine years had created.

He picked up her hand and kissed her knuckles before opening the car door. "I just want you to know that I rarely sleep with someone on the first date." He desperately wanted her to tell him the same thing. Why? She was a grown woman who owed him no explanations.

Still.

He wanted to believe she hadn't slept with anyone since him. Some kind of born-again-virgin-caveman bullshit.

She smirked. "Good to know. But," she said, "this is hardly our first date."

"Do you remember our first date?" he asked, stuck between not wanting to dredge up old memories and wanting to know she still thought about him, about them.

"Of course," she said, smiling. "High school gym, blue streamers, lingering haze of body odor."

Matt laughed. "That's right. The boys' basketball team had a game earlier that day."

"And I believe you scored the winning basket."

He laughed. "Could be. I wasn't any good, but I had my growth spurt before the other guys. Just stood under the basket and threw it in the hoop when someone passed it to me."

She cocked her head, a smile pulling up the corners of her mouth. "You don't remember?"

"No. I was preoccupied."

"With?"

"With the beautiful woman who'd agreed to go to the dance with me. I felt like the luckiest dude on the planet."

Avery's cheeks prickled with dots of pink. "And our first dance was to 'Put Your Records On.'"

Matt shook his head. "No, I'm pretty sure it was a slower one. 'Chasing Cars' by Snow Patrol."

"Nope. No way. Did you just see me crush that song game? It was 'Put Your Records On' by Corrine Bailey Rae."

Matt lifted one hand from the steering wheel in defeat. "I won't agree with you, but I surrender."

She smiled. "Smart man."

A couple of minutes of silence passed, each lost in thought.

He knew more about her than the other handful of women he'd slept with, but it was old knowledge. He wanted—craved— more. But how to get her talking?

He took her in, scanning from her feet to her forehead. "Tell me about the hair."

She ran a hand over the soft waves of raspberry hair. Blake had likened it to a red velvet cupcake. He wasn't sure she'd appreciate the comparison.

"It's part of the brand, I guess."

"The brand?"

"Avery Lind. When I started moving up through the Nashville radio scene, I wanted to stand out. Amy-Lynn McWilliams was a lost, grieving, small-town girl. I needed to leave her behind to find success."

And him too. Did she really believe she needed to leave him to find success? He'd always believed they'd been at their best together. Clearly, that was not a belief she shared.

"I cut my hair and colored it. Started wearing what became a uniform, jeans and a jacket, quirky, yet professional. You understand, no different from branding your band."

"I guess," he said, pulling into the driveway of his apartment complex and hitting a button above his head to open the door to the underground parking. "But there are five of us, so it's not all about me. Though the guys have taken to calling me Rhinestone Cowboy when I go a little over the top with the bling and belt buckles."

She looked him over, head to toe. "Always seeking attention."

More than she knew. "I've toned it down recently."

He killed the engine and rapped his fingers against the steering wheel. "This is it. You're still sure?"

She blinked a few times and chewed on the edge of a bright blue fingernail. "Kiss me."

He looked side-to-side, taking in the silent parking garage. Cold cement and exhaust fumes weren't exactly his idea of romantic. "What? Here?"

"Yes," she said, her voice even and matter of fact.

"Okay." He leaned across the console and placed a trail of kisses along her jaw. Her eyes fluttered closed. He moved to her luscious lips—god, she was beautiful—and kissed. Slow and easy, but with a longing he couldn't hide.

He pulled back, inches from her face, and let his forehead meet hers.

She bit her bottom lip and ran her hands up his arms. "Totally sure."

He chuckled. "Was that a test?"

She smiled. "Yes. But not for you. It was for me. You, Matt Taylor, have always known just how to kiss me."

Jesus. What was he supposed to do with that?

"Wanna go upstairs and see if you remember the other stuff?" she asked before he could finish his thought.

Hell yes, his body responded. His mind and heart couldn't help wondering if this was magic or mistake—either way he wasn't letting her get away this time. Even if it was only one night or a couple of hours. He would take whatever she was willing to give.

CHAPTER TWELVE

A<small>VERY WATCHED AS</small> M<small>ATT FUMBLED WITH THE KEY IN THE</small> lock. She wasn't the only nervous one. She reached out and wrapped her arms around his waist, laying her head on his back. She needed to touch him, or she'd chicken out. And she didn't want to chicken out.

She wanted Matt.

She'd deal with the consequences later.

She never did things like this. Everything in her life was planned and considered against the impacts it would have on everyone and everything in her life. That she was about to leap with no idea if a net would catch her was frightening, but it was also exhilarating.

She ran her hands up his chest, and he sucked in a shuttering breath. The key slipped out of the lock.

"I hope that's not a harbinger of things to come."

Matt coughed. "Again. So bold."

She let her arms fall. "You said you liked it. Did I take it too far?"

He pushed the key in the lock, turned the handle, and

opened the door, standing aside for her to enter. "Not even a little bit."

"Then what?"

"It's just that when you say things like that, I'm reminded that I'm getting to know you all over again."

"Have I changed so much?" Was she asking herself or him? Until tonight, she realized she'd thought of herself as two people. Avery Lind, strong and confident radio host and Amy-Lynn McWilliams, the woman saddled with anxiety and family responsibilities. Standing on Grace and Andrew's balcony, saying brash things, those two sides of her personality had grown a little closer together.

"Yes, you've changed. We both have. But one thing hasn't. You are still the most beautiful, sexy, driven woman I have ever known."

She settled on his sofa, pulling her legs beneath her, trying to let his compliment sink in. She watched his eyes travel up her leg to where her fingers wrapped around the hem of her dress. "Have you *known* many women?"

He opened a beer and lifted it, asking if she wanted one.

"Water?"

He grabbed a glass and filled it from the refrigerator. "Are you asking me how many people I've slept with?"

She nodded. "I know it's not the sexiest thing to ask, but safety first, right?"

He looked up at the ceiling, presumably counting. "Including you?"

"Yes." She took a long drink from her glass, instantly regretting refusing the beer.

"Four."

"Four?" she said, nearly sending water spraying across the room.

He sat down beside her, pulling her legs across his lap. He

drew tiny spirals up and down her leg, each touch sending sparks flying.

She shivered but forced her attention back to their conversation. "Is that all? I mean, your reputation would lead a woman to believe . . ."

He smirked. "What do you know about my reputation?"

She sighed. "Fine. I might have followed Storyhill for a while."

He laughed and squeezed her calf. "I knew it."

She brushed away his hand. "Smug doesn't look good on you, Matt Taylor."

His smile dissolved. "You know better than anyone that not everything is as it seems in this business. Don't get me wrong, I've had plenty of offers. But it's not a super casual thing for me. I wasn't lying earlier when I said I've never slept with someone on the first date. And I've *never* taken someone home after a concert, no matter how much they offer at the signing table."

He slipped a finger under the hem of her dress, pulling his thumb across her thigh. "What's your number?"

He really needed to stop that if he expected coherent answers. "More than four."

"How many, Mac?"

She shrugged. "Ten-ish?"

"Ish?"

"A quick scan of history brings up nine names." When he simply stared at her, she said, "That's only one a year since we broke up."

"I'm not here to judge you. And I can't expect you to have been celibate . . . though I must admit, I'd have preferred it," he muttered just loud enough for her to hear it. "Anyone serious?"

"No. I'm all work and no play, remember? Most guys don't want to come second to my job." *Or deal with my family. Or my anxiety.*

She inched her bottom closer to him and with one quick move, straddled his lap.

He grabbed her hips, digging his fingers in. "Done talking, Mac?"

"I don't want to talk about my job or the past. I just want to feel."

"If I recall, you started this line of conversation."

"And now I'm finishing it." She leaned down and brushed a kiss across his lips. Her body thrummed with just a single kiss.

He pulled at the fabric sash around her waist, and the dress fell open. "Wow, what magic is this? It's like a ripcord on a parachute."

"It's called a wrap dress. Only one lever," she said with a soft laugh, kissing his neck and sinking her teeth into his earlobe.

"Easy now. Actions like those have consequences." He flipped her on her back and hovered over her. His eyes darkened as the mini dress flipped further open, revealing her black lace bra and panties. "I'm going to pretend you wore these for me." He traced a finger over the top edge of the bra before rasping his thumb over her nipple, giving it a pinch.

She moaned and arched up into him. She pulled at his shirt, yanking it over his head. "Need skin," she nearly growled. He helped her the rest of the way. She took advantage and unbuttoned his pants while he was struggling with his shirt.

"Wait," he said, causing her to protest. "Do you want to do this here? Or should we move to the bedroom?"

"Bedroom's too far away."

"Okay, but I need to stand up for a second and get some protection."

Protection. How could she have forgotten? After everything. She covered herself up as she watched him walk toward the bathroom, his pants hanging dangerously low on his hips.

She should leave. She wasn't thinking correctly. She had started to tie the sash around her waist when he returned holding a condom—and wearing absolutely nothing.

Her mouth watered and the panic left her body. She wanted —needed—her hands on that body. Something deep inside her knew he was her lifeline, and she had to hold on, no matter the cost.

"Hey," he said, kneeling between her legs, "you're all tied up again." His smile fell, nearly wrenching her in two. "You change your mind? Because if you did, it's totally okay."

Yes, she'd changed her mind. And then changed it back.

She slid her hands down and circled him, squeezing while moving her hand up and down his shaft.

"God, Mac."

His eyes fell to half-mast and a groan slipped from his lips. One small sound that said it all. Gratification. Pleasure. Need. An unfamiliar feeling unfurled in her chest. Power. *She'd* pulled that sound from him. With a single touch. Something so intense from something so simple.

"You're not the only one who remembers things." She leaned up and drew her tongue across his nipple. She wanted to hear that sound again. She hungered for it.

"But your dress . . ." he managed between groans.

Think fast, Avery. "I thought maybe you'd like to unwrap me again."

He smiled and tugged. A part of her sagged under the weight of half-truths. He deserved more from her. She should tell him. Before any more clothes came off.

But he'd unhooked her bra and sucked a nipple into his mouth. She squirmed at the sensation. *I'll tell him later. I promise.*

He continued his path down her body, pulling her panties

down as he kissed her hips. His mouth slipped into the valley between her leg and torso, and he ran a finger over her core.

"Christ, Mac, you're so wet."

"Put your mouth on me, Mr. Taylor."

He arched an eyebrow.

"Please," she breathed out impatiently.

He licked up her crease, and she screamed, shattering into a million pieces. Wow. That went from match strike to full-on forest fire in no time flat.

He didn't stop caressing her until the last aftershock faded into a whisper of warmth.

"Now you," she said, grabbing the condom from the back of the sofa, ripping it open, and sliding it on him. She could feel his heavy gaze on her the entire time.

"I want to see your face when you come a second time." He sat back on the sofa and lifted her over him. She slid down over him inch by inch, allowing time to adjust to his size. His breath hitched, and then he moved inside her.

She followed his rhythm. And it was like they'd never stopped doing this. The physical pleasure was unbelievable, but the connection between the two of them was . . . was . . . What was it? She had no words.

His head fell back to the sofa. "I'm so close, Mac. Are you close?"

She took the hand clutching her thigh and moved it six inches to the right. "Help me," she whispered.

He circled the spot just north of where they joined, and they screamed out together and she collapsed forward on his chest. Sweat making their skin slick. Exertion making their chests heave.

"I gotta say, that is not the way I expected this evening to end."

"Is it over?" she said into his chest.

He chuckled softly, burying his head in the crook of her neck. "Not if you don't want it to be."

"Got another round in you?"

"Or two."

"Two more?" she said. "Sounds like someone's been reading romance novels. I think three times in one night only happens in fiction."

"That sounds like a challenge. Give me five minutes for a snack and water and then move over Nora Roberts."

Avery laughed. "You know Nora Roberts writes romance?"

He shrugged, biting back a smile. "My mom had a stash, and I might have scanned to get to the sexy bits."

"Okay, sign me up for the snacks too."

Matt stared at the ceiling as Avery slept beside him. How many times had he imagined this? He ran a finger down her bare arm just to make sure she was real. She moved but didn't awaken.

Was it everything he dreamed it would be? Yes. And in some ways, it was so much more. They weren't kids anymore, and the fumbling sex they'd had in the beginning had been replaced with something so much better, so much hotter.

But in his dreams, it had only been about the physical act. He never thought about anything else. But now, here in the dark, his body was satisfied, but his heart ached.

Was this just one night? Was it just sex? Did he want it to be more than that? If he did, could he convince her to give them a chance in less than ten days?

They had years of history and yet time was running out.

He knew he'd take whatever she'd give him. A few more nights like this. A few days spent together. His heart squeezed. He'd ask for all those things—and more.

He reached for his phone. Yes, it was the middle of the night. But time was short. The stability of the band was good. The radio gig helped. But he needed more. He needed to prove he was a man she could rely on. Smart. One that people respected.

He shot off a quick text to his manager and agent. Surely there was more out there for him.

She rolled over and her eyes fluttered open. "What are you doing?" she asked, her voice heavy with sleep and, he hoped, satisfaction.

"Taking care of some business," he said, brushing her hair away from her face.

She bolted upright, leaving the sheet behind. His eyes followed. He knew her nipples were hard from the cool night, but damn if the sight of them didn't send a bolt of lightning to his groin.

"Business? Is it morning?" she asked, panic in her voice, as she scanned the room.

"Not yet, love," he said, kissing her shoulder and reaching to pull his thumb across a nipple.

She batted his hand away. "I need to go."

He smirked. "I haven't delivered on my three times yet."

She looked back to him, desire flaring in her eyes, but only for an instant. It was quickly replaced with something entirely different. Panic.

"I need to get home. What if they realize my bed is empty? What if something has happened to one of them?"

He pulled her tight against his chest. "You told me you've had several sexual partners."

She swung her legs off the bed. "Yes, but I never stayed the night. I don't stay the night. It's too . . . too . . ."

Something deflated in his chest. He'd hoped this was differ-ent. He hoped *he* was different. "Personal?"

She strained against his embrace. "Yes, and Momma and Jess and Wyatt are my responsibility."

He kissed her shoulder and let his arms fall slack. "Isabel and Jessica are grown women."

Her chest heaved and her breath came faster. "You don't understand."

He rose from the bed, opened a nearby drawer, and threw a t-shirt at her. She'd feel more comfortable, and her naked body wouldn't be a distraction. "Explain it to me."

He climbed back into bed, set her pillows against the headboard, and pulled her back to lean against them—and him. Her shoulders dropped, but just.

"Something might have happened to one of them," she repeated. "Where's my phone?"

Matt pointed at the side table. "I grabbed it last night." He turned the screen toward her. "See? Nothing."

She grabbed the phone and opened her text app. And then her email. Her fingers shook as she navigated between the apps. She let the phone drop, screen-side down, to her thigh, but she maintained her grip on it.

He pried her fingers up. "Can I have this?" he asked softly.

She nodded but said nothing. He set the phone beside her on the bed.

"Mac." He turned her head to face him. "Look at me." When she finally raised her eyes to his, he asked, "What's going on?"

"Ever since daddy died, they've been my responsibility. I can't leave them alone." She said it so quietly that he wasn't certain if she was talking to herself or him.

He stroked her hair, trying to calm her. "Mac, you're the only one in that house that's not a parent."

She looked up at him as if it was the first time she'd thought about that.

"Why are you responsible for them?" He knew, from the moment they met, that she'd been protective of her family. She'd had to shoulder extra duties after her father passed. But this panic, in the middle of the night, was new—or maybe just more intense? It was breaking his heart to see this brash, confident woman reduced to this.

"Do you have your medication with you?"

She shook her head, causing the waves in her hair to bounce against her cheeks. "Don't take it anymore."

"Okay, then you need to talk to me. Are you upset about what happened between us?"

Her eyes flew to his, something inscrutable passing behind them. "No," she whispered. "But I never expected to still be here"—she looked at her phone—"at three in the morning."

"I'll take you home whenever you want, but let's wait until this passes. Okay?"

She nodded.

He wanted to take this from her, to help shoulder the burden of whatever was pulling her down into the depths. But he knew that wasn't the way this worked. "Are you ready to tell me why you think your mom and sister are your responsibility?"

She pulled the sheet up to her neck and held it there. He could tell she was trying to regulate her breathing. He waited. If memory served, she'd talk when she was ready and not before.

She ran her thumb over her clavicle. Back and forth. Quickly, then slowing. She looked at him, pain dancing in her beautiful eyes. "They are my responsibility because it's my fault Daddy died."

His gut clenched and he wanted to scream, "What the hell are you talking about?" but he calmly said, "Tell me more."

He eyed the dresser. This was a conversation that called for pants, but he didn't want to leave her.

"Momma got pregnant in high school, and their families forced them to marry."

This was not new, but the guilt dripping from her voice was something he hadn't heard before. How long had she been carrying this around? Forever, he guessed. How had he missed it before? He thought he knew everything about her. But even at twenty-two, when they broke up, they were still basically kids.

"And?"

"They never should have gotten married. It was my fault they did," she whispered.

"Mac, honey." He laced his fingers with hers. He had to touch her. "It was their choice to have unprotected sex. Yes, you resulted from that, but that doesn't make their unfortunate marriage your fault."

"Yes, but they were only together because of me. And it got him killed."

"He was serving his country, across the world in Iraq, when he died."

She shook her head. "He kept signing up for more tours. He was running from a family he never wanted . . . and it got him killed. I got him killed, so it's my duty to take care of them now. Because he can't."

His heart shattered. He kissed her temple. "Is this why they all live with you?"

She nodded, quiet tears running in rivulets down her cheeks.

He swiped at them with his thumb. My god, she'd been carrying this burden for over fifteen years. Is this when the anxiety started?

Something else clicked into place. Could this be part of the real reason she broke up with him? He shook the thought from his head. One issue at a time.

"Mac," he said, and when she didn't look at him, he placed a finger under her chin and softly turned her head to face him.

She closed her eyes. "I'm so embarrassed."

Wait, what? "Why are you embarrassed?"

"I never want anyone to see me like this," she said.

"What? Naked and sated?" he said, trying to make her laugh.

She didn't laugh, but at least she smiled. She ran a hand up his chest. "Make love to me again."

"There is nothing I would like more, but I think we should talk about this a little more." Plus, it didn't help his already shaky confidence that perhaps tonight's activities had less to do with her wanting him and more to do with her wanting to block out her life for a while.

"So, I've got daddy issues? Who doesn't?" she said, forcing out a fake laugh.

"Darlin' this is more than your run-of-the-mill daddy issues. Have you talked to anyone about this?"

"You mean like a therapist?"

Matt nodded.

"About my anxiety? Yes. A long time ago. But about Daddy? No. I can handle it."

"Really? Because I'm going out on a limb here and say that having a full-blown anxiety attack right after the best sex of your life is not a good sign."

She smiled a genuine smile. "Someone's full of themselves."

"Mac," he whispered. "You are not responsible for your mom and sister—or your father's death. It's great that you want to help them. A family that supports each other is a rare gift. No one gets that more than me. But support is a two-way street, and it needs to come from here." He touched a finger to her chest, above her heart. "It's not about atoning for something you had nothing to do with."

She slumped into him, and he inconspicuously felt for her pulse at her wrist. Normal. "Promise me you'll see someone. Talk through it. I know Grace sees a therapist in Nashville. Do you want me to get her name?"

Her eyes widened. "Grace sees a therapist?"

"When she started writing with Andrew, she was still dealing with some very real grief issues from the loss of her husband."

"And she told you this?"

"Grace's mantra is, 'We can't remove the stigma of mental health issues if we don't talk about them.'"

He felt her nod against his chest. "Promise me, Mac."

"How about a deal? I'll promise to call someone if you promise to do that thing with your tongue again."

He laughed softly. She was still making jokes, but it was a start—and he had no problem making good on his portion of the deal. "You don't want to go home? I meant what I said. Anytime you want to go, we'll go."

"Thank you," she whispered, her hands roaming over his chest again. "But I'd like to stay. You're right. Momma or Jess would call if there were any issues."

He wrapped his fingers around her hand, stopping her motion. "I'm sorry? Could you say that again?"

She tipped her head up, a smirk playing at the corners of her lips. "Momma would call?"

"No, the other part."

"You're right," she said, planting a kiss on his pec.

"Those are some magical words, Avery Lind."

She started planting kisses from his neck down his torso to his belly. He wanted to ask her about the break-up. If what she'd just shared had something to do with it. But her mouth was distracting. And he didn't want to upset her again so soon. He knew how exhausting each anxiety event was for her.

Once again, he let his body take the lead. He captured her shoulders and flipped her underneath him.

Were they both using sex to forget about all the things they should address? Highly likely.

Did he care? Nope. He had a promise to keep. He couldn't very well let Nora Roberts down, could he?

CHAPTER THIRTEEN

AVERY ROLLED OVER AND BURIED HER FACE IN A PILLOW. It smelled like cinnamon and leather. Matt. Her eyes popped open. She scanned the room. Not her bedroom. So last night wasn't a dream.

She patted the space beside her. Empty. And cold.

She stretched and parts of her twinged that hadn't ached in a long time. Then she remembered the anxiety attack. And what she'd said about her father.

What would he think? Would he treat her differently this morning?

Her phone pinged and she reached for it. Two messages. One from Momma, making sure she was okay. How was she supposed to answer that? Guilt rumbled through her. She should have let Momma know. But is that what grown women did? Check in with their mother before having sex with their ex? She rubbed her forehead. This was all kinds of messed up.

The second one was from Jess. Were they sitting across the breakfast bar from each other, texting her? No words from her sister, just a single emoji. Winky face. Ugh. She couldn't get mad. It was her fault that they were all up in each other's business.

She typed a response to her mother that said, 'I'm okay' but immediately deleted it because that wasn't even close to the truth. She felt so far from okay, she couldn't even see it from where she was standing. 'I'm fine' and 'I'm good' also felt wrong. She followed Jess's lead and sent back the thumbs-up emoji. She'd have enough questions to answer when she got home. No need to get into things now.

She rolled from the bed, pulling the t-shirt Matt had given her last night over her head, and wandered into the bathroom. Lying next to the sink was a new toothbrush and a tiny tube of toothpaste. Her eyes misted over. Seriously? Was she crying about a baby-sized Crest?

It had been so long since someone had taken care of her. She sighed. It'd been so long since she'd *let* anyone take care of her.

She brushed her teeth and wiped away the faint smudges of yesterday's mascara. Who knew tears were such an effective make-up remover?

She padded into the living room and stopped, silently sucking in a breath. Matt stood at the stove, wearing nothing but a pair of low-slung jeans. She'd bet her annual salary that he had nothing on under those jeans. She watched as the muscles in his back rippled as he stirred what looked like cheesy scrambled eggs.

"See anything you like?"

Damn him, the cocky SOB, he always could sense her.

"Those eggs look fantastic," she shot back.

He laughed. Deep and full. And it made her stomach flutter. It made her remember the first time she saw him walking down the hallway in high school. Only three months after Daddy died, her mother had packed them up and moved them to Marla. Her mother said they needed a change, but Avery knew the truth. After her father's death, base housing was no longer an option.

Huddled next to her locker, trying to make sense of her schedule, Matt had been one of the first people to talk to her. "You must be the new girl," he said, flashing a smile that made her feel like snow in the sun. "Matt Taylor," he said, thrusting out a hand. "You know where you're going next?"

"Not really." She handed him her schedule. "Oh," he mock grimaced, "you have American History with old man Paulson next."

"Is that bad?" she had asked.

"It could be, but I'm in that class too, so it'll be good." He'd winked at her. *Winked.*

"Are you sure there'll be room for me *and* your ego in the classroom?" she'd retorted. She expected his smile to drop, but it only got bigger. It was like no one ever challenged him, and he welcomed it.

"Earth to Mac," he said, setting a plate of bacon and eggs in front of her and sliding a glass of OJ next to her plate. "Where were you?"

"Thinking about the day we met."

He ran a hand down his sculpted chest. "Because you were thinking about what I looked like without a shirt the minute we met?"

"No. But it's good to know your ego is still intact." She smirked. "And I'm pretty sure washboard abs were not part of sixteen-year-old you."

He winked at her and chuckled. "Some things get better with age."

"I've never complained about your body."

His smile dropped. "No one ever has," he mumbled.

"What?"

"Nothing." He sat down next to her and shoveled eggs into

his mouth. "I suppose you'd like to get home," he said after swallowing. "You finish up and I'll jump in shower, then we can leave."

"Matt," she said, touching his arm, "what did I say? You seem upset."

"Nothing," he repeated. "It's just I'm sure you have plans for today."

She sucked in a breath. This was another moment to channel confident Avery Lind, not tentative Amy-Lynn. "And if I don't?"

He set his fork down and turned to her.

"What if I'd like to spend the day with you?" So maybe it would be one night *and* one day.

"What about Isabel and Jess?"

"I texted them. I'm sorry about last night's overreaction."

He ran his thumb along her jawbone, and his eyes searched her face. "I told you the other day that you're safe with me. And I didn't mean only in the studio."

"Thank you," she said, getting very interested in her eggs. God, how she wanted to trust him. To let him in. To have him help shoulder her burdens.

But she didn't deserve that.

She needed to tell him. Now. It was bad enough she'd slept with him while still carrying her secret.

"Matt, there's something we need to talk about." Her stomach turned over, and it felt like the eggs were climbing back up her throat. She couldn't do it.

But she had to.

He deserved to know.

"I already know," he said, pulling her from the stool.

She winced. "I don't think you do."

"You don't have to be shy about it, Mac," he said, nuzzling his face into her neck. "If you want to shower with me, just ask."

Her shoulders sagged. She couldn't drop a giant, steaming truth bomb right after he'd suggested shower sex. She was sure that was a rule.

Coward, the little voice chided.

I'm the worst kind of coward. The selfish kind. She wanted a little more of him. And the truth would change everything. She'd been carrying around this particular skeleton for years. What was a few more days?

A few more days to get attached all over again.

Screw it. Selfish or not, she was taking this for herself. She rubbed the spot on her clavicle and willed the guilt and anxiety away.

She pulled the t-shirt over her head and watched his eyes go wide. "I am feeling pretty dirty."

"Jesus, woman, you are going to kill me." He stepped up to her and scooped her into his arms and didn't let her down until the water ran over them.

Matt ordered two iced coffees from the vendor in the park and turned to watch Amy-Lynn. She was sitting on a nearby swing, hanging on to the chains, pumping her legs, trying to propel the swing higher. They'd stopped by her gym this morning, and she'd changed into a pair of jeans and a t-shirt she kept there. Said it was too risky to stop at home—they wouldn't let her out of the house without answering one hundred questions.

It was hard to believe this was real. A few days ago, she was only a memory and now she was here, spending the day with him, after spending the night with him.

It was just the two of them. Together. Not because of Story-hill or the radio show, but simply because they wanted to be together. His heart climbed into his throat when she waved at him with a small smile.

Should he tell her he was still in love with her?

No. Not yet.

He'd put feelers out for another gig—something to do between tour dates. Something to show her he was more than just a part of a band. Something that would match her impressive drive and ambition. Something that would prove he was worthy of her.

He checked his phone. No messages from Brad or his agent. Rationally, he knew it was Sunday, but he was still disappointed. He needed another gig lined up before he shared his feelings . . . and asked her if she felt the same way.

He'd waited nine years. He could be patient a little while longer.

He walked back to her, stilling her swing, and handing her a coffee. "Want to walk?" He pointed to the paved trail that led through the park.

"Yes," she said. She closed her lips around the straw, and his mind immediately flashed to sitting on his sofa while she kneeled in front of him. All his blood rushed southward. He needed to get a grip. The nine days left in the studio would be painful if he didn't.

"Lead on," he sputtered, trying to dislodge the memory.

"Matt," she said, swirling the straw in her coffee.

She seemed nervous. "Yes?"

She bit her lip and opened her mouth and closed it again. "Did you get the notes I sent you for Monday's guest?" she asked.

He laced his fingers through her free hand. Was she still worried about the show? "Devin Penney?"

She nodded but kept her gaze on her shoes. "Yes, that's right."

"I scanned them, but I had planned to review them today."

She sighed. "And I ruined your plans."

Why did he get the sense that she was talking about more than show research?

"No worries. There's plenty of time for that." He lifted her fingers to his mouth and kissed each one softly. "How about no show talk for the next couple of hours?"

She sucked her bottom lip under her teeth again but agreed. "What should we talk about instead?"

She'd given him the perfect opening to discuss the elephant in the room. They needed to talk—*really* talk. But, right now, right here, with the sun shining and her hand in his, the words wouldn't come. Maybe some easier questions, first? Ease into the bigger stuff.

Ease in or chicken out?

He pulled her to a park bench and nestled her under his arm. "You've lived an entire life I know very little about. How about we get to know each other a little better?"

Chicken out it is.

She laughed. "Sounds like an interview."

He smiled. "Since you've already interviewed me, I think it's my turn."

"I'm not very comfortable in the spotlight," she said.

"I've noticed. Why is that?"

"I guess that inside I'm still that shy girl who showed up in Marla. And, frankly, my life is not all that interesting." He started to protest, and she held up a finger. "Not when you compare it to the lives of the people I interview."

"I'll be the judge of that—after I interview you."

A nervous laugh trickled from her lips. "Be gentle."

"Always," he said, his eyes softening. "I'll start with easy questions."

She glanced over at him from the corner of her eye. "Like?"

"Like, what's your favorite color?"

She laughed. "You know that."

"Maybe it's changed?"

"Nope, still pink."

He mocked pulling out a pen and paper and straightening an imaginary tie. "Okay, Ms. Avery Lind. You know my first full-time job was at Dollywood. What was your first job out of college?" How was it that he didn't know such simple things about her?

"Um," she said, her fingers clenching and unclenching, "well, I moved back to Marla for a couple of months. After . . ." —she cleared her throat— "after I saved some money, I moved to Nashville. I've worked in radio ever since. I did traffic reports and research at my first station. Not super glamorous, for sure."

He tugged on her fingers, pulling them straight. "See? Those questions weren't too hard, right?"

A smirk pulled at the corner of her lips. "No. Celeste would say you're asking softball questions. Not a compliment, by the way."

He touched his chest, feigning offense. "I'd prefer to call it 'warming up the guest.' But I can make it more challenging if you'd like."

"Um, okay."

Strange that they'd bared themselves to each other, but she was still reticent.

He pulled the sleeve of her t-shirt up to reveal the tattoo he'd noticed—and kissed—last night. Three birds in stages of taking flight. "This is new. To me, anyway." He ran a finger over the ink. "Does it have a special meaning?"

She searched his face, as if seeking an answer to an unreadable question. She sucked in a deep breath and worried her bottom lip.

"It's a reminder."

"Of?"

She sat in silence. He could almost hear her warring with herself, debating whether to tell him. "To not forget."

She was dancing around the question. "That is the definition of a reminder. What's so important that you put a permanent reminder on your body?"

She stood and put a step between them. He could feel her slipping away. He grabbed for her hand. "I'm only asking because Celeste would expect me to," he teased quietly.

A tiny smile danced over her lips. "Well, you know how I feel about disappointing Celeste."

He chuckled. "I do."

She sighed, resigned. "It's a reminder that sometimes the right answer is to let things go."

"Like?"

She rubbed her fingers over the three birds and met his gaze. The look in her eyes spoke volumes.

"Like me?" he whispered, not sure how he wanted her to answer.

She nodded. "And other things." She swallowed. Hard. "The first one is for—"

His phone buzzed and they both jumped. He pulled it out to silence it, because he really, really wanted to know what the birds meant, but a familiar name flashed across the screen.

"It's Brad. I really should take this."

She nodded, and he was expecting her to be annoyed, but unless his Mac radar was way off, it was relief that flashed across her face.

He nodded and hit Accept. "Hey, Brad." He stood and walked back toward the sidewalk.

"Got your text," Storyhill's manager said. "And your request couldn't have been more serendipitous. I got a call from CTV yesterday. They'd gotten wind of the radio show and want to talk to you about hosting a new singing competition that's currently in beta."

He slapped his thigh. Yes! This is exactly what he'd been hoping for. A gig on national TV? Amy-Lynn would finally be proud of him, be proud to be *with* him. "That's awesome." Wait. "Won't something like this interfere with touring?"

"Maybe. Don't know. But I think you should talk to them. See what the timing is. Even meeting with the execs will help Storyhill's visibility." Yes, it would help Storyhill—and him.

Brad could not have called at a better time. He could tell Amy-Lynn about it right away. And then he'd tell her how he felt. Everything was about to change. For the better.

"Great, let's do it."

"I'll get back to them and get a meeting on the calendar. Preferably before you leave on tour."

"Sounds good. Just make sure it doesn't conflict with the radio show."

Brad laughed. "You're really enjoying that, aren't you?"

He looked back at Amy-Lynn, now engrossed with her phone. Yes, he was—in so many ways. Ways he would not share with his manager. "Yep, I am," he answered. "Thanks, Brad, for hooking me up."

He ended the call and jogged back to Amy-Lynn.

She looked up. "Everything okay?"

"Better than okay." He was so excited to tell her. "CTV reached out to Brad. They want to talk to me about hosting a new country music singing competition."

He waited for her smile. Or the words, "I'm proud of you." But none of that came.

Her eyes narrowed and her lips thinned. Pretty much the opposite of a smile. "CTV?"

He cocked his head to the side, his brows pulling together. He didn't understand her reaction. "Country Mu—"

"I know what CTV is, Matt," she snapped, shoving her phone into her pocket. "I just can't believe it."

His spine stiffened, and he hoped he was misinterpreting her reaction. "I can't believe it, either. But my 'not believe it' is happy. You sound upset. I thought you'd be happy, too."

She blinked her eyes. Several times. In rapid succession. "Everything is so easy for you."

"What?"

"Must be nice to be pretty. All you have to do is smile and things fall in your lap." She started to pace. "You leave OU and, like, a week later have a starring role at Dollywood. Your band found you on YouTube, for pete's sake. And you waltz in for an interview and three hours later you have a co-hosting gig—on a nationally syndicated show. Do you work for anything?"

Where was all this coming from? I mean, she'd always teased him about being born under a lucky star, but he thought she'd been kidding. God, she thought even less of him than he'd realized. Anger sizzled up his arms and shot directly into his core.

"I worked my ass off for all of that."

She stopped and looked up at him, her eyes flashing. "Did you? Did you really?"

"Yes, I did! And you would know that if you hadn't kicked me to the curb. If you'd have taken that journey with me—*like we had planned*."

They stood staring at each other, chests rising and falling.

Matt lowered his voice. They were drawing the attention of passersby. "I can't help what I look like. I had nothing to do with that. But I've been judged by it all my life. Every time I run into a problem, people say things like you just did, 'It's a good thing you're pretty' or 'Don't worry about being talented, your looks will get you the job.' It makes me feel like shit—like no one ever looks beyond the surface. I'm more than a plastic toy. And you, of all people, should know how commenting on my looks and maligning my efforts makes me feel." He stepped away from her and ran his fingers through his hair.

How did this day careen off the tracks so quickly?

He thought she'd be impressed. That's why he'd reached out to Brad. To show her he was more. And she still saw him like all the others, one-dimensional.

He startled when she placed a hand on his arm. "I'm sorry," she whispered.

"For what? Insinuating I don't work for the things in my life or for letting your real feelings show?" He knew he was being harsh—and childish—but her words stung. No, it was more than that. They dug into a place he tried to keep hidden. The part he hid behind big smiles and manufactured confidence.

She wasn't entirely wrong. He played into the stereotype, used his outward appearance to his advantage when necessary. But that was to sell a few tickets. Not the big stuff. He worked his ass off for the big stuff.

Her words hurt, for sure, but he was angry with himself, too. He was exploiting the very thing that he was fighting against. Having it both ways. Having his cake and eating it too. And all the other cliches his father parroted.

"Matt," she said, gripping his arm tighter. He turned to her. Her gaze was steady. "I really am sorry."

"I think it's time I got you home," he said, weary from their exchange, weary from his thoughts. "We both need to prepare for the show tomorrow."

Sadness filled her eyes before she blinked it away. "If that's what you want."

"It's not what I want, Avery, but I think it's the right thing to do."

"You called me Avery."

"Isn't that what you prefer?"

"Not when you use it to put distance between us."

"Putting distance between us, now that's something you're an expert at."

She sighed. "You're right, maybe it's best we call it a day."

Avery walked to the back door, giving Matt a small wave goodbye. The last twenty-four hours had been quite the ride.

She quietly slipped her key into the lock and slowly opened the door, trying to avoid the squeak the old house usually offered, announcing arrivals.

She tiptoed in. Was she really sneaking into her own house? Doing the walk of shame at thirty-one years old?

In the end, it didn't matter. The house was empty, and a note was on the kitchen island.

Jess, Wyatt and I went to the park. There are some left-over cinnamon rolls on the counter. ~M

She grabbed a knife and carved out an enormous chunk of gooey, bready goodness. Seems eggs and bacon only held out so long. Used up from a fight . . . or a night filled with mind-blowing sex.

She looked at the clock. Lunch or a nap? She grabbed another chunk of cinnamon roll, deciding on a nap. Then she'd prepare for tomorrow's show.

She grabbed a pen and turned over Momma's note, ready to tell her family she was home and resting for a while. But she didn't even have the cap off the pen before Wyatt burst through the door, his hair plastered to his forehead and a streak of mud across his cheek.

"Tía," he yelled, running to her, wrapping his chubby arms around her knees, and squeezing.

She couldn't help laughing. If only everyone was so happy to see her.

"You're in a good mood," her sister said, winking.

"I was just thinking, what if everyone greeted me as exuberantly as Wyatt? Then a picture of Celeste and Ajay popped into my mind. I think I'll save those kinds of hugs for Wyatt."

"And Matt?" Jessica said.

Avery's smile fell and she slumped onto a barstool, shoving the balance of her cinnamon roll into her mouth.

"Oh," Jess said. "Please don't tell me you accidentally fell asleep on his couch or something equally lame."

"Doesn't your child need a bath?" Avery said around the cinnamon roll and pointing to the muddy handprint on her jeans.

"Bath!" Wyatt yelled, spinning in a circle. Avery wasn't sure if he was excited or upset until he added, "Get dinosaur toys, Mommy."

Excited it was.

"Fine," Jess said, "but I'll be back in twenty minutes, and I want every juicy detail." She grabbed Wyatt around the waist and ran upstairs. He opened his arms and squealed, "Airplane!"

"You can leave out the juicy details for me," her mother said, moving to the opposite side of the island.

"Good," Avery said, "because I didn't have any plans to discuss sex with my mother."

Isabel's eyes widened ever so slightly. "So you did sleep with him?"

Avery grimaced, funneling a hand through her hair. "Yes."

"Do you think that's a good idea given your history?"

"Too late now. It's done. But after this morning, I don't think I have to worry about it happening again."

"Because?" Isabel grabbed a dishcloth and wiped away the

crumbs Avery dropped. Her eyes appeared to be lowered, but Avery knew she was watching her.

"Things were said."

Her mother's head popped up. "You finally told him the truth?"

"Not those things."

"Amy-Lynn," her mother said, putting an entire conversation into two words.

"I tried to tell him last night and again this morning—twice, but we got interrupted."

"Did you get interrupted, or did you allow yourself to use something as a convenient excuse?"

"Wow, Momma, tough love this morning."

"The more you allow him back into your life, the harder it's going to be to tell him. If there's a relationship starting here, the longer it goes, the likelier it is that the truth will have devastating consequences."

"I'm not sure that's an issue anymore. He got a text about a job opportunity and I"—Avery grimaced and squeezed her eyes shut— "made a crack about him only getting ahead in life because of the way he looks."

"Oh, Amy-Lynn."

Avery dropped her head into her hands. "I know Momma. I hit him where it hurt. And to make matters worse, I couldn't make a full apology because I think part of me, deep inside, wonders if it's true."

"You're a beautiful woman, Amy-Lynn. What would you do if someone accused you of the same thing?"

"I'd scream about the patriarchy and how women are unfairly judged by their physical appearance," she grumbled.

"Exactly. Do you think your reaction had more to do with the simple fact that you thought Matt Taylor would never be back in your life? Yet here he is . . . and you've fallen back into old"—Isabel cleared her throat and lifted her fingers in air quotes— "habits."

Avery tried to suppress a giggle, but it burst out at her mother's euphemism.

Her mother chuckled but sobered quickly. She reached for Avery's hand and covered it with her own. "I just want you to be careful, Amy-Lynn. It took you a long time to get over him."

Avery nodded. Momma was mostly right. Having Matt back in her life, if only for a short while, unsettled her. But she was wrong about how long it took to get over him. Because she never had.

CHAPTER FOURTEEN

FORTY-SEVEN MINUTES TO SHOW TIME.

Avery had arrived early under the pretext of avoiding her family, but the truth was she had laid awake for hours. In the pre-twilight hours, she had mapped the contours of her bedroom ceiling while her comments to Matt played on repeat. What was it about anxiety that made the bad stuff loop over and over? Why couldn't her mind replay the good stuff? I mean, she'd had one of the best orgasms of her life just hours before losing her shizzle at the park. She'd gladly relive that. But no.

Eventually, she gave up any hope of falling back asleep and got dressed. That's how she found herself here, sitting in the studio, staring at the black and white analog clock hanging opposite her desk with an ache she hadn't felt in years wrapping around her lungs and squeezing. It was loss. Or maybe, more accurately, the fear of losing something so precious all over again.

The red second hand clicked loudly in the eerily silent studio. Forty-three minutes to show time.

Needing a distraction, she opened the blue file folder sitting six inches to her right. Blue folders were for show notes. She scanned the bullet points, seeing nothing but a jumble of words. No matter. She didn't need the notes. She had them memorized. Like always.

So why bring them into the studio every day? Routine. Precaution. Systems mitigated risk. Didn't they?

Sitting here, counting down the minutes in her perfectly adjusted ergonomic chair, she wondered if any of it mattered. It's not like her innumerable spreadsheets and to-do lists could wallpaper over the chaos in her mind.

She'd always told herself that her systems helped her remember all her responsibilities. But what if she'd put them in place to help her forget? Forget that no matter what she did, she couldn't bring Daddy back or make Momma well again. Forget that she'd walked away from the only man she'd ever loved.

Thirty-three minutes to show time. Twenty-three minutes until Ajay arrived. He didn't have any ridiculous pre-show rituals. He just calmly arrived, opened his computer, and was ready to take on the day.

Thirteen minutes until Matt arrived. If he showed up at all. The chances were fifty-fifty at best.

She pulled a sheet of notes from her blue file folder and flipped it over. At the top she scrawled, 'Will Matt Taylor show up?' Pros: he has a contract; he wants exposure for Storyhill. Cons: her.

Oh my god. Was there anything she didn't make a list for? She crumpled the paper and threw it in the bin. Almost. It didn't quite make it. It landed a few inches from the trash can mocking her—and she left it.

A groan-laugh-crazy cackle erupted from her. Her one act of defiance. A piece of paper on the floor. *You go, Avery. Really let loose.*

She laid her head down on her desk. She was tired of all of it. Tired of wanting the things she didn't deserve. Tired of believing she didn't deserve them. So tired.

"Avery."

Someone was tapping lightly on her back.

"Yes?" she said, raising her head, blinking, and rubbing at the corners of her eyes. Had she fallen asleep?

Ajay was standing next to her. "Eleven minutes to show." Even Ajay knew her proclivity for odd numbers.

Her eyes flashed to the door. "Is Matt here?"

"I haven't seen him, love. I'm sure he's on his way." He handed her an updated schedule, placed a copy on Matt's side of the desk, and wandered out. See? Calm. Not nervous at all. *Why would he worry? He had no idea that she'd had the best sex of her life, freaked out, and slung mean words at the co-host.*

A week ago, she'd have been thrilled if Matt decided not to show. Today she wanted him to walk through the door like she wanted her next breath.

Because she didn't want to explain his absence to Celeste. Or to her listeners.

Whatever you need to tell yourself.

She punched the talk button. "Ajay, I think it might just be me and you today."

The words were barely out of her mouth when Matt stepped into the studio.

"You came," she breathed out. She cleared her throat. "I mean I figured you would." *Lie.* "I made a pros and cons list." *Embarrassing truth.* She pointed at the balled-up paper. "Pro: you signed a contract, you wouldn't let Storyhill down—"

"Mac," he hissed.

That name. His name for her. It stopped her ramble in its tracks. He picked up the paper and deposited it in the trash. She

167

released a ragged breath she didn't know she'd been holding. Order restored.

Avery met his gaze, and the moment stretched between them. She should say something more. But what? *I'm sorry? I'm glad you're here? I'm an idiot that sometimes loses control of my mouth when I get stressed?* She'd say all three if her perfectly styled, I-always-have-everything-under-control boss hadn't just blown into the studio like a beautiful tornado.

Avery watched as Matt turned away from her and, in what felt like slow motion, morphed his frown into his 'nothing bothers me' smile.

She knew it was fake, but it still cracked her heart a bit. She wanted that smile.

Celeste smoothed a hand over her perfectly styled hair and once again expertly ignored the cloud of tension fogging up the room. *Could Celeste teach her how to do that?*

"I know it's only three minutes to air, but I'd like you to stick around after the show. There's an opportunity I'd like to discuss."

Great. Celeste's last 'opportunity' involved dropping her ex into her lap. At least nothing could be worse than that. She hoped.

"You know I never leave right after the show," Avery responded.

"Right, but I need to talk to both of you," Celeste said, waving a finger between them. "Matt, do you have the time? It should only take fifteen minutes."

He sat down in what she now considered *his* chair, picked up *his* headphones. "Sure, no problem."

"Fifty-nine seconds," Ajay said.

"Great," Celeste said, turning toward the exit. "I'll see you in my office after you wrap the show." She clapped her hands. "Until then, make some magic."

Avery inwardly groaned. Celeste really needed to stop saying that. Anyone who had a basic understanding of body language knew they were both fresh out of magic.

Avery peered over the top of her microphone, willing Matt to look at her. He didn't.

"Hey," she said, reaching over, tapping a pen on his side of the desk. He finally looked up at her. "We okay?"

He nodded, but the usual light was missing from his eyes. "I told you on day one, I'm here to help Storyhill. I'm not about to let them down. No matter what happens between us."

"But—"

He held up a single hand. "If you want to discuss last weekend, it's best we do that during non-working hours."

A shiver of unease slithered up her spine. His voice sounded icy and indifferent. If he was going for coolly professional, he'd failed.

She didn't want to go on like this, but Matt looked down and flipped open his file folder (not blue) and pulled out his show notes.

So that was it. Conversation closed.

The show intro played in her headphones. Time to push his arctic attitude to the back of her mind.

When the intro faded out, Avery pushed the microphone slider up. "Good morning, country fans! Grab a cup of coffee— or two—it is Monday, after all, and get ready for another great interview. In just a few minutes we're welcoming Devin Penney, fresh off tour, to the Avery Lind Show. But first I need to thank Matt Taylor for filling in for me last week. I hope y'all had the chance to listen to his interview with Grace O'Connor. If not, Ajay will have the replay up on our webpage by this afternoon." She turned to her producer. "Say good morning, Ajay."

"Morning lovies," he said, not missing a beat. "Really

looking forward to this week, we've got a great line-up. We're previewing the new album by Josie Tillman—early reviews say it's her best music to date."

"I got to hear the title track last week," Matt said, his voice revealing none of his earlier irritation. "It's amazing. It's all acoustic, a very unplugged sound. I think her fans are going to love it."

Avery breathed out a sigh of relief. He was not letting their personal life leak into the show. "Sneak peeks are one benefit of being Matt Taylor, folks." She smiled at him, but he stiffened.

He stared at her for a beat. "A benefit of knowing Grace O'Connor, Avery."

Ouch, he really punched her stage name.

"It has nothing to do with being Matt Taylor." He tried to sound self-deprecating, but she heard the reproach in his voice.

"That's right," she said, trying to keep her voice airy and light. "I'd forgotten Grace co-wrote the album. Sounds like, from your interview with her, that she has successfully made the move from pop to country."

Matt held her gaze and cocked a single eyebrow. "Grace knows who she is and isn't afraid to show up as herself. That plays in any genre."

She dropped his gaze and squirmed in her perfectly comfortable chair. "Right. Even more reason to tune in Thursday morning to hear the album. But let's not get ahead of ourselves. Today is about Devin Penney." She double-checked her screen to make sure the music was cued up. "Let's listen to the title track from her latest album. And be sure to come back after the break when we'll be talking to the singer. Send any questions you have for Devin to @TheAveryLindShow or email booth@ALShow."

The on-air light went dark, and Avery pushed her headphones down around her neck. "Was that a thinly veiled message aimed at me?"

"Nope," he said, still not looking at her. He punched the intercom. "Ajay, how much time do we have?"

"Seven minutes, mate."

Mate? Avery looked between the two men. When did they become mates?

Matt stood, laying his headphones on the desk. "I need to use the restroom and answer a text. I'll be back. And Avery, sorry about being late this morning."

With that, he left the studio. She never thought she'd ache to be called Amy-Lynn again. She tried to convince herself—again—he was just being professional, but it wasn't working. She knew she'd blundered with her accusations, but she'd apologized. *Mostly.*

In the past, he'd always been free with his forgiveness. She sighed. It was dangerous to keep thinking that Matt Taylor the man was the same person as Matt Taylor the boy.

Was Momma right? Had she said those things specifically to put distance between them?

Did it matter?

If he didn't bolt after she told him the truth, he only had nine shows—eight, after this one wrapped—left before he went on tour. A sadness settled deep in her belly.

Dammit. This was why having Matt co-host was a bad idea from the beginning. Good or bad, he was a distraction. To her job. To her schedule. To her heart.

Matt re-entered the studio as Ajay announced Devin Penney was patched in. She needed to put all this aside. And remind herself of her number one priority: making this show a smash success.

~

After the longest four hours of his life, Matt followed Amy-Lynn down the hallway. His eyes kept dropping to the sway of her hips. His fingers twitched. It took everything in him not to reach out and settle his hand on her hip. Apparently, his body didn't understand he was angry with her.

Amy-Lynn stopped, and he ran into her, his front plastered to her back. The warmth generated between them was instantaneous. He hadn't noticed they'd reached Celeste's office. Why did she have to be so distracting?

She shot a look at him over her shoulder and knocked on the door frame.

"Come in. Please sit," Celeste said, motioning to the chairs in front of her desk. "The show sounded good today."

Matt snorted, and Amy-Lynn shot him a death glare. He shrugged and rolled his eyes. He thought the show had sounded stilted, forced. But maybe that was just the way he'd been feeling.

Celeste jotted down a few things on a towering stack of paper before placing her notes in a color-coded three-ring binder. Who knew they made tabs in so many colors? He was beginning to understand why these two women worked together so effectively.

She grabbed a blue and black folder from the credenza behind her and opened it. "You know I've been working to get the show more exposure, and a unique opportunity has popped up." Celeste turned the promotional folder to face them. "Have you both heard of the Wounded Warrior Project?"

Matt looked out of the corner of his eye, watching for Amy-Lynn's reaction. He guessed, given her history, veterans' issues could be a trigger for her. Her fingers tightened over the edge of her chair's armrests, but her expression remained placid.

"Yes," they said in unison.

Celeste tapped a pen on the left side of the folder. It appeared to be a printout of an email. "A wounded vet has recently been transferred from Walter Reed to a local military hospital to be closer to his family as he recuperates. The Wounded Warrior Project is involved with him on several levels, and he mentioned being a fan of the show. They've asked if you'd visit him in the hospital and take a few photos."

"Both of us?" Matt asked. He had to admit he'd been enjoying not being "face forward" and Amy-Lynn's comments over the weekend had only intensified his feelings.

"Yes," Celeste said, nodding. "It feels like a win-win-win situation. It's excellent publicity for the charity and the show. And we'll make sure the PR people know you are a member of Storyhill," she said, lifting her pen and pointing at Matt. "What do you think?"

Matt's emotions ping-ponged in his chest. He wanted some space from Amy-Lynn. But he respected this organization. And, irritated or not, there was no way he was letting her deal with a wounded veteran on her own.

Matt jumped as Donna Summer's voice suddenly filled the room. Celeste's phone was playing "She Works Hard for the Money." Matt chuckled. Of course, it was. When she reached to silence it, Matt leaned toward Amy-Lynn, lowering his voice. "Will this be too hard for you?" He wouldn't answer Celeste until Amy-Lynn gave him the go-ahead.

Her eyes fluttered to him. He could almost hear the gears turning in her head. "Sounds great, Celeste."

"I guess I should ask when it is," Matt said, "just to make sure I don't have any conflicts."

"Wednesday. I built some time in for you to grab lunch, but they want you at the hospital right after that. That's the best time of day for the soldier. He's just been transferred here and is still working through some substantial injuries—I guess he's a bit of a miracle. They weren't sure he would survive."

Amy-Lynn flinched and curled her fingers into fists. Everything in Matt wanted to wrap her in his arms like he had when she confessed feeling responsible for her father's death. He wanted to tell her he'd keep her safe. And that she didn't need to do this. Celeste would understand. Unless Celeste didn't know Amy-Lynn's history?

He reached for her hand, and she tersely shook her head. Irritation flared. His chin dropped to his chest. *Yep. Emotional rollercoaster.*

"Can you send us the details via email?" When Amy-Lynn finally spoke, it came out strong and steady. And people thought he was the actor.

Celeste nodded and turned her attention to him. "Work for you?"

"I have practice this afternoon and Thursday, but Wednesday looks open," he said, consulting his calendar. Looking at his phone was a formality. He would have cleared his schedule for this. For her.

"Great!" Celeste said. "I'll send you all the information. Thanks for doing this."

Matt slid to the edge of his chair, his elbow grazing Amy-Lynn's. The single soft contact made his body yell, 'Yippee!' while his mind chastised, 'this is the reason you shouldn't have slept with her. You've got no willpower when it comes to her.' He really needed some space.

"Is that everything, Celeste? I have to get to practice."

"That's it," Celeste answered. "Let me know if you come up with any questions."

Matt nodded and exited the office, heading toward the door.

"Matt," Avery called from behind him.

He stopped and turned back to her. His heart, and parts lower, clenched. "Yes?"

"Do you think we should talk about what happened this weekend?"

"The sex or your feelings about me being the living embodiment of a Ken doll?" He knew he was being unfairly harsh—and clearly cashing in his tickets for a second ride on the emotional rollercoaster.

"I don't think you're a Ken doll. Sometimes stress makes me say stupid things. Momma thinks I'm trying to drive a wedge between us."

"Are you?"

She transferred her weight from her right foot to her left and back again. "I don't know. Everything this weekend was so intense. I didn't expect that to happen. And I didn't expect all the feelings that came with it. It scared me."

A little of the ice around his heart melted. "It scared me too. And it would have been so much easier if you'd simply told me that."

"I know," she whispered. She looked over his shoulder. "Can we talk about it over lunch?"

He wanted that. He did. But. "I'm expected at practice, and our weekly meeting, in thirty minutes."

Her gaze dropped to the floor.

"Mac," he said, putting a finger under her chin and tipping her face back up. "I agree we need to talk, and I don't want to rush it. And honestly, I'm not in the right place to talk yet. What you said yesterday really threw me. Raincheck?"

She nodded. "Okay. I'll see you tomorrow then?"

"Tomorrow," he repeated. "And I'll be on time."

She reached out but pulled her hand back. She tried for a smile, but it withered before it really got started. "Bye Matt. Have a good practice."

He nodded and turned to leave. *Screw it.* He spun back around and brushed his lips over hers. He couldn't help it. Even with bruised feelings. Even standing inside their place of employment.

"Goodbye, Mac," he said, smirking at her stunned expression. No need for only one of them to feel unbalanced.

CHAPTER FIFTEEN

I'm here, Avery texted Matt from the parking lot outside his building.

Be right down.

Only five shows to go. After the uncomfortableness of Monday, yesterday and today's shows went smoothly. So smoothly, in fact, she was wondering what returning to just her and Ajay in the studio was going to be like.

And what life outside the studio was going to be like, too.

She jumped when Matt opened the car door.

"You were expecting me, right?" he asked, chuckling at her physical response.

She tapped her fingers against the steering wheel in beats of three. "Sorry, lost in thought."

His eyes followed the motion. "You worried about this appearance?"

Her fingers stopped mid-beat and she curled them in. Her thumb tapped the final two beats against her fingers. "Not really."

"Have you interacted much with vets?" he asked tentatively.

"No." She put the car in reverse, checking her mirrors. "But not because I've avoided it. More because it's never come up before."

"Do you do much charity work?"

She hesitated, pulling out into the traffic. "A little. How about you?"

"Nothing really on my own. I'd like to do more, but my schedule is tough with all the travel. Storyhill makes regular contributions to MusiCares and Blake does a lot of work with a few animal charities in New York City. I've joined him a couple of times. It's pretty cool. Do you donate time or money?"

"Both," she said, turning left, following the GPS instructions. She reminded herself he wasn't digging, just making conversation. Still, what happened to the 'what's your favorite color' type questions?

"Anywhere specific?"

She didn't want to answer the question. But it wouldn't take long for him to realize she was avoiding the question. "Women's shelters and transitional housing, mostly."

"That's great. What made you choose those types of organizations?"

Penance.

She shrugged. "There's just something about helping women and families find a new beginning."

He nodded. "Admirable."

Not the word she'd have chosen. But she couldn't very well tell him she too had once needed a new beginning. Not without opening a can of worms.

"Mm-hmm," she said, pulling into the hospital parking lot. "We're here." *Thankfully.* She flipped her phone over. "And right on time, they're expecting us in five minutes."

．　．　．

"We're here to see Wayne Massey," Avery said to the young receptionist sitting behind a large mahogany desk inside the front door. "Avery Lind and Matt Taylor."

She smiled. "I know who you are," she said shyly.

Avery smiled and opened her mouth to say thank you.

"I was at the concert at the Ryman. I just started medical school and don't get out much, but I couldn't miss Storyhill. You guys were amazing."

Avery's smile faded and she mentally rolled her eyes.

The young woman looked side-to-side and leaned into the desk's raised counter. "I'll probably get in trouble for this, but could I have your autograph?"

Matt laughed and winked at her. "It'll be our secret."

The poor girl looked like she might pass out.

He scrawled his signature across her notebook and handed it to her.

"Thank you," she wheezed out.

Avery shoved an elbow into Matt's ribs.

"You're welcome, Jenny," he said, reading her nametag. "Would you give us directions to Mr. Massey's room, please?"

"Of course." She clicked the space bar on the large desktop computer. "The staff sergeant is in room B125. Down the hall. Take two lefts."

Staff sergeant? Same rank as her father. Avery closed her eyes and sucked in a ragged breath. She could do this. Her father had been gone for fifteen years. And this was an entirely different situation.

Matt rapped on the desk. "Thanks Jenny. And thanks for coming to the concert. Have a good day."

She smiled, went pink again, and nodded vigorously.

"We should go, Matt," Avery said. The sooner they got started, the sooner this would be over. Plus, she didn't have it in her to watch another woman fawn all over Matt.

Was she jealous? Seemed so. Surprising. She'd never been jealous in the past.

Maybe that's because you knew where you stood then, and now, you have no idea.

"Mac?" Matt said, watching her closely.

"Huh?" She shook the thoughts out of her head. "Yes. Yes. Ready. Let's go."

They followed the receptionist's directions and wound through the halls, locating the staff sergeant's room. The plain white door served as a backdrop to a sign with a rainbow of sliders protruding from it. Fall risk. No Flowers. Visitors must check-in at reception. No Latex. No outside food and drink.

"That's a lot of rules," Matt said, staring at the sign.

She chuckled and some of the tension slipped from her shoulders. The Matt Taylor she remembered had an aversion to rules. "Well, unless you have pockets full of posies and peanut butter cups, I think we're good."

He laughed, turning out his pockets. "I'm clean." He knocked and a quiet "Enter" welcomed them in.

Staff Sergeant Massey was propped up in his bed, one arm in a sling, one leg missing. Avery swallowed. She would honor her father's memory by being strong. He would want that. He would want her to honor this man's service.

Matt ran a hand down her spine and stepped forward. "Matt Taylor," he said, reaching out his hand, "and this, which you likely already know, is Avery Lind. We heard you're a fan of Avery's show and want to thank you for your service."

Avery was suddenly very thankful not to be doing this alone. Having Matt here gave her space to collect herself. She'd teased him a lot, but his smooth, charming personality had its uses.

The soldier's smile broadened. "Nurses told me you might pay me a visit. This is turning into a big day for me."

"Were you also asked whether a photographer would be okay?" Matt continued. She should be the one asking the questions. And she would as soon as she could catch her breath.

Sergeant Massey nodded. "Wounded Warrior Project, right?"

"That's correct," Avery said, finding her voice.

"Ma'am," Sergeant Massey said, looking at Avery, "your show was broadcast over American Forces Network. You've got a lot of fans in the military. You can't imagine how much hearing something like your show helps."

"Really?" Avery asked, overcome with emotion. She never imagined she could be of assistance to soldiers, to men and women like her father.

"Really. It gets us through the tough times, provides a slice of home, and gives us something to do in the down times. Sometimes those long stretches with little activity can be the hardest. Gives us too much time to think."

She wanted to ask about his injuries, but how did one do that tactfully? "You were stationed in Afghanistan?"

"Yes, ma'am."

"There's no need for 'ma'am.' Avery will do."

"Avery," he repeated with a smile.

Matt laughed. "You clearly rank higher than me. She still makes me call her ma'am."

Sergeant Massey chuckled. "I'm guessing it's not my rank, but this sexy hospital gown."

Avery smirked. "You got me. Baggy, backless sleep shirts and the faint smell of antiseptic are my weaknesses."

The soldier sobered. "Thanks for not ignoring the elephant in the room. Most people have no idea what to say to me. And certainly don't feel free to make jokes."

The corners of Matt's lips switched. "Enjoy it, sir. Avery Lind jokes are a rare sighting."

"Then I'll take it for the gift it is."

Avery smiled but before she could say more, the photographer hired by WWP stepped into the room and after introducing himself, took a few photos, got a statement from the staff sergeant and one from Avery and Matt.

The photographer stepped toward the door but was blocked by a nurse pushing a wheelchair. A woman sat in the chair holding a baby that couldn't have more than a day or two old.

The staff sergeant beamed. "See what I mean about this shaping up to be a great day?" he said to Matt and Avery. "That, there, is the reason I was transferred from Walter Reed. Matt, Avery, this is my wife, Laurie Massey, and the daughter I thought I'd never meet."

Avery stepped back, and her pulse jumped. The child he never thought he'd get to meet. Her breath quickened. Her fingers tingled. Her stomach spun. She needed to get out of this room before she had a full-blown panic attack.

Her eyes flew to the door. Getting there meant conquering a medical-themed obstacle course. It was a small room, and she'd have to get around a giant hospital bed, the wheelchair, the nurse, and the photographer, who had the camera back up in front of his face.

Mrs. Massey looked at Matt. "Are you afraid of babies?"

"Not unless they need changing," he quipped.

She laughed. "Can you hand Olivia to my husband?"

"It's okay?" Matt asked the nurse. She nodded.

Matt reached for the baby, and Avery's knees almost buckled. She felt like a rocket on the launchpad, and the countdown was on.

Matt laid the newborn on the staff sergeant's healthy arm, and both men's eyes were wet.

"Excuse me," Avery blurted out, maneuvering herself around medical equipment and people. She needed air and fast.

She got out of the room and collapsed against the wall, sliding down until her butt hit the floor.

She squeezed her eyes shut. *Calm down, Avery.* Think of the last three things she saw. She rocked. That wouldn't help. The last three things she ate. Bacon Cheeseburger. French fries. Diet Coke. The last three three things . . .

Suddenly, Matt was next to her, pulling her into him. "I suspected this would be too hard for you."

"You did?" she choked out.

"A staff sergeant deployed to the Middle East? You'd have so many memories. Painful ones. And then when his family came in. More memories of losing your father while he was so far away and not having a chance to say good-bye."

As terrible as it sounded, she wished it were that.

A nurse came down the hallway and stopped. "Are you okay?" she asked Avery.

"Hospital smells do this to her every time," Matt said, showering the nurse with his signature smile. "I tried to warn her, but she never listens." He shrugged and winked at the nurse, who turned the color of a ripe raspberry. "She just needs a couple of minutes and she'll be fine." The nurse nodded and walked off.

She rubbed her forehead, willing away an emerging headache. "You don't have to keep making excuses for me. I can handle things."

"Baby, you are one of the strongest people I've ever met. I'm not saving you, just offering a helping hand. It's what friends do."

"We're friends again?" she said, trying to steady her breathing and voice.

"We never stopped being friends. I was just upset. Friends get upset with each other once in a while." He brushed the hair from her face. "And I'd be lying if I didn't hope we could be more than friends."

God, how she wanted that. But she knew it wasn't possible —not until she cleared the air.

"Think you're okay to stand?"

She nodded, and he helped her into a standing position.

"Okay?" he asked, bending to look directly into her eyes.

"Okay," she answered.

"Think you can come back into the room with me?"

She looked at him. "Is his baby—I mean, his family—still in there?"

His eyes narrowed. "Yes."

Avery dropped her eyes. She needed to power through this.

"I think the photographer got everything he needed. We only need to say goodbye. He'll want to spend this time with his family. Sixty seconds, Mac. That's all it will take."

She could do sixty seconds. She'd do it for the job. And to show Matt she wasn't a complete basket case. "Okay," she repeated. You'd never know she made her living speaking. She couldn't manage more than one-word answers.

Avery calmed with every step away from the soldier's room. They'd made their excuses and he'd thanked them profusely for coming. She forced her attention on the soldier, avoiding looking around the room, and they'd been able to exit gracefully.

They climbed into her car.

"Do you want me to drive?" Matt asked, concern still lining his face.

"I'm fine now." Well, mostly fine. Dammit, she couldn't keep doing this. "Matt, can you have dinner with me?"

He smiled. "I'd love that, but I have plans tonight."

"A date?" The question blurted out before she could stop it.

"Why? You jealous?"

"No," she lied.

He reached for the hand that clutched the console between them and slowly ran his fingers over her knuckles. "I think it's time for us to be honest with each other, Mac."

Her eyes flashed to his. "What?" *Here? Now?* The fear that consumed her in the hospital room rushed back.

"I meant it earlier when I said I wished for more than friendship. We're good together. The show feels natural. Being together feels good. And what happened the other night wasn't just two people fumbling toward release."

"It wasn't?" *Again, so eloquent with the words, Avery.*

"No, it was the intimate love making of two people who once knew everything about each other. I think you felt it, too."

Whoa. Maybe he should be the one making his living with words.

"I want more," he admitted. "I want to try again. But I don't want to go any further until I know if you'd consider the possibility. I don't think I can sustain another broken heart."

Now would be the time to tell him. But she couldn't bring herself to do it, sitting in her car, in a hospital parking ramp. "But you're still going to be traveling all the time." She'd fallen back on the same bogus excuse she'd used all those years ago.

And his face said he knew she wasn't being honest.

He sighed. "Do you know why I agreed to do this radio gig, Mac?"

She dropped her gaze, staring at his knees. "Exposure for Storyhill."

He lifted her chin. "Yes, but more than that, I wanted to do something that didn't involve my face. I thought it would be a way to show everyone that there is more to me than a pretty package."

"Oh, Matt." Lines creased her forehead. How was it that someone so skilled couldn't see his own talents?

185

"That's the reason I said yes, but the reason I stayed was you."

Her eyes flashed wide. "Me?"

"Yes. When you left me, I was destroyed. And everything in me said you weren't being one hundred percent honest with me. I told myself if I ever got the chance to talk to you about it, I'd get to the bottom of it." He studied his fingers.

She tried to say something, but nothing came.

"I wanted to show you that I was worthy of you. I wanted to kick this radio thing out of the park so you'd see I was the kind of man you could count on—that I have skills and abilities. That we could be equal partners. If I did that, you'd stop doubting me."

Oh my god. It suddenly became crystal clear to her. He thought she broke up with him because he wasn't enough. That's why he kept repeating things like 'all flash and no substance.'

How had she not seen this? He'd always hated it when people thought all he needed was his looks. She knew that. And she'd played right into it. He hadn't bought her reasons for breaking up with him—and he'd carried the burden of thinking she thought so little of him. *For nine years.*

Enough. She was going to tell him. And if he walked away from her, so be it. At least he'd know she had always believed in him.

She reached over and squeezed his fingers. "We need to talk. But not here. Tomorrow after the show?"

"I won't be in the studio tomorrow—it's the day I negotiated off, remember? I have a full day with Storyhill tomorrow. It's our second to last practice before we leave on tour."

"Right," she said, nodding. "I forgot about that. Lunch after the show on Friday? Come to my house. I'll cook. Momma and

Jess will be at work. We'll have the house to ourselves. We'll talk and afterwards if you still want to give us a shot, I'm in."

"Really?"

"Yes, Matt. Just because we broke up doesn't mean I stopped caring about you."

He leaned over the console and placed a kiss right below her ear and whispered, "I never stopped loving you, Mac."

She sucked that in and pushed it into a safe space in her heart. She'd keep it close if he walked away. A speck of hope bubbled up. He seemed to want her. He just admitted he still loved her. Maybe after she explained, he would understand—or try to.

When he slid back into his seat, she started the engine and pulled out of the parking space. "So, lunch on Friday?"

He squeezed her shoulder. "Friday lunch."

CHAPTER SIXTEEN

MATT LET HIMSELF INTO THE PRACTICE SPACE GRACE HAD arranged. Apparently, it *was* all about who you knew. He scanned the space. Overlapping Persian rugs covered the pine floor, and a stone wall ran the length of the space. There was no doubt it had been a warehouse before the current owners carved it up into studios for musicians, visual artists, and writers.

He was early, but he'd been pacing around his apartment. He'd become so used to being at the station on weekday mornings, he didn't know quite what to do with himself.

A single guitar was hanging from the wall. Having seen better days, it was for decoration, not playing. But he pulled it from the wall, strummed the strings, and did his best to tune it.

The strings felt rough on his fingers. He flipped over his right hand. The calluses he'd worked so hard for were gone. It had been years since he'd picked up an instrument to do anything but figure out a few chord progressions.

Gone were the hours he'd spent playing. Working out his feelings with nothing but a pick and a pen.

Storyhill didn't use instruments. That was his excuse.

The real reason was more complicated. He'd played every

free moment after Amy-Lynn left him. The guitar became synonymous with heartbreak and as the years passed, he picked it up less and less.

And there was the fact that he'd let the show get too big. He'd become wrapped up in the performance, in his brand, and the purity of the music had faded.

He didn't want the heartbreak back, but he did need to reconnect with the guy who left for Pigeon Forge—who used music as solace rather than solution. The guy who performed for the love of it.

Amy-Lynn's comments made him realize that.

He couldn't get angry about people making assumptions when he'd been using the very things he claimed to hate.

He hung the beat-up guitar back on its pegs and scrubbed a hand down his face. Time between tours usually meant downtime. Unpacking his bag. Sleeping in his own bed. Outside of the concert at the Ryman—which felt like a lifetime ago—relaxation was the priority.

But instead, he'd chased a chance to prove himself. And run headlong into a brick wall of memories. And unresolved feelings. And so many unanswered questions.

"Mattie!" Blake yelled, letting the heavy steel door slam behind him.

Matt jumped, and his hand flew to his chest. "Having a heart attack was not on my to-do list today. Holy shit."

Blake laughed and clapped Matt on the shoulder. "You the only one here?"

Matt held up a hand, motioning to the emptiness. "It appears so."

Blake let a large duffel drop to the floor. The sound reverberated through the cavernous space.

"What you got in there? A dead body?"

Blake smirked. "Props."

Matt groaned. "For what?"

"You'll see." His smirk turned into a full-blown grin. "Let's just say, they'll help you return to your roots."

"Oh, hell no, Blake. I am not dressing up as a pirate ever again." Matt pursed his lips and shook his head.

"Someone role playing in the bedroom again? Who's the lucky sea wench, Mattie?" Andrew said, walking in, an eyebrow climbing his forehead.

"Seriously, dude, you really need to stop arriving mid-conversation." Matt blew out a breath. "Blake brought props."

"That's a hard no," Andrew said.

Matt lifted his hands out to his side and dipped his head in a mock bow. "Thank you. That's what I said."

"But—" Blake stammered.

"No, buts. Joe and Nick are right behind me. Let's get these numbers blocked and get out of here."

Matt stumbled through the blocking of the last song—again. It was like his brain couldn't handle one more thing.

"Mattie," Andrew grumbled, "you still with us? I have a beautiful fiancé I want to get back to and that's going to be impossible if your head's no longer in the game."

"I think a beautiful woman is likely his issue, too," Blake said, biting back a smile.

"Hilarious," Matt growled.

"Wow, dude," Joe said. "I didn't even know your voice went that low." Joe swung his head from one band member to the next, his eyes wide. "It's definitely a woman."

"Or he's finally going through puberty," Nick deadpanned.

Joe walked to Matt and threw his arm around Matt's shoulder. "Tell Uncle Joe all about it."

Matt rolled his eyes. "You are four years older than me. Hardly puts you in the 'uncle' category."

"Yes, but I've been married forever."

"Exactly why you're not the one to give advice." Matt looked up at the rest of the group and pointed his finger at each man. "And I'm not taking advice from any of you other dopey dwarfs either."

"Dopey dwarfs?" Andrew asked, smirking.

"Yeah. Happy," he pointed at Andrew. "And Resentful," pointing at Nick. "And Unwilling," he finished, pointing at Blake.

"Hey," Blake retorted, his palms out in surrender. "I'm not unwilling."

"I'm not talking about your dick. I'm talking about your heart," Matt retorted.

Andrew laughed. "He's got you there."

Blake shook his head and rolled his eyes. "Yeah, well, we can't all walk around dripping with sappy love. We're all tiring of your blissed-out attitude, Andrew."

"Hey Joe," Andrew called over his shoulder. "You tired of my happiness?"

"Naw," Joe said. "It's been a long time coming."

"How about you, Resentful?" Andrew shot a look at Nick.

Nick sighed and ran his fingers through his short hair. "While I'd rather be practicing than doing this, no, I'd like to think if Andrew can find love, it can happen to any of us."

Andrew laughed. "Guess it's just you, Unwilling."

"How'd this become about me?" Blake said. "Matt's the one acting like it's his first day. Whatever it is, Mattie, get it off your chest so we can get out of here."

Matt walked in a circle and rubbed his temples. "I think she loves me."

"Avery?" Blake asked.

Matt snorted. "Yes, you idiot, Avery."

"You're saying that like it's a bad thing," Joe said, his expression turning serious. "Do you not feel the same way?"

Matt fisted a hand in his hair, making it stand straight up. "I've loved her since high school."

"So the problem is?" Andrew asked.

"She's hesitant to admit it or even to give us another chance to see if we still work." He thought about how she kept trying to talk to him and how they kept getting interrupted. And each time he'd been relieved. He knew he was being a coward, but he was pretty sure he wouldn't like what she had to say.

"And you're hesitant to trust her again," Nick said. "I get that," he mumbled, just loud enough to be heard.

Matt's head snapped up. He'd been telling himself it was because he wanted resolution of the past, but Nick was right. "My gut is screaming that there's still a wall between us. And I guess I'm unwilling to give her my whole heart until I figure that out."

Blake laughed. "Did you just say you are *Unwilling*?"

Matt rolled his eyes and threw one of the absurd props at Blake. "You're a comedian today."

Andrew picked up the foam sword that Blake insisted they use while singing their medley of sea shanties. He poked it into Matt's stomach. "If I learned anything in the past few months it's that you need to talk about it—not with us, but with her."

Matt nodded. "Yeah. We're having lunch after the show tomorrow, and she promised we'd talk."

"That's good," Andrew said.

"Is it terrible to admit I'm scared out of my mind? What if she yanks my heart out and stomps on it again?"

"Then you have your answer," Nick said. "The only thing worse than having your heart stomped on is having no answers at all."

Matt looked at his buddy and realized, for the first time, they'd been in the same boat all this time.

"All right, dopey dwarfs, thanks, let's finish this song and wrap things up," Matt said.

~

Avery sipped her coffee and confirmed her show notes were in the proper order. For the third time. If she went through them enough times, maybe she'd forget what waited for her after the show.

"Two weeks down. Only four shows left after today," Celeste said, popping her head into the studio, causing Avery to jump. "Pretty soon you'll have all this back to yourself. You excited?"

No. Not even a little bit.

She'd been so focused on getting here, to a place where she could support everyone in her life, that she never even considered having a co-host. She had to admit she liked it. Someone to riff with, someone to laugh with, someone to support her on the days where she felt weighed down.

But would any co-host do that, or was it just Matt?

She'd been looking forward to yesterday when it was going to be just her and Ajay in the studio. But the studio had felt empty, cold. Damn it, she'd missed him.

"This queen never left her throne," Ajay said, saving her from having to answer. "Matt Taylor could never be more than a court jester."

Ajay meant to be funny, but she knew the comment would wound Matt. He was more than studio dressing. He'd proven himself to be a capable, clever co-host.

"Court jesters made sure no one got too bored by the queen," Matt said, sauntering into the studio.

Avery whirled toward him. "Ajay was only joking."

He smiled a soft, private smile. "Being an entertainer is all I've ever dreamed of, Mac. I'm choosing to take it as a compliment. Though I draw the line at wearing one of those striped poufy costumes with some weird hat."

Celeste laughed. "Good thing this is radio. No costumes required."

"Good thing," Matt echoed.

"Avery and I were just discussing that you've banked two weeks of shows and only have four more to go. You excited to get back on the road?"

"It is my favorite place to be," Matt said, before lifting his eyes to meet hers. "Though this has turned out pretty great too."

Her heart kicked hard against her ribs. It *had* been pretty great, and it was likely to be very different in a few hours. Once she told him the truth, even if he didn't immediately bolt, she knew beyond any doubt that the easy camaraderie they'd finally managed would disappear.

Why had she waited this long to tell him?

If she told him that first day, he'd have left immediately. Her show would have stayed solely hers. And she wouldn't have fallen in love with him all over again.

But that's not what had happened.

In two short weeks, she realized she'd never fully be over Matt Taylor. Ever.

But maybe it'd be like Momma said, she'd finally feel better when she came clean with him. Maybe.

"Five minutes," Ajay called through her headphones.

She nodded at him.

"You ready?" she asked Matt.

"I am. Are you?" he said, his eyes finding hers.

She knew instantly that he wasn't talking about the show.

Or that wasn't the only thing he was talking about. But she couldn't think about that now, she had a show to do.

She cleared her throat before bringing up her mic. "Good morning, country music fans. This is Avery Lind and—"

"Matt Taylor. I'm still here," he said, laughter lacing his voice.

She laughed with him. She couldn't help it. "And he's Matt Taylor. With us today and for four more shows before Storyhill goes back out on the road. Where is your first stop, Matt?"

"Calgary."

"A Canadian tour?" she asked, already knowing the answer. It's not as if the information was hard to find.

"Yes. Our fans north of the border have been so supportive, we wanted to take this new album to them first. And speaking of Canadians, I believe our guest this morning was born in Toronto, right?"

She smiled. A smooth transition. And given the opportunity to publicize his own band, he deferred to the show.

"That's correct. And it's one of the first questions on my list —how did he get from Ontario to Nashville? Seems like there might be a story there."

"Let's get to it then. We ready Ajay?" Matt said.

"We are mate."

"We still on for lunch?" Avery asked tentatively as Matt organized his side of the desk at the conclusion of the show.

"Yep." He stood and walked over to her side of the console, leaning his long frame against the desk. He brushed a stray piece of hair from her face. "Are we still going to be alone?" he asked softly and winked.

Her core clenched. She looked at Ajay's window. He wasn't paying them any attention.

She'd like nothing more than to take him home and push him down on her bed. Her bed. How long had it been since a man had been in her bed? Not since Momma moved in.

She shook her head, shaking out the vision of Matt naked on her sheets. That wasn't what this lunch was about. Though it would be far more enjoyable.

"We will, but we need to talk. Clothing is strictly required."

He nodded, and his smile fell a little. "We do. There's a lot to talk about."

More than you know, Matt Taylor. More than you know.

He slipped his messenger bag across his chest. "Should I ride with you? You can bring me back to get my car or I can Uber back."

She shook her head. "I think it's best if we drove separately."

He cocked his head, his eyes questioning, but said nothing.

"Can I pick up anything on my way over?"

She'd been obsessing about this lunch ever since she'd suggested it. She didn't need anything but sending him on an errand would buy her some time. She could get home, make sure the house was empty. She had asked Momma and Jess to stay away, but you never knew. They'd both be at work, but plans change. And this couldn't be interrupted. She'd never find the courage again.

"I made soup—well, Momma made soup. I froze it. And will unfreeze it. Could you stop by that bakery on George Street and get a sourdough loaf?"

"Done. See you at your house in a few." He moved to leave the studio but turned back to her. "I'm glad we're finally doing this, Mac. I have a feeling things are about to change for us."

Truer words had never been spoken.

CHAPTER SEVENTEEN

MATT PUT HIS TRUCK IN PARK AND GRABBED THE BROWN paper bag from the passenger seat. He grasped the door handle and stopped.

Leaving the station, he thought he was ready for this. Now he wasn't so sure.

He was going to tell her he was still in love with her. He knew how she felt about his lifestyle—or at least he thought he did. Lying awake last night, he'd come up with every excuse she might offer and his response to each one. His argument was solid.

But he would not push himself on her. He only wanted her in his life if she wanted him in hers. The thought that she might not want him sent a cold ripple through his body.

Nick's words ran through his head. *At least you'll have an answer. No more wondering.*

He sucked in a breath and opened the door. It was now or never.

He strode up the front walk and smiled, remembering Amy-Lynn tipsily kicking over a pathway light—and asking him to kiss her. He'd be totally okay if she asked him again today. And this time he wouldn't say no.

He knocked on the door and she yelled, "It's open."

He opened the door, pulled his boots off, and took in a giant breath. The house smelled amazing. Isabel's Pozole. He hadn't eaten it for over a decade. But he'd know that smell anywhere. Funny how those things stuck with you.

Amy-Lynn came around the kitchen corner. She'd changed from her work 'uniform' into a loose sundress, her hair down, curling toward her neck. Casual. And beautiful.

He handed her the bag. "If I'd known you were serving Pozole, I would have tried to find some bolillos."

She smiled, but it was clearly fake. Was she trying to figure out how to let him down easy? No. She didn't know what he intended to tell her, to ask her.

"Sourdough is close enough," she said, taking the bag from him. "Thank you."

He followed her into the kitchen. "I really like your place," he said, taking in the Craftsman design and the bright colors.

"I forgot you've never made it past the entryway." Her eyes flashed around the room, as if taking it in for the first time. "The soup needs a few more minutes. Do you want a tour?"

"Sure," he said. "How long have you lived here?"

"About three years."

"And Isabel?"

"About a year. And Jess moved in shortly thereafter."

"I'm impressed. I can't imagine buying a house." He dipped his head, rubbing the back of his neck. "Neither can my bank account."

Her throat bobbed and she ran her fingers over her exposed collarbone. "I got a little help. When Jess and I reached twenty-five, Momma gave us a portion of daddy's death gratuity. I used mine for a down payment."

"And Jess?"

Her eyes met his, and a flash of something flickered in her eyes. "A baby."

He lifted a brow. "Huh?"

"She had Wyatt . . . and was uninsured."

"Wyatt's dad is not in the picture?"

Amy-Lynn visibly stiffened. "No. They didn't have a relationship, and he didn't want to be a dad. Jess considered all her options, but ultimately decided to have the baby."

"That's—"

"So, this is the living room," Amy-Lynn said, cutting him off.

Huh. So that subject was off-limits. So many of her walls were crumbling, but so many remained intact. Maybe after he told her how he felt, she'd let the rest fall. Sadness bubbled up. She'd always had a lot of walls, but never with him.

Floor-to-ceiling bookcases flanked a vintage fireplace. He wandered over and ran his hands over the spines of the books. Jane Austen. Virginia Woolf. Ayn Rand. Toni Morrison. Stephen King. And Nora Roberts. He laughed and pulled it off the shelf.

"I think I've read this one."

Her lips twitched. "Or at least the sexy bits."

His eyes widened. "Wait. There are other parts?"

She smiled a half smile. "If those books are where you learned your moves, remind me to send Ms. Roberts a thank-you letter."

He licked his lips and let his eyes slide down her body. "I learned all my moves with you, Mac. Trial and error."

Her cheeks went pink. "I don't remember the errors," she breathed out, her voice rough.

He smiled, reminding himself that he was here to talk. Or at least talk *first*.

He placed the book back on the shelf, a collection of framed photos catching his attention. The first one a chubby baby with a mop of dark curls, laughing with abandon, ice cream running down his cheeks. He picked up the second one. Two teenagers. The girl smiling at the camera. The boy looking down at the girl like he couldn't bear to take his eyes off her. "I haven't seen this one."

Amy-Lynn lifted up on her toes to look over his shoulder. "That's shortly after they met. Momma had just moved from Mexico. She said Daddy was her first friend."

He turned, brushing a stray hair from her face. "Sounds familiar."

She grunted. "Yeah, history repeating itself."

He frowned at her negative response and waited for her to continue. She didn't. He set the frame down and his eyes landed on another photo, tucked in the back. "Is that our prom picture?"

A nervous giggle escaped her lips. "Momma's sentimental."

He grinned and nodded. "It's always Isabel." He wrapped an arm around her waist and pulled her tight into his body. She stiffened before melting into him.

"That guy," he said, tapping a finger on his face in the photo, "had no idea what was coming later than night."

She rolled her eyes. "So cliché. Losing your virginity on prom night."

He kissed her forehead. "Seventeen-year-olds aren't known for inspired ideas. Good thing we've learned a thing or two since then."

Her face flushed from pink to red, and she unwound from his embrace. "Do you want the rest of the tour?"

He wiggled his eyebrows. "Does it include your bedroom?"

She playfully swatted his chest. "Maybe lunch is a better idea. I'm sure the soup is hot by now."

She turned back toward the kitchen. Something was up.

She'd been the one to initiate sex the other night, but ever since then, she'd gotten uncomfortable any time he even hinted at a repeat performance.

Was she reluctant to do it again because he was leaving? Did she think he'd wrap up his gig at the station and never look back? If that was it, he'd remedy that this afternoon.

An all-too-familiar nagging feeling crawled up his spine. Or maybe she still didn't think he was a good long-term bet? He shook his head, trying to dislodge the thought. He couldn't ask her for more if he kept doubting himself.

Remember, talk first, Matt. Get everything out in the open. Then they could move on to other, more satisfying, things.

"Matt?" she called from the kitchen. "Are you coming?"

"Coming," he said, doing his best to ignore the doubts. He turned into the kitchen. She'd set bowls on colorful woven placemats at the bar. His bread lay sliced on a cutting board, butter in a crock to the side.

"Hope you don't mind eating at the bar. We rarely use the dining table. This floor is easier to clean with a toddler just learning how to hold a spoon."

"I've been using a spoon for a while now."

She laughed. "I meant Wyatt."

"Oh," he nodded, biting back a smile, "okay." He slid onto a bar stool and watched her efficient movements as she poured a glass of amber liquid. She held up the pitcher. "Sweet tea?"

"Now I know you've been in Nashville for a while."

She pulled a face. "Do you want some or not?"

He held a glass out to her. "Yes, please."

She placed the glasses in front of their bowls and moved around the bar, climbing onto her stool. She placed a napkin in her lap and moved her spoon and knife, turning her bowl to the left three times.

She looked up, finding his eyes on her, and blushed. "I . . . I . . ."

"Mac," he said, sliding his fingers over hers. "I've known you for a long time. You don't need to explain yourself. The way you move through this world is uniquely you and nothing that needs an apology."

"Thank you," she said, staring at her bowl. A beat passed. Then another before she lifted her head, confidence back in her expression. "Now eat. Before it gets cold."

He dipped a spoon into the bowl. The smell was embroidered into the memories of his youth. How many times had Isabel fed him this specific meal?

He took a bite and groaned. "It's good to know some things never change. This is exactly how I remember it. It's amazing."

"Momma will be happy to hear that."

"Did you tell her I was coming here today?"

"Yes." She looked back down at her bowl, her spoon aimlessly moving through the soup. "They're both working today, but I also asked them not to come home, so we'd have some time to talk—just the two of us."

"About that," he said, after swallowing another bite of Isabel's creation. "There're some things I need to tell you."

"Yeah?" she said, still not making eye contact with him.

"Mac, please look at me."

She turned her head, her eyes still squeezed closed. She slowly opened them with a shake of her head. "I have things to tell you too."

Could she be ready to admit she loved him, too?

"Can I go first?"

She drummed her fingers on the counter. "I'm not sure that's the best thing."

"I need to get it out before I lose my nerve. Mac," he said, grabbing her hand. "It's always been you. No one ever —"

"No," she said, standing up and walking to the other side of the bar.

"No?" he said, his hopes deflating.

"Before you go any further, there is something you need to know."

"Mac, I know you've always had reservations about us. About my job, but . . ."

"That's not it."

"Then what?"

She opened her mouth to speak just as her phone played "We Are Family" by Sister Sledge. She looked from him to her phone. "That's Jess's ring tone. I really should get that."

He sighed. He wanted to throw the phone out the door, but that wouldn't be honoring all the things she held most dear.

"Family first," he said, gesturing to the phone.

She nodded and hit Accept. "Jess?"

He could hear rapid talking coming from the other end but couldn't make out words. She walked into the other room, and he tucked back into his soup. This was not going at all like he planned.

When she finally reappeared, her mouth was pulled tight. "I'm sorry to cut this short—I wanted to talk to you—but I need to go get Wyatt. Apparently, he spiked a fever and the daycare called Jess."

"And she can't get him?" He knew he sounded uncaring, but this was supposed to be the day they cleared the air. The day they started the next part of their life—together.

"She just started a new job."

He shook his head. "You do too much for them."

She straightened, turned to him, and gave him a serious look. "This is different."

He set his spoon down and rubbed between his eyes. "How?"

She grabbed her keys from a hook on the wall. "I don't have time to argue with you. I need to go pick up a sick little boy. We'll need to reschedule."

"No."

Her eyebrows arched. "Excuse me?"

His posture softened, and he attempted to douse the irritation swirling in his stomach. "I'll go with you. We can get Wyatt. Settle him back here and then continue our conversation."

"It might not work that way."

"I know." He grabbed her hands and laced their fingers together. "But you carry so much burden, let me help you with this."

She nodded. "Fine. Can you move your truck? It's blocking me in."

"I can drive," he offered.

"The car seat is in my car."

He snapped his finger. "Right. Forgot about that."

Matt grabbed his keys and headed out the back door. Maybe it wasn't the right decision to continue after this interruption, but he wanted this done.

If she rebuffed him, he'd have the weekend to lick his wounds before he was due back in the studio on Monday. Because, dammit, he would see that through to the end.

But more than that, he wanted to start his life with Amy-Lynn as soon as possible.

"Tía and Dad!" Wyatt yelled when Matt and Amy-Lynn walked into the daycare center.

Amy-Lynn stiffened, and her eyes flashed to his face. Was she embarrassed?

"I didn't know Wyatt's dad was in the picture," the daycare

provider said before Matt could reassure Amy-Lynn it was okay. In his experience, toddlers could say far worse.

Amy-Lynn's mouth opened and shut, no sound coming out. Matt reached his hand out. "Not dad. Matt," he said, pointing at himself. "I'm a friend of Avery's."

"Oh, I see." She smiled knowingly. "Little ones are often confused. He hears all the other kids call adult males 'dad.' He hasn't grasped the meaning of the word."

Amy-Lynn walked over to the little boy, pushing back the hair that was plastered to his sweaty forehead.

"His fever is about 100," the daycare worker said. "Not super high, but his nose is running a bit, too. Take him home and tuck him in for a nap, and he should be good to go by Monday."

"Thank you," Amy-Lynn said, moving to pick Wyatt up.

"No," he said, his little forehead crinkling. "Want Dad," he said, pointing at Matt.

"Wyatt," she said, light admonishment in her voice.

"I got this," he said, pulling on Amy-Lynn's arm.

"But . . ."

"No, we can't have the star of the Avery Lind show getting a cold, can we?" Matt dipped his large frame to the child. "Do you want to walk, or should I carry you?"

"Carry," Wyatt said, raising his arms.

Matt picked up the child. "Okay, but there is one thing we need to talk about first."

Wyatt's forehead crinkled, and he tipped his head, fixing his eyes on Matt.

"If I'm going to carry you, you shouldn't call me 'dad.' My name is Matt."

"Matt," the toddler repeated.

"Yes. Can you do that? Can you call me Matt?"

"Matt," Wyatt repeated.

"Okay, Tía," Matt said to Amy-Lynn, "lead on."

When they got to the car, he placed the little boy in his car seat and expertly buckled him in. He turned to find her staring at him.

"You're very good at this."

Matt shrugged. "I don't see them as much as I would like, but I have seven nieces and nephews and then there's Henry, Nick's son, he's been the honorary sixth member of Storyhill pretty much since his birth. Since it seems they need some sort of car seat or booster until they're fifteen, you get pretty good with the contraptions. Plus, it's good practice for when I have my own kids."

Her eyes skittered toward him as she rounded the front of the car and slipped into the driver's seat. "You want kids?" she asked while buckling her belt.

His eyes narrowed. "Not everything has changed since we last discussed our future. At least not for me."

She nodded, three lines appearing between her brows—a sure sign the gears were moving in her head.

"Go home," Wyatt chirped, breaking the moment. "Matt," Wyatt added, making them both laugh.

"Yes, sir," Matt said, turning to Amy-Lynn. "You heard the man."

She turned the car toward home. "So Nick is a single dad?"

He ran his hands down the length of his thighs and nodded. "Yes. He has sole custody."

"What happened to Henry's mom?"

Matt let out a sigh. "She disappeared shortly after Henry was born. She had some substance abuse issues."

Amy-Lynn tapped her fingers on the steering wheel. One. Two. Three. "Were they married?"

Matt nodded. "Still are."

She signaled into the alley behind her house. "*What?*"

"Nick doesn't like to talk about it."

Her lips twisted and she exhaled a sputtering breath. "Relationship fails are difficult to discuss."

"But you and I are going to change that today, right?"

She killed the engine. "I hope so," she whispered.

CHAPTER EIGHTEEN

Avery unbuckled the car seat and reached for her sleeping nephew.

Matt placed a hand on her shoulder. "Let me get him."

"He's hot and sweaty."

He winked at her. "I like hot and sweaty."

She sucked her bottom lip under her teeth, biting back a smile. "Have you always been this much of a flirt?"

"Not with you. Didn't figure I needed to. You were so besotted with me."

She snorted. "Besotted? Really?"

He tipped his head back and laughed. "I've upped my language game too."

"Too?"

He waggled his eyebrows at her, and she rolled her eyes. "Get the baby."

Matt negotiated Wyatt out of the seat and laid him gently on his shoulder. Wyatt never opened an eye.

Avery tugged the hem of Wyatt's t-shirt down. "Impressive, Mr. Taylor. Just how often do you see your family?"

"Not as often as I would like. They're spread around the

country. Mom and Dad are still in Marla. Miranda is in Kansas City. Emma moved to San Francisco. And Dan is in Oklahoma City. I try to see them when Storyhill passes through one of their cities, and we're together for Mom's birthday and Christmas. But you know, digital age, I'm getting videos all the time."

"How old are they now?"

"Anywhere from fourteen to eighteen months."

"Eighteen months?"

"Emma got her PhD and settled into a teaching position before considering kids."

"Here, let me grab the door." She unlocked it and held it open. "Why don't you sit with him in the living room—there's a rocking chair in the corner—while I grab some clean, dry clothes and start running a bath. Let's see if we can get his temp down a little. If we can, we can tuck him in his bed and resume our conversation."

"Do you have any Children's Tylenol?"

Avery snapped her fingers. "Good call. I'll get that too. Meet you upstairs in five minutes?"

Matt nodded.

She didn't need five minutes. She needed a moment to collect herself. He was so good with Wyatt. So careful. So steady. He would be such a wonderful dad.

She pulled a fresh pair of shorts, a t-shirt, and a Pull-Up from Wyatt's small dresser. He'd object to the Pull-Up. He was a 'big boy' after all, but since he was sick, she didn't want to take any chances.

She set the Tylenol on the counter and started the bath.

"I'm ready," she hollered down to Matt. A lie of epic proportions, on every level.

She could hear Matt gently cajoling Wyatt awake. "What's your favorite tub toy?"

When he climbed the stairs, he sat Wyatt on the counter and Avery gave him a dropper of the pain reliever.

"Arms up little man."

Wyatt put his arms in the air, never taking his eyes off Matt.

"I have a penis," he announced as Avery removed his bottoms.

She bit back a laugh. This was it. This was when Matt finally ran out of the right thing to say.

Matt leaned down close to Wyatt's ear. "Can you keep a secret?"

The little boy nodded earnestly.

"Promise not to tell anyone."

Wyatt nodded again, his eyes wide.

Matt looked side-to-side and cupped his hand around his lips. "I have one too."

Wyatt's mouth fell open. "You do?"

"Yep."

"Me see it," Wyatt said, grabbing for the button on Matt's pants.

Avery laughed, and Matt inched back, just out of Wyatt's reach.

Matt ruffled Wyatt's hair. "I only take my clothes off for baths. And that bathtub is not big enough for both of us. How about you show me your bath squirts instead?"

The little boy seemed appeased, and Matt swung him into the bath.

"You okay by yourself for a bit?" he asked, stepping away from the tub.

She raked her eyes down his body. "You worried you're going to have to take your clothes off?"

He leaned down, whispering in her ear. "This will be the only time I'll say no when Avery Lind asks me to take off my clothes. But as you said earlier, we have some things to talk about before *bath time*."

Avery wet a washcloth and gently wiped the toddler's cheeks. "Where are you going?"

"I got some little man goo on my shirt. I have a gym bag in my car. I'm just going to run out and change."

When Matt came back, Avery was toweling off Wyatt, and the little boy's eyes were drifting shut. "How about we put your clothes on and then tuck you in for a nap?"

"Matt nap," Wyatt said, pointing his finger at Matt.

"Okay, little dude, I will rock you for five minutes, and then you have to sleep in your big boy bed. Deal?"

"Deal," Wyatt said with a serious nod.

Matt carried him down the stairs, and they reclaimed their spot in the rocking chair.

Avery watched as Matt laid her nephew on his shoulder. This was going to be even harder than she had expected.

"If you're good," she said, her voice catching in her throat, "I'm going to call Jess and then clean up the kitchen."

"I'm good," he said, rubbing small circles on the little boy's back.

She nodded and slipped into the kitchen. The clock chimed just as she finished cleaning out the soup bowls and getting everything in the dishwasher. Momma would be home soon. They'd have to move their discussion to another location. Maybe his place? Or better yet, a public space where he'd be less likely to yell at her.

She walked back into the living room to tell Matt exactly that, but they were both out cold. Wyatt snored softly, some crusty bits developing under his nose. Matt's head tilted back.

Seriously, he had to be one of the most beautiful men she'd ever seen.

"Matt?" she called softly. Nothing.

She stood and watched them until her heart melted into the floor. Maybe she shouldn't tell him. It might be better to just go their separate ways.

Except that's not what she wanted.

"Well, would you look at that," Isabel said from behind her.

Avery gasped and clutched her heart. She hadn't even heard her mother come in, so lost in her thoughts.

Avery circled the depression in the center of her clavicle and tried to swallow the emotions growing thick in her throat. "Jess called in the middle of my lunch with Matt."

"See, I told you, he would have made a great father," Isabel said.

"Momma, shush," Avery said, pulling her mother back into the kitchen.

"Lunch must have gone okay. What did he say when you told him?"

Avery sliced her hand back and forth in front of her throat. Movement caught Avery's eye and she whirled to find Matt standing just behind her, Wyatt still draped on his shoulder.

"*Would have* made a great father? Like past tense?" Matt ignored Isabel, his full attention focused on her. "On Wednesday, you said once we talked, you were in. Did you change your mind? Did you bring me here to tell me we don't have a future?"

She dropped her gaze to the floor. She couldn't bear the look in his eyes. "That's not *exactly* what I said. And Momma just misspoke. She meant you *will* make a good father."

Isabel looked between them and shrugged. "You know my English isn't always so good."

Matt's eyes narrowed. "Isabel, your English is as good as mine."

"I'll take Wyatt upstairs," Isabel said, taking the small boy from Matt. She turned but stopped on the first stair.

Avery rushed to her side. "Momma, is he too heavy for you?"

"Not at all, mi hija." She patted Avery's cheek with her free hand. "This has gone on too long. I'll grab a book and sit in Wyatt and Jessica's room. Let me know if you need me."

Avery sucked in a long, deep breath and turned back to Matt.

"Mac, what's going on? What did Isabel mean? What's been going on too long? And why would you need her?"

She sighed, resigned. This was not how this was supposed to go. She had a whole speech planned. "Have a seat, Matt."

His chest rose and fell with a giant exhale. "I think I'd rather stand."

"Um, okay. So. Well. I've wanted to tell you this since that first day in the studio." She paced around the island and back. She didn't know if she wanted to be close to him when she finally told him or if putting the island between them was a better strategy. "Actually, longer than that." She looked down, unable to make eye contact with him.

"So, tell me now."

"I'm not sure where to start."

"The beginning is always a good place."

"You sure you don't want to sit?"

He fisted his fingers in his hair. "Mac."

"It's about why we broke up."

"We?" he scoffed.

She rubbed her collarbone, but it only seemed to spread the fire burning in her chest. "Fine, why I broke up with you."

"I'm listening."

Avery stopped pacing and lifted her eyes to Matt's. "First, I really was worried about you being gone so much. I saw what each deployment did to my parents' marriage. But that wasn't the only reason."

"Go on," Matt said, circling a shaky hand in the air.

Here goes nothing. "About two weeks before graduation, I found out I was pregnant."

Matt's eyes widened, and he stumbled. He gripped the back of the bar stool. "What?" he hissed out.

"Must have been a faulty condom." *Nice one, Avery. That's not what he cares about.*

He wasn't screaming, so that was good, right?

"You're telling me you broke up with me because you were pregnant with my child?" He rubbed his temples, pacing back and forth, stopping abruptly. "Unless it wasn't my baby? Is that what you're trying to tell me?" His voice was rising.

"God, no, Matt. Of course, it was your baby."

"So, let me see if I have this correct? You and I had planned a life together. Hell, I got down on one knee and asked you to marry me, and you said no and broke up with me *because you were pregnant*. I thought your previous reasons were ludicrous, but you're going to have to help me with this, Mac."

The fire spread through her arms and legs and her fingers convulsed. She gulped air and grabbed her thighs to stop the shaking. "I couldn't do it," she said, her voice breaking on the last word.

"Couldn't do what?" He was pulling at his hair, making it stand straight up. "Have a baby? Tell me I was going to be a father? What?" The last word was loud enough Momma was sure to have heard.

He stopped moving, his body reverberating as if a thought suddenly smashed into him. "Where is this baby now? Did you have an abortion? Did you give the child up for adoption? Am I going to have some kid showing up on my doorstep claiming I'm its father?" He slammed a hand on the counter.

She reached for him, but he pulled his arm away like her touch burned him. "No, none of that. Matt, if you calm down, I'll tell you the whole story."

"Calm down? *Calm down?* I thought you left me because I wasn't good enough and now, I'm learning you didn't think I could support you and be a good father. Good god, Amy-Lynn, did you think so little of me? *Do* you think so little of me?"

"No." The tears she'd been holding back leaked from the corners of her eyes. "It was because I thought so much of you."

"You're going to need to explain that."

"I didn't want to trap you."

"Trap me? I was already committed to you."

She lost all control of her emotions. The tears started in earnest. "I didn't want to trap you into marrying me, like what happened with my mom and dad," she yelled. "Then you'd resent me just like my parents resented each other." She tried lowering her voice, but it wasn't working.

"They got married because of me. I was the unplanned pregnancy. I'm to blame for their terrible marriage. I told you, I'm to blame for my father's death!"

"Stop being ridiculous! He died serving his country!"

Ridiculous? She reared back as if he'd struck her. "If I hadn't been born, he would still be alive! I couldn't do the same thing to you!" She was nearly panting now, tears dripping off her chin. "I didn't tell you to save you from all that."

"You made decisions for me."

"I know, I know," she sobbed. "I'm so sorry. I was stressed and scared. I wasn't thinking straight."

His face went blank and his voice froze over. "And if hadn't walked into your studio, you'd never have told me?"

"I'd like to think I'd have told you, eventually. But I don't know." Now was not the time to shrink from the truth.

"You let me make love to you. You let me think we might have a chance again. Was that part of your plan?"

"No, no. No! I just knew that the minute I told you, this"— she waved between them— "would happen. I never stopped loving you, and I wanted a little time with you. I was selfish. Please try to understand."

"I'm not sure I can. Amy-Lynn, we were twenty-two, not seventeen like your parents. We'd planned a life together."

She sniffled, wiping her nose with her hand. "I know, but . . ."

"But what?"

She sucked in a breath, trying to slow her breathing, and yanked a paper towel from its holder, running it over her face. "I was protecting you."

His eyes popped open and flashed with anger. "*Protecting me?* What if I didn't want to be protected?"

She slumped into a chair at the breakfast table and covered her face with her hands.

"What happened to the baby, Amy-Lynn?"

The memory ripped through her, and she sucked in a shuttering breath. "I miscarried at eleven weeks. That's the other reason I never told you. The baby was gone. You were already working in Pigeon Forge."

"What about the, wait let's see if I can do the math, five weeks in between?"

She gnawed her thumbnail. "I picked up the phone every day. Knowing I should tell you, but all I could think of was the way my parents became strangers. It was a marriage that never should have been."

He slumped onto a barstool like every ounce of energy had drained out of him. "But I asked you to marry me without knowing."

She frowned at the tabletop. "I know it doesn't make sense."

"No, it doesn't. And you know what else doesn't make sense? You going through the trauma of a miscarriage alone. I don't know what makes me angrier."

Her head popped up. It had never occurred to her that he'd care about that. "I had Momma."

"Does Jess know?" he asked, his voice soft.

"No. Only Momma knows—and now you." She swallowed and prayed for a miracle. "Can you forgive me?"

Matt hung his head, his chest rising and falling like he'd just finished a marathon. "I don't know, Amy-Lynn. I've always thought there was more to our break-up than the reasons you gave, but this is on an entirely different level. I suppose I could come to forgive you. We were still basically kids. But I'm not sure I can ever trust you again."

"Matt," she pleaded, reaching out for his arm.

He pulled it away. "No. I need some time to think." He grabbed his keys from the counter and turned toward the door.

"Matt," she said, softer this time. He stopped but didn't turn. "Will you be at the show on Monday?"

He whirled around and locked eyes with her. She expected anger, but all she saw was hurt and disappointment. That was so much worse. "Fuck, Amy-Lynn, you drop a bombshell like this, and you're worried about your goddamn show?"

"No, I just meant . . ."

"Forget it," he said, yanking open the door and letting it slam behind him.

"Wyatt's asleep," Isabel said softly. How long had she been sitting at the table? It felt like hours, but likely it had only been minutes.

"You mean he didn't wake up when World War 3 broke out

down here?" Avery attempted a smile that she knew just twisted her lips into a grimace.

"You okay?" her mother asked, sliding into the chair opposite.

"Not even a little bit. But at least it's out in the open. It's one less piece of baggage to carry around. Though I suppose I could replace it with guilt, for all the pain I caused him."

"About that baggage," Isabel said, her voice still soft, like she was trying to communicate with a spooked animal. "Apparently, you and Matt are not the only ones who need to clear the air. You and I need to talk about a few things. About your father and me. And some things you said."

Her grimace deepened. "You heard that?" She'd hoped that only the sound had carried, not the actual words. She'd never spoken to Momma about any of this.

"Honey, the people getting gas at the corner mart heard it."

Avery winced. "Sorry."

Isabel rubbed Avery's back. "I can't believe you have been carrying the burden of our marriage—and your Daddy's death around. How long have you felt this way?"

"Pretty much since I did the math and figured out you were pregnant with me when you got married. So, since I was nine?" She laughed a mirthless laugh.

Isabel rubbed her sternum. "That hurts my heart." She looked up, realization dawning. "But it does finally explain the anxiety. Did you tell your therapist about this?"

"Not exactly. I told her about feeling responsible to be the second breadwinner in the house once Daddy passed."

"Why didn't you come to me with this? Yes, finances were tight, but I had a budget. We had Daddy's military benefits, and I worked as many hours as necessary to pay the bills."

Avery shrugged. "I didn't want you to work so hard. I

wanted to give you and Jess more. And since it was all my fault . . ."

"Okay, *enough*." Isabel grabbed both of Avery's hands and squeezed. "Look at me. It's time—well past time—we talked this out. I will not watch you continue to punish yourself for things you had no control over."

"But —"

"No buts. Yes, I got pregnant. Your father and I decided together to get married. Even before my parents' ultimatum. It was our decision. We thought we could make it work. And yes, it didn't work out the way we planned. Unfortunately. But do you remember any fighting?"

Avery searched her memory. Not a single fight manifested in her mind. It felt far more like apathy than anger. "No. But I remember a lot of deployments. I figured Daddy just left every chance he got."

"Those deployments were joint decisions, as well. Whatever you imagined they meant, it's not the truth. You're right about the love. It did die. But not because of anything sinister. We just grew up. We got married at eighteen and by the time we were adults, after a second baby, we just didn't have a lot in common anymore. The love may have died, but the respect never did. He was a good father, mi hija. And we figured out a way to co-parent. We figured out how to share a house. For you and Jess.

"Your father's death was a wartime tragedy and had nothing to do with you. Yes, his choices were because of you. But because he loved you so much and wanted to provide a good life for you—for all of us, not because he was running from a family he didn't want."

"Was Jess planned?" She had no idea why she wanted to know that. She just did. Searching for all the pieces of the puzzle, maybe?

"I know we McWilliams women do not have an impressive track record of planned pregnancies, but yes, she was planned. We made the mistake that so many couples make, that maybe another baby would rekindle our relationship."

Avery wiped her tears on her sleeve.

Isabel smiled a sad smile and pulled a tissue from her pocket. She dabbed at Avery's tears like she was eleven instead of thirty-one. "I'm so sorry you've taken on so many burdens and lost so much of your childhood—and if I really think about it, given up your early adulthood to provide for me and Jess. And I'm sorry I didn't put the pieces together sooner."

"You've had a lot on your plate," Avery said, laying her head on her mother's shoulder.

Isabel shook her head. "It's no excuse."

"I like taking care of you and Jess—and Wyatt."

"I know you do, but it can't be at the cost of your own life," Isabel said, patting Avery's leg.

Avery snuffled, and her pulse finally dropped from hare to tortoise. "Thanks for telling me all this."

Her mother nodded and then grabbed her shoulders, squeezing. "There's one more thing."

Avery stiffened. "Yes?"

Isabel locked eyes with Avery. "Yes, you made some decisions you regret, but it's time to forgive yourself. For my marriage. For Daddy's death. For your pregnancy. And for not telling Matt."

Avery's eyes widened. "But you've always chided me for excluding him and not telling him."

"Yes, I've always believed he deserved to know, but that is separate from you beating yourself up about it. And here's a little more tough love. I think pushing him away—then and now —is just another way you're punishing yourself."

Avery's first response was to deny it, but it rang true. She

220

thought she'd pushed Matt away to save him, but had she really been protecting herself? Did she push him away before he walked away first?

Did she trust relationships so little?

"Oh, Momma, I've made such a mess of things." She should have told him when he asked her to marry him. She should have told him after that first day at the station. And she certainly should have told him before they slept together.

"Do you love him, Amy-Lynn?"

Avery sniffled and nodded. "I've never stopped."

Isabel clasped Avery's fingers in her own. "Does he love you?"

"Does it matter? It's not like he'll trust me again."

"I know I may not be the one to give advice on this subject, but the heart is a very resilient muscle. Do you think he still loves you?"

"Yes," Avery whispered. "He's hinted at it." He'd done more than hinted, but if Avery admitted it out loud, her heart would surely shatter. Right here. Right now. In a million little pieces.

"Then there's a chance."

Avery raised her eyebrows at her mother.

Isabel smiled. "It might be a slim chance, but it's still a chance. Try explaining again. Tell him how you feel."

Avery twisted her hands in her lap. She desperately wanted to believe in that tiny chance. "How do I even get him to hear me out?"

"You are one of the strongest, most resourceful women I know."

"In my professional life. My personal life is a giant clusterfuck."

Isabel chuckled. "Maybe it's time to tell Amy-Lynn to take a back seat and let Avery Lind take charge."

How many times had she told herself the same thing? "But —"

"Matt!" Wyatt yelled from upstairs. "Matt come!"

Isabel laughed. "Seems like you're not the only one who's taken with Mr. Taylor."

Avery rose from her chair.

"No," Isabel said. "I'll get him, and Jess will be home soon. It's time to start taking care of yourself."

She circled her fingers around her mother's arm. "But Momma, he's getting heavy, you shouldn't be lifting him."

Isabel sniffed and waved Avery off. "Nonsense. The doctor said I should keep as active as possible, especially in periods of remission."

Avery cocked her head and pursed her lips. "Momma."

Her mother mimicked her expression. "Amy-Lynn. We've all leaned on you too long. That stops now."

Avery watched her mother walk to the stairs. *Take care of myself? Where would she even begin?* She was pretty sure the answer wouldn't be found on a to-do list or a spreadsheet. The answer existed in only one place.

Her heart.

CHAPTER NINETEEN

MATT STUDIED THE BEADS OF CONDENSATION MAKING tracks down his pint glass. He'd spent the last twenty-four hours going over and over Amy-Lynn's admission.

She'd been pregnant with his child.

She'd chosen not to tell him.

She'd walked away.

The panic attack at the hospital hadn't been about the soldier. It had been about the baby. Should he have seen it? He tipped his head to his right shoulder, cracking his neck, but the tightness remained.

No. Never in his wildest imagination would he have imagined this scenario. He'd only wanted confirmation of his suspicions—that she'd left him because he was 'all flash and no substance,' the proverbial class clown. Hell, when he drove to her house that day, he'd considered letting it all go. So what if she'd thought that nine years ago? He was a different man now.

Hadn't he been in for a surprise?

He pounded a fist against his chest. He never knew his heart could ache like this. He thought the worst pain he'd ever experienced was when Amy-Lynn broke it off, but he'd been wrong.

"Hey."

Matt looked up to find Nick standing at the edge of the table. "You made it."

"You sounded desperate. Sorry I'm a little late. It took me a few phone calls to find someone to watch Henry."

A vision of Wyatt flashed in Matt's mind, and his heart squeezed again. He really didn't think about the support system a single parent needed until Amy-Lynn was called into duty. "Sorry man."

Nick slid into the booth, raising an eyebrow. "For?"

"For being selfish. I didn't think about childcare—or the fact that you can't really bring a kid to a bar on a Saturday night."

Nick laughed. "Or any night."

Matt shook his head. Maybe he really couldn't think about anyone but himself. "I should have suggested a diner, or something."

Nick scratched his beard and scanned Matt's face. "It's fine. It's not like you do this regularly. Plus, I can honestly say I've never seen a guy more in need of a drink."

Matt nodded and took a long draw off his beer.

"When are the other guys getting here?" Nick asked, scanning the small pub.

"They're not coming. Didn't invite them," Matt muttered while rubbing circles over his temple.

Nick's eyes narrowed. "It's just me?"

Matt nodded and spun his glass on the paper coaster provided by the bar. "I need a dad's perspective."

Nick's eyes flew open. "Oh shit, is someone pregnant?"

Matt frowned. "Not anymore."

"What does that mean?" Matt opened his mouth, but Nick raised a single finger. "Hold that thought. It's becoming clear that I'll need a beer for this discussion."

Matt watched his friend walk to the bar. Nick had been the

right call. Any of the guys would've showed, but Nick would understand that making jokes wasn't the way to make him feel better. Tonight was not the night for ribbing about the 'Matt Taylor Charm' or how his smile was his 'get out of jail free' card. Neither charm nor a perfect smile was going to help him through this.

Nick slid back into the booth, careful not to spill his drink. "Shit. You look worse than when I left. What is going on? You said someone was pregnant."

Matt nodded. "You remember how I told you that Avery and I dated seriously throughout high school and college and then she broke up with me out of the blue?"

"Mmhmm," Nick said, siphoning the top of his beer. "On the day you proposed."

Memories of that day flashed in front of his eyes. Her expression—first elation, followed by something cold—finally made sense. "I always thought the excuses she gave seemed off. And I was right. She broke up with me because she was pregnant."

"What?" Nick asked, his eyes popping wide. "With some other dude's baby?"

"That's what I initially asked too, but no, it was mine."

"Whoa." Nick scrubbed a hand along the back of his neck. "When did she tell you?"

"Friday."

"Friday? Like yesterday, Friday?"

Was it only yesterday? It felt like a year ago.

"Yep," Matt said, popping the P.

Nick picked up his pint, slid a cocktail napkin underneath it, and folded up the corners. Nick was a fiddler. He once told Matt that he thought with his fingers. If they were in motion, you could be pretty sure his brain was too. "So you have a kid?"

Sadness crackled like lightning through Matt's chest. "No. She miscarried."

Nick folded the napkin again. "And all this happened, like, nine years ago? And she's just telling you now?"

Matt was pleased he wasn't the only who thought it was odd. "Pretty sure if the radio gig hadn't happened, I'd have gone the rest of my life not knowing."

The server stopped at their table, pointing at their glasses and raising an eyebrow. "He's going to need a second one," Nick said, pointing at Matt. "And I'll take an order of onion rings."

"Got it. One O-ring. And another IPA. Coming right up." The server turned away, but not before winking at Matt and exchanging a piece of paper with his phone number on it for Matt's empty glass.

"Wow," Nick said, watching the server walk away. "That was bold."

Matt blew out a breath. "Seriously. Does something like that ever work?"

"I'm confused," Nick said.

Matt smirked for the first time since Amy-Lynn dropped her truth bomb. "What? You don't get hit on like that?"

"No, not about that. And, no, I do not get hit on like that. I'm pretty sure the neon 'single dad' sticker on my forehead scares people away. I'm confused because you were ready to marry her."

Matt balled up the server's phone number and stuffed it under his thigh. "Yes."

"So why wouldn't she tell you? I know it would have changed your plans, but you were graduating and planning on spending your life together."

"She said it was because she didn't want to trap me into marriage and have me end up resenting her because I'd have to give up my dreams. She'd seen that happen with her parents."

Nick rolled his eyes and clicked his tongue. "People making decisions for other people with no consultation really pisses me off."

Matt knew Nick wasn't only talking about Amy-Lynn. But one issue at a time.

"She said she tried to call and tell me, but never found the courage and then she miscarried and figured what was the point."

"Do you believe that?"

"I don't know. It feels like she pushed me away because she didn't think I had what it took to be a father. She wasn't protecting me but protecting herself and the baby from me."

"Dude, how can you say that? I've seen you with Henry. Kids love you."

Matt sighed. "Probably for the reason everyone else loves me. Giant clown. Just a big kid himself. Nice to look at, but nothing else."

Nick's eyebrows shot up. "Jesus, is that what you think of yourself?"

Matt pulled out the scrunched-up napkin from under his leg and lobbed it at Nick. "That's the way the world sees me. Matt doesn't have real emotions or struggle with things, because look at him. People that look like him don't have problems."

Nick stared at him for a long time.

"Spit it out," Matt said.

"I think her reasons for pushing you away are hers, but if not, do you think she doesn't believe in you because you don't believe in yourself?"

Nick's words landed with a thud in the middle of his chest. "I believe in myself!"

"You sure? I think you might be projecting."

A humorless laugh leaked out of Matt. "Projecting? Where did you pick that up?"

Nick shrugged. "Most of the magazines in the pediatrician's office have a female bent—there are a lot of personal development articles in those magazines."

A smile lifted the corners of Matt's lips. Nick—big, burly, bearded Nick—had more layers than anyone knew. And as much as he wanted to tease him, Matt couldn't help wondering if he wasn't right.

"So, let's just say you might be right—which I'm not conceding—but if you are, what do I do?"

Nick tapped his fingers on the table. "Well, you probably shouldn't take relationship advice from me, but I can tell you one thing: if you love her, don't let her walk away without a fight."

"Even with a lie this size?"

"I know her lie was a doozie, but she was scared and, it sounds like, carrying around a truckload of baggage. Finding out you're about to have a baby is a scary experience, even when you're already married. And can you imagine her dilemma when she miscarried? She would've had to decide which would cause you more pain—telling you there was a baby or telling you there wasn't."

Matt considered his words. Had she really thought she was being selfless? Putting his needs and dreams ahead of her own?

Nick emptied his pint, turning the glass upside down. "You're an open, giving guy and one of the best things about you is you always let people make amends. Yes, maybe this will prevent you from getting back together, but I think you need to let her explain—in a non-heated moment—so you don't have to carry this around with you forever."

Matt pinched the bridge of his nose. "Maybe."

"Sleep on it."

"If only I could. I didn't sleep one wink last night."

"You want to come over and hang with me and Henry tonight? We can ride to practice together tomorrow."

"Shit. I forgot all about practice."

"Dude, we moved it to Sunday for you, so it wouldn't interfere with your final week at the station."

Matt closed his eyes and shook his head. "The station. How do I go back there?"

"You don't have to."

"I signed a contract and . . ." Matt stuttered to a stop.

"Is the radio gig about proving to everyone you're more than a pretty face?"

Matt snorted. "Damn self-help magazines."

"And Matt?"

"Yes, oh wise one?" He was glad he'd called Nick. He might still not know what to do about Amy-Lynn, but at least the vise that was strangling his heart had loosened a little.

"Work out what you need for yourself, but don't think for a minute that you need to prove anything to the band."

Matt's smile faltered. "Sure, whatever."

Nick tapped his fingers against Matt's glass. "I'm serious. If the teasing bothers you, tell the guys."

Matt snorted. "Right. Then they'll tease me about being all touchy-feely."

A smile broke across Nick's face. "Better you than me, brother."

"If they start in on me, I'm totally throwing you and your magazines under the bus."

"Go ahead, it's not like anyone will believe you."

"Grace would. She's like some sort of clairvoyant."

Nick chuckled. "And yet, she's willingly living with Andrew."

"Wonders never cease." He clinked his empty glass against Nick's. "Thanks, man."

"You bet. Meet me at the house?"

Matt nodded. "Yeah. I'm just going to run home and grab some clothes."

Nick slid to the edge of the booth and stopped, turning back to Matt. "Think about what I said. I often wonder, if I'd been more understanding, whether Kirsten and I would still be together. I'm still upset with the way she acted, but I miss her more."

Matt nodded. Did Amy-Lynn's lie trump how much he wanted to be with her? His heart knew the answer. His mind was going to need a little more convincing.

Matt threw a t-shirt, boxers, socks, and jeans into a duffel bag. Add in a couple of things from the bathroom and he'd be good to go to Nick's place. He flipped on the light and stared at the man reflected in the mirror.

That face. His face. It sounded ridiculous, but it was both a blessing and a curse. It opened doors. He couldn't deny that. But it also kept people from looking deeper. People, like the server at the bar tonight or women at the signing table, made assumptions. They didn't bother finding out who he was as a person. They didn't care.

But when did *he* stop caring?

When did he start believing he was nothing more than the way he looked?

When did he start doubting his talent?

Was it when Amy-Lynn walked away? Or was her rejection just an easy excuse? A way to play it safe and never have to try too hard?

It didn't matter anymore.

Amy-Lynn hadn't left him because he wasn't enough. Nick

told him he had nothing to prove to the band. The radio station had done nothing but compliment his work.

No one was going to bury the doubts for him. That was a one-man job. And it started now. He tossed deodorant and a toothbrush into his bag and flipped off the light.

He locked his apartment door and, walking down the hallway, texted Nick. *On my way.*

He'd figure out what to do about Amy-Lynn tomorrow.

Tonight, he was figuring out what to do with himself.

CHAPTER TWENTY

Avery had spent the last forty-eight hours thinking about what she really wanted from her life. She'd forced herself to take long walks so there was no chance of getting caught up in lists and color-coded spreadsheets. She needed to listen to herself without all her organizational crutches.

When Jess had asked for her assistance with Wyatt, she'd said no. And only felt guilty for a few minutes. Okay, maybe an hour. She'd replayed her conversation with her mother and saw her parents' marriage through a new lens. She'd stumbled upon a southern red oak—her father's favorite—and sat cross-legged under its sprawling branches. She closed her eyes and asked him for forgiveness, for assuming he was running from his family.

She cried for the baby and the man she lost.

And finally, she asked herself the million-dollar question: did she simply want forgiveness from Matt, or did she want him back in her life as her partner?

The answer had roared through her, nearly knocking the breath from her.

She'd run home. And that brought her to where she was now, rinsing out a cereal bowl, impatiently waiting for a return text. Not much of a lunch, but her stomach refused most everything.

She needed help, and she needed it today. She wanted matters settled with Matt as quickly as possible. Grace's loyalty was undeniably with Storyhill, but she hoped she would still help.

Had Matt told anyone about her secret? What would they think?

She shook out her shoulders. It didn't matter. It's not like she could change her decisions now. The first step in jettisoning her baggage was to stop worrying so much about what other people thought.

Her phone pinged and she ran to grab it.

Storyhill is in a closed practice today, Grace wrote. *But I know someone on the inside. ;) Text me when you get here and I'll meet you at the door. I don't know what happened, but Matt looks terrible. And I love grand gestures.*

Too bad Avery didn't have a grand gesture. She couldn't offer him her heart. She'd given it to him fifteen years ago, and he'd had it ever since.

Thanks, she texted back to Grace. *When I told you it'd be cool to collaborate, this is not what I had in mind. C U soon.*

She laid her phone back on the counter and ran up the stairs. She rummaged through her drawers until she found it. Her OU sweatshirt—or rather his. She'd never been able to part with it. She pulled it over her head, and it dropped nearly to her knees.

It was a little warm for a sweatshirt today, but she had a feeling she was going to need to pull out every trick in the book.

Would he be angry that she was interrupting practice? Would he blame Grace? In the end, it didn't matter. She needed to get to him as soon as possible, and especially before tomorrow's show.

Avery descended the stairs to find Momma, Jess, and Wyatt making lunch.

"You feeling okay, Sissy?" Jess asked. "It's kinda toasty for a sweatshirt."

Avery tried to steady her quaking fingers. "I've felt better."

Jess felt Avery's forehead. "Oh no, did you get Wyatt's cold?"

"No, it's nothing like that," Avery said, shaking her head.

"It's the nauseousness you get when you decide to go after your dreams," Isabel said, a smile playing on her lips.

"What?" Jess said, before understanding dawned. "Oh. *Oh.*"

"There's a reason people stay inside their comfort zones," Avery said, rubbing her belly. "It feels terrible out here."

"Comfort zones are boring," Jess said. "Welcome to the technicolor side of life."

"Boring!" Wyatt echoed, slamming his chubby fist on the counter.

It was just enough to break the tension. Avery laughed, and the colony of butterflies in her stomach stopped fluttering so fast.

"I'm proud of you, Amy-Lynn," Isabel said.

"What if he doesn't forgive me?" Avery whispered.

"Then you can finally move on," Isabel said.

"Forgive you for what?" Jess asked, looking at Avery and Isabel.

"It's a long story. I'll tell you later."

"How bad can it be? It's not like you've ever done anything wrong in your perfect life."

"I'm far from perfect."

"Really? Because from where I stand, you're the perfect one and I'm the screw-up. You're the perfect daughter, the perfect sister—always taking care of everyone else. And don't even get

DON'T LET THE MUSIC DIE

me started on your job—you set a goal at twenty-two and achieved it in less than ten years. What did you do? Out perfect him?" Jess chuckled but stopped when she looked at Avery's face.

A dam burst inside of Avery. She didn't want to be that perfect girl anymore—or rather, the woman who thought she needed to be perfect to atone for her sins. She was exhausted. And empty. She'd made keeping up the facade and beating herself up a full-time job. Suddenly what Momma just said felt like a lifeline. Yes, she wanted a life with Matt, but if he couldn't forgive her, she'd be free of the secrets.

And here was her chance to take a baby step. She turned to Jess and blew out a giant breath.

"I was pregnant and didn't tell him."

Jessica's mouth dropped open, and the spoon she was holding clattered to the counter. "Wait, what?"

Here goes nothing. "I got pregnant shortly before college graduation and didn't want to repeat Momma and Daddy's mistakes." She looked at her mother, and Isabel nodded, encouraging her to continue. "So, when he proposed, I said no, and never told him about the baby. Until Friday."

"He proposed? And not because you were pregnant?"

"That's correct."

Jess spun on her stool toward their mother. "Did you know about this?"

Isabel nodded. "I did, but not until after the miscarriage."

"A miscarriage? Oh, Sissy." Jess's face fell. "Did you go through that alone?"

Avery dropped her eyes to the floor and nodded.

Jess jumped off the stool and threw her arms around Avery. "Why didn't you tell me?"

"You were just a kid."

Jess scoffed. "I was twenty. That's hardly a kid."

Avery steadied herself on the kitchen island. "I made some bad decisions."

"Like not telling Matt," Jess said, stepping back from Avery.

"Like not telling Matt."

"Matt Daddy!" Wyatt yelled.

"Wyatt knows Matt was the daddy?" Jess asked.

"No, Wyatt called Matt 'Daddy' when we went to pick him up on Friday. The daycare teacher said it was because most of the other kids call the men that come in Daddy," Avery explained.

"Want Matt!" Wyatt said.

Avery kissed her nephew on the head. "Me, too, Wyatt. Me too."

"Then go get him," Jess said, as if it was easy as going to the grocery store for a loaf of bread.

"It's not that easy, Jess."

"Well, it's not if you keep standing here. Go." She gave her a little push in the back. "Follow my lead and take a step into the unknown. Who knew my life would ever be an example to you, Sissy?"

"Let's not get too cocky," Avery said, managing a small laugh.

"I agree, mi hija. If doesn't work, I'll make a key lime pie this afternoon, and it'll be waiting for you."

Jess strung her arms around Avery's shoulders. "We'll all be waiting. Me, Momma, and Wyatt. You don't have to go through this alone."

She squeezed her sister's hands. "When did you grow up?"

"I think it happened when my perfect sister threatened to throw me out."

Avery sucked in a breath and looked up at the ceiling. "I think I just demonstrated I'm far from perfect."

"You're perfect for me. For us," Jess said, pointing to her son and mother.

"Thank you," Avery croaked out.

"We don't judge you, Sissy, we just love you."

If only she could have internalized that years ago. Avery planted a kiss on each of their cheeks before turning toward the door. "Wish me luck," she said as her hand stilled on the doorknob.

"You don't need luck, you're Avery-fucking-Lind," her sister said.

"Avery-fucking-Lind," Wyatt echoed.

Jess squeezed her eyes shut. "Say a prayer he doesn't repeat that at daycare."

Avery steepled her fingers, smiled, and forced herself out the door.

I'm here, Avery typed, but her finger hovered over the send arrow.

She could do this. She'd told her sister, and she'd been nothing but supportive. She checked in with her body. No signs of an impending anxiety attack.

She hit send on the text.

Grace's response was immediate. *There's a stage door on the north side of the building. Meet me there.*

Avery's stomach rolled and flipped. *Stage door?? I don't want to end up on the stage.*

Her phone pinged. Grace had fast thumbs. *Sorry, bad choice of words. It leads into the main floor seating. But in fairness, there's nowhere to hide in this venue.*

Nowhere to hide. Maybe she should do this at a different time—and place. She knocked her fist against the steering wheel. No. Hiding had gotten her here. She needed to do this.

Momma's words played in her head. Today had value. Whether it was a beginning or an end, it was an important step.

The fact she wasn't having a panic attack spoke to that.

Getting out of the car. See you in a few. This time, she didn't hesitate.

She swung her legs out of the car. It really was too hot for her outfit. Hopefully, the auditorium would be air-conditioned. Let's just hope it wasn't Matt freezing her out.

She located the door and knocked softly. Grace swung the door open and smiled. A good sign. Or at least Avery was going to take it that way.

Avery could hear music coming from the stage. This is not the way she thought she'd first hear Matt perform live.

"Your timing couldn't be more perfect. The guys are taking a break after this song, probably in about ten minutes. Until then, let's step in here."

Grace led her down a small corridor that emptied into the venue's lobby.

"I know we've just met, but if you need to talk about this, I'm a pretty good listener."

"Matt says you're clairvoyant."

Grace laughed. "I'm hardly clairvoyant, but I do spend a lot of time paying attention to the small details. It's the songwriter in me, I think. Watching people's behavior helps me write with more emotion."

"Makes sense," Avery said, shaking out her hands and looking at the double doors leading to the auditorium.

"Nervous?"

"Incredibly."

"I don't know what's going on with you and Matt, but in the time I've known him, I've never seen him happier than he was that night at the party. And I've never seen him less like himself than today. You bring out the best in him."

"And the worst, I'm afraid."

Grace tipped her head back and laughed. "Been there."

"Really?"

Grace smiled and shook her head. "Really. When I realized I was in love with Andrew, I got so freaked out that I pushed him away with some really bogus excuses. In retrospect, I was a little unhinged."

"What did you do?"

"My best friend gave me a healthy portion of tough love," she leaned in and added in a whisper, "she basically told me to pull my head out of my ass. I did and asked for forgiveness."

"And he obviously forgave you. I don't think my situation is so easily resolved."

Grace placed an arm around Avery's shoulders. "Never underestimate the power of love."

"How do you know I'm in love?"

"If you weren't, you wouldn't be here." Grace turned toward the looming doors. "The music has stopped. It's showtime, Avery Lind."

Grace pulled open a door and held it open. Avery threw her shoulders back, straightened the sweatshirt, and marched into the auditorium. Matt hadn't noticed her entrance, deep in conversation with two other bandmates.

Nick, if she was remembering right, tapped Matt on the shoulder and then with a speed belying his size, hustled the other three men off stage.

Grace squeezed her hand and whispered, "Good luck." She slipped up the side stage stairs and stopped to say something to Matt. Avery couldn't hear it.

"Hi," Avery breathed out. *What happened to her voice?*

"Mac," he said, standing center stage, not moving. "How did you get in here?"

"I had some help."

"Oh," Matt said, nodding, "that explains Grace's comment."

"What did she say?"

"That I shouldn't be angry with her, she did it in my best interest."

"I hope you agree with her—or will."

"Is that my sweatshirt?"

Avery pulled at the hem of the oversized shirt. "I could never bring myself to get rid of it. I was wearing it on the—"

He frowned. "The day I proposed."

"I so wanted to say yes. I've spent nine years wishing for a do-over, the chance to make a different choice. I'm so, so sorry."

"For what?"

"For everything. For saying no. For not telling you about the baby. For losing nine years. Years we could have spent together."

"I still don't understand." He looked at her directly in the eyes. "But someone recently made me realize I should try to."

Her eyes widened. "You told someone?"

Matt ran his fingers through his hair, rubbing a spot directly behind his ear. "Only Nick knows the details."

She stepped closer to him, wanting to close the gap, but knew to take it slowly. "You're close with your bandmates."

He nodded. "They are my brothers."

"What did Nick say when you told him?" *So much for not caring what other people thought.* Baby steps, she reminded herself. Change doesn't happen instantaneously.

"That fear makes people do things they otherwise wouldn't. And that sometimes love trumps mistakes—no matter how big the mistake."

"Huh. Grace just said something similar."

"Not surprising. Grace is always going on about the power of love."

She lifted her fingers to rub her clavicle and pulled them back. She wouldn't let panic cloud this moment. "Love?"

"Yes, Mac, love. I've loved you since the very moment I saw you, all nervous, walking into that new class in a new school. But I'm going to need a little more."

"I don't have a grand gesture. And I can't even offer you my heart because I gave it to you fifteen years ago and never got it back."

"So that's what I've been carrying around." The edges of his lips lifted upward. "Think of the late fees."

She smiled. "I don't think hearts work like books."

"Well, that's good, because at a quarter a day that's," he looked up to the ceiling, his mouth moving slightly, "I'd owe the library nearly fourteen hundred dollars."

"Wow, that's some quick math."

"Proving I'm not just another pretty face."

Avery took three steps closer to the stage. "I've never thought that about you."

Matt arched an eyebrow. "What about that day in the park? With the job offer?"

"That was about me, not you."

Matt bit his bottom lip, sucking it under his front teeth. "You sure?"

"Matt, all of this has been about my fear—and my misunderstanding about my parents' marriage."

He paced the edge of the stage. "Misunderstanding?"

"Will you come down here?"

"Don't like looking up at me?"

At least his lame attempts at humor hinted that he wasn't immediately going to dismiss her—and maybe that he was softening a little.

"I want you to look into my eyes when I explain."

He jumped down from the stage. Lucky it wasn't a sunken pit. He walked toward her, and she made up the difference, reaching for his hands. He didn't pull away. Another good sign.

"First, I want you to know that I figured out I put fear ahead of us. And I came here to tell you I'm putting us ahead of fear." A nervous laugh gurgled out of her. "Well, maybe it's closer to 50/50, because I'm scared out of my mind that I might lose you again."

"This seems like it's going to take some time," Joe yelled from backstage, "we're going to get some lunch at Wheezy's. You want anything?"

Matt squeezed his eyes shut. "Joe, why is that you always have such impeccable timing?"

"Well, if people in this group could dial down the drama, I wouldn't have to keep interrupting."

"Do you want anything?" Matt asked her.

"Pitcher of margaritas?"

Matt laughed. "Another rare sighting of Mac humor?"

"Yes?"

"Get two number threes, one without tomatoes," Matt yelled over his shoulder, his eyes never leaving hers. "And get out."

Avery listened until the footsteps faded away. "Can we sit?"

Matt dropped into a chair a row in front of where Amy-Lynn stood. It was his only defense against touching her. He'd heard what Nick had said yesterday, and he'd been doing a lot of thinking.

He just wanted to forgive her and haul her into his arms. But. He needed a few things from her first. He needed to hear her out when anger and disappointment weren't raging through him.

Amy-Lynn followed suit and plopped into a chair, pulling

her legs up underneath her. "Ask me anything. Whatever you need to know."

He pushed his fingers through his hair, tugging at the roots before turning his eyes on her. "Why are you here?"

"To ask for forgiveness and to ask for another chance."

"Not because of the show?"

"What?" Her voice rose in incredulity, but softened. "No. Not because of the show. Yes, it would be awkward to explain to Celeste why you're not finishing your contract. But, for once, I'm not worried about my job—or what it means to Momma and Jess. I'm here solely for us."

"You didn't have to tell me about the pregnancy. Why did you?"

"Because I couldn't start something with you again and have this secret hanging between us. And, mostly, because you deserved to know."

"I deserved to know then."

"I know. And trust me, I've lived with years of overwhelming guilt. But Momma helped me see I can't change the decisions I made then. All I can do is try to right my wrong by being honest with you now."

He nodded. The words sounded good, but . . . "I told you on Friday that I might be able to forgive you, but how do we rebuild trust?"

Her eyelashes fluttered, and he realized she was trying to hold back tears. "It sounds cliché, but one day at a time, I guess. If you give us a second chance, I commit to honesty. It's not like I ever wanted to lie to you. There was no conspiracy. In my twenty-two-year-old head, I really thought I was protecting you. I was helping you achieve your dreams, but . . ."

"But?"

"But I realize now that I was protecting myself. I never ever wanted to be a burden again. I loved you so much that I felt like curling into a ball every time I thought about you resenting me, resenting our baby. I couldn't do it."

"It doesn't make sense to me, Mac. You knew I loved you. I was ready to marry you."

She stood and paced the aisle. "I know. But my mom and dad. Losing my dad so young. I believed I was to blame for all of it. Their marriage. His death." The tears started in earnest, dripping down her cheeks.

Damn it. He couldn't just watch this. He stood and pulled her into his chest. He didn't have words. But he could hold her. Even if they didn't get back together, she'd been alone through too many hard times, and he wouldn't let that happen again.

She pushed back against his chest. "No, no. I'm not done yet. There's more." She walked back across the aisle and fished a tissue from her handbag. "I made an appointment with a therapist. I see her for the first time on Monday—after the show. I did it for me. But I also did it for us. I needed to show you I'm serious about dealing with my issues."

"Is there anything else you're not telling me?"

"That's the only thing. I know my words may not mean a lot right now, but I've got nothing to lose at this point. Momma knows. I told Jess this morning. And you know. You either give me a second chance or you don't. I'm prepared to live with either decision."

"Either way, there's a pitcher of margaritas in your future?"

Avery let out a tremulous laugh. "Close. Momma's key lime pie."

Matt groaned. "It might be worth it to get back together just for Isabel's key lime pie." He smiled and it slipped away. "If we agreed to take another go at this, I leave for tour in four days. Will that freak you out?"

"I think you know by now that was never the real issue."

"You made me doubt myself."

Avery straightened in her seat. "I will take the lion's share of blame for the way our relationship ended, but not that. No one can make you doubt yourself except you."

Matt grimaced. He'd had the same thought last night. He knew he was falling back on old excuses. Deflecting instead of dealing with his issues head-on. She hadn't made him doubt himself, but her rejection did rub salt in the wound.

"Matt," she said, breaking into his thoughts. "I didn't believe in myself, but I always believed in you. I didn't know how much all this bothered you. I thought you knew I was teasing when I called you my golden boy."

Matt sighed. "How is it we knew so much about each other, but failed to recognize how much the other one was struggling with this shit?"

"I suppose we tried to hide it from each other, always wanting to show our best side to the ones we loved the most. There's not many people who fall in love at sixteen and are still in love at thirty-one."

"No, I suppose not."

"Are you?" she asked.

"Am I what?"

"Still in love with me?"

"Love has never been the issue."

"No, I suppose not."

They sat in silence for minutes until she rose from her seat.

"I suppose I should go. I came here to say my piece, and I'm grateful you let me. See you at the studio tomorrow?"

"Before you go," he said, grabbing her wrist.

"Yes?" she turned to him, undisguised anticipation in her eyes.

"Let me get your sandwich."

"Oh, okay," she said, her voice falling.

He ran up the stage stairs, taking two at time and skirted

around tables and cables to the green room. He pushed through the door, and all the chatter stopped.

"You get things settled?" Nick asked.

"You got our sandwiches?" Matt asked, ignoring Nick's question.

Joe pushed two packages wrapped in white butcher paper to the end of the table.

"Thanks."

"Mattie?" Andrew called after him. "We're knocking off for today, so you're free to do—whatever."

"Okay, sure." If only he knew what he wanted to do.

He re-traced his steps back to Amy-Lynn. "Here you go," he said, holding out the sandwich that read "No Toms."

She took it. "Thanks."

"Can't have you going hungry." He wanted to tell her so many other things, but the words wouldn't come.

"So tomorrow?"

He nodded. "I'll be there."

"Okay." She turned up the aisle.

"Mac?"

"Hm?"

"Thanks for coming today." His words couldn't have been any lamer if he tried.

She moved to the edge of the aisle. "Thanks for listening. I guess I should go."

"I'll see you tomorrow, Mac. We'll talk more then."

She nodded and walked up the center aisle. He wanted to call after her but thought better of it.

"She's leaving."

Matt turned to find Grace standing next to him. "Yep."

"Why?"

"I need some time to think."

"I get that, but if I might offer some unsolicited advice?"

"Can I stop you?"

Grace laughed. "Probably not. I'm not sure how it happened, but I feel like I've become the Storyhill den mother."

"We should be so lucky," he said, imbuing the statement with as much vintage Matt Taylor charm as possible.

"It's a good thing I'm not affected by that smile."

He laughed. "Your advice?"

"When Jax died, I really believed I'd never get a second chance at love. And I almost didn't. I almost let the specters of the past color my future."

"Meaning?"

"Meaning you can't change the past." Grace tapped his left pec right over his heart. "But if your heart tells you she's the one, there are very few things you can't work out. The key is that you're committed to working things out. Today and tomorrow. Together."

Matt nodded, taking in her words.

"And Mattie?"

"Yes?"

"I've never seen a woman that much in love. If you don't feel the same way, let her know as soon as possible. Give her the gift of being able to move on."

Move on. Why did those two words pierce his heart?

"You ready, babe?" Andrew said, slinging an arm around Grace's shoulders. "Or do you need to stare at the door with Mattie for a while longer?"

"I wouldn't get too cocky, Cowboy. I've heard the stories of you mooning around practices not too long ago."

Matt chuckled. "Truth."

"Engaged two weeks and you're already turning on me, Gracie?"

Matt looked at the newest member of his family. "Your title

is getting long. Songwriter, clairvoyant, den mother, and ego manager," he finished looking at Andrew.

"You good?" Grace asked Matt, lightly placing her hand on his arm.

Matt nodded. "I'll get there."

"Think about what I said," Grace said.

He nodded and watched Andrew and Grace walk up the aisle, disappearing through the same door Amy-Lynn had just exited.

He collapsed into a chair and scrubbed a hand through his hair.

Should he have stopped her from leaving?

Should he have told her he wanted to try again?

Trust could be rebuilt, right?

He leaned forward and his head fell into his hands. Nick said to give her another chance. Grace, too. And his heart was certainly on board.

He felt terrible. She'd come here and poured out her heart, and he'd given her a sandwich. What an idiot.

CHAPTER TWENTY-ONE

AVERY PACED THE STUDIO. IT WAS 5:45, AND MATT WASN'T here. Had he changed his mind?

"Avery, love," Ajay said through the speakers, "you're going to wear a hole in the carpet."

"Sorry," she mouthed through the glass that separated them and forced herself into her chair. But what to do? Everything was exactly the way she liked it.

She stared at the pens to her right. Always the same colors, always in the same order. Damn it, she was so tired of her careful life. Yes, she dealt with anxiety, but if the last few days had taught her anything, it didn't have to define her. She could manage it, even use it to her advantage, but she didn't need to fear it.

She moved the green pen to the left side of the console and then laughed. This would not be what Jess would define as "living the technicolor life" but decades of behavior didn't change overnight. So, moving the pen it is. Baby steps.

"Avery, you okay?" Ajay said into her headphones

Was she? She checked in with her body. She felt free. Free

from the past. She wanted Matt in her life, but she also knew—in her bones—that if he didn't want her, she would survive.

She had Momma and Jess and Wyatt. And she had a new understanding of who she was. Flawed, but whole. A little broken but loved. She would heal.

"Avery?" Ajay repeated.

"Yep. Okay."

"Good, because I'm not accustomed to you pacing, followed by laughing. I thought maybe you'd finally cracked."

Two weeks ago, that comment would have unsettled her, as if people thought she couldn't handle the job. But now she knew he was teasing her—because he cared.

Yep, she had her family. And Ajay. And Celeste. All people who respected and cared for her. People she knew would keep loving her, even if she told them all her ugly truths. And it was time she let them know. Time she let them in.

Ajay was correct. She *had* finally cracked. Cracked open. These past three weeks with Matt helped her see her walls were unnecessary and she'd be forever thankful.

She hit her talk back button. "Hey, Ajay, thanks for always caring. In case you don't know, I love you."

His mouth fell open, and he gaped at her through the glass. "Like a brother?" he said, finally regaining his composure.

She chuckled. "Yes, like a brother and like the best damn producer in the business."

She thought she saw a tinge of pink blossom on his dark cheeks.

She glanced at the clock. "Should we get started?"

"But Matt's not here," he said, eyeing the empty chair.

"I'm here. I'm here," Matt said breathlessly, sliding into his chair and slapping on his headphones.

He was here. And she was thrilled. Because she hadn't

scared him off. And because she'd been ready to go on without him. Look at her rolling with the punches.

He met her gaze. "I'm sorry I'm late, but I had some business to attend to."

Her eyes narrowed. "Before 6 a.m. on a Monday?"

He smiled. A full force Matt Taylor smile. God, how she'd missed that smile. She couldn't help but return it and notice the way her stomach flipped and squeezed when he said, "Yep" and winked at her.

"On in fifty-nine seconds," Ajay announced.

She pushed down the talk-back button, still holding Matt's gaze. "You mean *sixty* seconds?" She turned her head to her producer to see his mouth hanging open. Again. She cocked her head and shrugged, smirking.

"Baby steps," she said, turning back to Matt. She knew that anxiety wasn't something that disappeared overnight. Or ever. But she was committed to thriving alongside it.

"Good for you, Mac," Matt mouthed.

"*Twenty* seconds," Ajay said, punching the even number.

She laughed. Ajay was testing her. Because he believed in her. Because he was her partner.

She pulled up her mic slider. "Good morning country fans and welcome to a brand-new week."

She looked up at Matt and hoped it was also a brand-new beginning.

"As usual, we are going to fill our morning with great music and a great interview. But first, let's check in with our co-host. Mr. Matt Taylor, I understand you had a lengthy practice this weekend. Are you nearly ready for the tour?" She couldn't bring herself to ask how his weekend had been. She was finding her strength, but it was still a little too soon to rip off that Band-Aid.

~

Matt sucked in a deep breath and switched his mic on. She'd given him the perfect opening. All he had to do was step into it.

She was circling her hand as her eyes widened.

Dead air. He smirked. She was more relaxed this morning, but not *that* relaxed.

"Good morning, Avery," he said, his voice cracking ever so slightly. He guessed the listeners wouldn't notice, but she did. "Storyhill did, in fact, have a practice this weekend. We normally don't have three weeks off between tour dates, so it's important to run through the songs and touch base with each other at least once a week."

Avery jumped back in. Their give and take smooth and easy now. "This tour will be all about your new record. What should your fans expect?"

"If the audience at the Ryman was any indication, I think people will enjoy it. It's a mix of traditional country, a couple more upbeat tunes, and of course, a few love songs."

Avery laughed. "That is what Grace O'Connor is known for, right?"

He sucked in a big breath. *Here goes nothing.* "Indeed. In fact, Grace and I co-wrote a song recently." Recently meaning last night—after some serious begging on his part.

"Really?" Her eyes widened. "How is it that you've been here for three weeks and we're just learning this?"

Shit. He hadn't anticipated that question. *Think, Mattie.* "I wasn't entirely sure it was ready. Grace convinced me to let the guys perform it—take it for a test drive—at a few tour stops." Another deep breath. If he wasn't careful, he was going to hyperventilate. "If you're amenable, I brought it along"—he waved a thumb drive in the air— "and would love to play it, for the first time, for your listeners."

Her eyebrows rose. He knew she didn't like surprises, but he was hoping she'd make an exception.

"Well, you know I love exclusive reveals." Emotion passed over her face. She didn't seem mad, but her shoulders were tight.

"Baby steps," he mouthed to her. She rolled her eyes and circled her hands, giving him permission to move forward.

"Great," he said. "Ajay, anything special I need to do?"

"Easy as pie, mate. Slide it into the USB drive on your left and I'll bring it up."

He did as told, and his earphones filled with the opening notes.

Her head tipped to the side. "This isn't *a cappella*."

"It's not. It's just me on vocals and Grace on the piano. It's an acoustic version of something I wrote several years ago. Grace helped with the music."

His voice started and Amy-Lynn pulled her second head-phone over her ear with a snap.

Here I am, thinking of you
Why did you leave, I wish I knew
We fell in love so long ago
It feels like my heart always belonged to you

I wish I could hear your voice, take your hand
Why did you leave, help me understand
You know we're meant to be
It should be us against the world, you and me

If I could turn back the clock, I'd make you see
That your heart belongs with me
Come back, let's give it another try
All I'm asking is, please don't let the music die

He watched as realization dawned on her face and color

bloomed across her chest and up her neck. At first, he thought he triggered a panic attack and then he realized she was trying with all her might to hold back tears.

The song faded just as the first tear rolled down her cheek.

He didn't have to tell her the song was for her. She knew. But did she know what it meant?

He paused for only a second. She was an immensely private person, but something inside told him he had to do this on air.

He opened his mic and collected himself.

He held her gaze and spoke directly to her. So what if thousands of people were also listening? "That song was a little different from typical Storyhill stuff. When we take it on the road, we have an arrangement that will feature all the guys. I want to say a big thank you to Grace O'Connor who stayed up until the wee hours of the morning putting notes to my words."

Surprise crossed her face, but he continued.

His stomach flipped, but he continued. "If you listened to my interview with Grace O'Connor, you know Avery and I met long before she interviewed me two weeks ago. We met when we were sixteen years old in a tiny town in Oklahoma. What I didn't say in that interview was that it took me less than three minutes to fall hopelessly in love with her."

A few more tears fell, but she didn't take her eyes off him, and she didn't stop him.

"And I've been hopelessly in love with her ever since. We took different paths after college, and it took fate to bring us back together. It's like the universe knew the only way we could heal old wounds was to force us to sit across from each other for three weeks.

"Avery, you had the courage to tell me how you felt and ask for forgiveness, and my response was to give you a sandwich."

A laugh gurgled out of her chest, thick with emotion.

"But I'm here now, and I want you to know that I'm betting

on love. Betting that our love is stronger than any mistakes we've made. Let's not let the music die. What do you say?"

Avery opened her mouth, and nothing came out.

"Christ, love," Ajay said from the booth, "how can you say no to that? I've already gotten seventy-three emails saying that if you don't want him, any number of listeners would be more than happy to make music with him."

"Avery?" Matt said.

"Yes. I say yes! I love you too, Matt Taylor."

"And with that," Ajay interjected, "we are going to commercial and then some music. I think our host needs a moment to collect herself."

Avery slid her headphones around her neck. "Do you mean it? Do you forgive me?"

Matt stood and walked to her side of the console, crouching down beside her. "I do. After you left yesterday, after berating myself for the sandwich thing, Grace said something that finally made everything clear."

"What did she say?"

"That if your heart tells you she's the one, there are very few things you can't work out. And my heart has always known you are the one. But no more secrets, okay?"

She placed her hand on his cheek, and he leaned into it. "No more secrets. I promise."

He leaned in to kiss her as Celeste burst into the studio.

"You two are ratings gold!"

"That's not what this was about, Celeste," Matt said, without taking his eyes off Avery.

"I know, but if you think I'm not going to capitalize on this, you are so wrong." She waived a piece of paper in front of Matt's face. It had three lines of typed text.

"What's that?" Matt asked.

"It's a very crude extension of your contract."

He finally turned and looked at Celeste. "But I leave for tour in three days."

"I want you to call in from the road. We can't lose this momentum. What do you think?"

"It's not my choice," he told Celeste. "This is the Avery Lind show. It's her choice. What do you say, Mac?"

Avery smiled softly. "A chance to spend every morning with Matt Taylor, whether here or away? I'm all in."

"Partners?" Matt held his hand out to her.

"Forever," she said and kissed him, "in every way."

"We're in, Celeste," Matt said, not letting her hand drop.

Celeste clapped her hands. "Magic!"

They laughed. "She's been telling us that from the beginning. Maybe we should have listened," Avery said.

Matt dipped his head, touching his forehead to hers. "I think there is only one thing left to do."

"Oh yeah, what's that?"

"We need to send Addison May the biggest fruit basket we can find—or maybe a puppy."

Avery laughed. "I love you, Matt Taylor."

"I love you too, Amy-Lynn Avery Mac Lind McWilliams."

THE END

Not ready for Matt and Avery's story to end?
Want to find out what happens next?

To claim your
FREE BONUS EPILOGUE
and sign up for Annmarie's newsletter, go to
https://www.annmarieboyle.com/dltmd-epilogue-sign-up/

ABOUT THE AUTHOR

Annmarie is a connoisseur of yoga pants, Sharpies, and fancy coffee drinks.

She loves to create stories about strong, smart, and sexy women tackling some of life's biggest issues—while finding their happily-ever-after along the way. Throw in a lot of laughter and a fabulous supporting cast of characters and you've got the stories she both loves to write and read.

She enjoys traveling the world but spends most of her time in a sleepy Midwestern town overlooking a lazy river with her husband, who, after 20+ years, still makes her believe in happily-ever-afters.

Connect with Annmarie at:

instagram.com/annmarieboyleauthor
facebook.com/AnnMarieBoyleAuthor

ACKNOWLEDGMENTS

Early in my writing journey a seasoned author told me to, "Enjoy writing your first book. It's the only one people aren't waiting for." And now I understand exactly what she meant. A second book brings with it a whole set of new challenges and pressures.

So it is with utmost gratitude that I thank the people who carried me through this journey:

To Najla and her amazing team at Qamber Designs and Media, for creating the covers of my dreams.

To Jolene Perry, my editor, for always knowing the perfect balance between tough love and cheerleading.

To Deb, Emily, Niomi, Sharon, and Tricia, thank you for taking time away from your busy lives to proofread this book. As a former copywriter, I'm mortified to find typos in my books. Thank you for saving me from that fate.

To Sandy and Tami, for always knowing exactly how to talk me down from the ledge.

And to my husband, my best friend and my most ardent fan, it's been a hard year. Thanks for hanging in there with me.

And, as ever, a great big thank you to the readers. I appreciate your support and kind words more than I can say!

Made in the USA
Monee, IL
11 July 2022

99451413R10155